CM DAPORTO

THE SAME SIDE

UNIVERSITY PARK SERIES BOOK 2

The Same Side
Book 2 from
The University Park Series
By CM Doporto

http://www.cmdoporto.com
Cover design by Cora Graphics
Edited by Monica Black
Copyright 2014 by CM Doporto

Acknowledgements

I'd like to thank my husband for his continual support. I can't do this without you, babe. To my son, for allowing me to write when I should be giving you more attention.

A huge shout out to my critique partner, Sam. Your help has been wonderful and I'm glad we work well together. Many thanks to my street team, CM Doporto's Heroes and Heroines. I appreciate your dedication and time with supporting my books and getting the word out. A big thank you to Smexy Fab Four for managing my street team. Thanks to Cora Graphics for creating another beautiful cover! Many, many thanks to Monica for the edits on this book. You're awesome! A big salute to Barb. Your coaching and advice makes me a better writer. Love you!

I would be remiss if I didn't mention the bloggers and reviewers who take the time to read and post reviews. Your support of indie authors helps get the attention of readers we work hard to obtain.

A huge thank you to you, the reader. Without you there would be no one to read my story. I appreciate you taking the time to read it. I hope you enjoy it as much as I did writing it.

Most of all I want to thank our Heavenly Father for providing me with the opportunity to do what I love, write.

Dedication

To my Aunt Dorelia.
Thank you for telling me all about
those vampire books.
If I'd never read them, I doubt this story
would have been written.

Chapter 1

Raven's head tilted to the side and his eyes captured every part of me with finite detail. My breathing stilled and the incessant hunger that was building inside of me begged for release. I had fought the feeling for way too long and I refused to wait another second, minute, or day to experience what he had to offer.

I wanted him to kiss me.

No. I needed him to kiss me.

Kiss me and take my lips captive.

My heart pumped faster, waiting anxiously as he moved closer to me.

A tender smile played on the edge of his lips. "Are you sure you want me to kiss you?"

I nodded, unable to speak as my eyes zeroed in on my target. His lips called to me, pulling me in until I breathed in all of his air.

His mouth pressed to mine and my eyes fluttered closed. He kissed me softly, touching my lips in a gentle motion. I melted when the warmth of his hand caressed the edge of my face. My lips parted and his tongue slid in effortlessly, and every muscle in my body relaxed. Our tongues swirled together and I devoured his sweet taste. The kiss was everything I'd ever dreamed of and more. Raven was a damn good kisser. If his lips could reduce me to a puddle of water, I could only imagine what the rest of his body could do to me.

He pulled away slowly. "Lexi?"

"Hmm?"

"Look at me."

I didn't want to let the feeling go and even though he had stopped kissing me, I held on to it for as long as I could. Slowly, I opened my eyes.

Holding my gaze, he said, "You have no idea how long I've wanted to kiss you." He brushed his thumb across my lips and it took every bit of my strength not to barrel into him and beg that he take me.

I took a deep breath and counted backwards from five, pacing the beats of my heart. "I've been dreaming about you kissing me since the day I met you."

For several seconds, we simply stared at each other. The hunger in his eyes knitted me tighter in his trap and I was truly helpless. If he was intuitive, I'm sure he knew what I wanted. And even though every hormone in my body screamed his name over and over, I refused to rush in to this. The last thing I wanted was to become another one of his hoes.

"How about we go grab a bite to eat? I'm starving and if I don't—"

He stopped and smiled. He didn't have to finish for me to know what he thought. I nodded and relaxed back in the seat. "That sounds like a good idea."

"I'm really craving Mexican food."

"Perfect."

We exited the parking lot of Park Hill University's stadium and headed down the street. Raven reached over the console and took my hand, holding it in his. His rough skin felt good against mine and through his touch, I could sense that he missed me just as much as I missed him. Being with him made me so happy. It took my heart to a place where it finally felt free to beat on its own. My only fear was Raven destroying it. But I had to take that chance, otherwise, I'd never know.

He pulled up to a Mexican restaurant off 7th Street and a slight heaviness hit me. The last time I had been to that area was with Collin and my friends when we went bowling. I internally shook off the hurtful memories and concentrated on getting to know Raven better.

Spanish Christmas music filled the air and colorful lights decorated the hodgepodge of 1950s car parts scattered throughout the restaurant. For a Saturday night, the place was empty. The hostess led us upstairs to a booth in the corner and we sat opposite of each other. I looked over the menu and decided on a light dish, since I hadn't been eating too much over the last month.

"Did you have a nice Thanksgiving?" Raven glanced up from his menu.

I closed mine. "No, not really."

"I'm sorry." He frowned. "Why not?"

Shifting in my chair, I considered what I would tell him. Did I really want to admit how pathetic I was? "I, um..."

"If you don't want to talk about it, I understand."

I shook my head. "It's okay." Leaning against the table, I confided in him. "I actually stayed in bed instead of going home to eat with my family."

His eyes widened and a look of sympathy settled on his face. "Were you sick?"

"No." I looked at the table, ashamed to reveal the truth. "I mean, I told my family I was sick." I grabbed my napkin and unrolled it. "But I wasn't. I didn't want to be around my mom. She won't stop hounding me about my breakup and..." I took in a deep breath. "So to save myself from the agony, I chose to lie to them instead."

"Wow. I'm sorry." He placed his hand on top of mine and the tension released.

For some reason, I wanted to tell him everything. Explain to him how screwed up my life was and how I was dying to find a new one. He was so easy to talk to, and it was like I had known him my entire life. "Thanks. It hasn't been easy." I grasped his hand for support. "I basically grew up with Collin and everyone expected us to marry. I just went along with it because he's all I've ever known. But deep down, I knew we didn't love each other."

"It takes a lot of courage to admit that and do what you did."

"Yeah, it does. I just want to be happy and... well, loved."

"I understand. I'm sure there are women who just go with it and then several years later find themselves in a nasty divorce."

"Exactly. And Delaney helped me realize that."

I wanted to tell Raven that he was the one who opened my eyes, but I refrained. I wasn't sure if that was something he was ready to hear.

"Thank God for that. Otherwise, we might not be having this conversation." He grinned.

"Yeah, I guess you're right."

"So, why are your parents so overbearing?"

"My mom got pregnant with my older sister when she was in high school. I guess they felt that if they directed all our steps, that wouldn't happen to us. To be honest, I never really thought I was missing out on much." I stalled for a moment. "I just did what I was told, wanting to be a good daughter." My throat tightened and I pushed the lump down with a tough swallow.

"Sometimes it takes a rude awakening to realize there's more to life. Believe me, I know."

I nodded, quickly wiping away a stray tear.

A tall, skinny guy stopped at our table. "Sorry to keep y'all waiting. Can I bring you something to drink or are you ready to order?" He had on short-sleeve shirt and shorts, as if it were summer time, and a purple ball cap that he wore backwards.

"Do you know what you want?" Raven hesitated, as if unsure if he should tell the guy to come back.

"Yeah, I'll have the chicken fajita salad with the dressing on the side."

The waiter nodded. "And to drink?"

"Water with lemon, please."

"No problem. And for you?" The guy didn't bother to write anything down, committing it to memory instead.

"I want the beef fajitas, tortillas, refried beans, and rice. The whole works. And a tall glass of sweet tea."

"You got it. And by the way, great game." The waiter patted the table and smiled at Raven.

"Thanks, man."

"If you need anything, just holler. My name is Brock."

"Thanks, Brock." Raven handed the guy our menus and he walked off.

I couldn't help but smile. Being recognized and appreciated by total strangers had to be thrilling, not to mention, ego boosting. "Do you ever get tired of that?"

Raven shrugged. "Sometimes. Especially if I want some privacy." He leaned forward, keeping his gaze steady on me. The restaurant buzzed with a low chatter but the way he looked at me, it was as if no one else existed.

The waiter promptly returned with our drinks. He placed a basket of chips in front of us along with hot sauce, guacamole, and cheese dip. "It's on the house."

"Thanks." I grabbed a chip, unable to resist the tempting food that I'd deprived my body from over the past month.

"Thanks, Brock. I'm starved." Raven immediately took a chip, dipped it in the guacamole, and shoved it in his mouth.

"It's kind of nice to get special treatment." I dipped another chip in the cheese sauce.

"I won't deny that." Raven loaded a chip with everything. "But right now, I want to give you all the special treatment you need." He winked and I nearly choked.

Kill me, why don't you?

"You alright?"

"Yeah." I gulped my water and patted my chest. "Just went down the wrong way." After the food cleared, I said, "If I seem a little hesitant or tell you I'd like to take things slow, you'd understand, right?"

He swallowed and then took a drink. "Of course I do. I just want to get you to know you, Lexi. Explore everything about you. From the sweet dimple that forms on your right cheek when you smile, to the curl in your pinkies when you play the piano, and the little shake of your hips when you walk."

"I wiggle when I walk?" I bypassed all the sweet talk and focused on the last part. "Is my butt that big?"

"Relax." Raven laughed and he tilted back his head. "Baby, your ass isn't fat. In fact, it's tight," he growled low in his throat, "and looks too damn good."

"Oh, well, um... thanks." His gaze lingered on me and the air suddenly became thick, making it hard to breathe. A new warning sign told me to proceed with caution, but I zipped past it. Why did his words strike a fire in me? The muscles in my rear tensed and I made a mental note to tell Delaney I wanted to try that Yogalates class with her. If Raven was checking out my butt, I had to make sure it looked good. Saggy cheeks dotted with hail damage would surely scare him.

He leaned back in his chair and rested his arm along the top of the booth. "But don't worry. Like I said, I won't do anything unless you ask me."

Would you take me right now, on this table?

"Lexi?"

"Huh?"

"Did I say something wrong?"

I shook my head, trying to think past the tempting thoughts that cluttered my mind. "I promise you, I'm good. In fact, I'm better than good."

The waiter appeared with our food and I was glad. I was an emotional train wreck. One moment, I was excited about being with Raven, and the next, I was mad that Collin hadn't fought for me. But after a month of not hearing from him, I knew I had done the right thing. He didn't love me enough to marry me. Despite knowing that, it still hurt, and the pain told me that I wasn't over Collin, at least not completely. But I couldn't deny my feelings for Raven. There was something about him. Not only was I happy with him, but also sensed a connection like I'd never experienced before.

We ate our food, chatting a little more about my overbearing parents and how they ruled my life as well as my brother's. Raven sympathized with me and assured me that I didn't need to feel guilty about wanting to live my life. His support gave me the confidence that I had made the best decision.

I placed my fork and knife across my plate and relaxed against the seat. "We've been talking all about me and I really haven't asked you anything."

Raven scraped the last of his beans from the plate with a tortilla. "Go ahead, shoot. I'll tell you what you want to know."

"For starters, how was your Thanksgiving? Does your mom make a big feast?"

"Actually, my granny does. My mom and her sister help with the side dishes and pies. She lives in New Orleans and we usually go there every year. This year I missed out because of the game."

"Oh, I'm sorry."

With a slight mouthful of food, he said, "It's no big deal." He cast a flinty expression, but I could tell it bothered him. "I actually went to my friend Josh's house."

"That's good. So you were able to have turkey and all the fixings."

"Yep. His dad makes fried turkey and it's the best."

"Hmm. Never tried it."

"Well, you're missing out."

The waiter appeared again and took my plate. "Can you bring the check when you get a moment?" I pulled out my wallet from my purse, prepared to fulfill my promise of paying for the next meal.

"The manager said it was on the house."

"Wow, thanks." I was slightly disappointed that I wasn't able to pay but grateful for the act of kindness.

"Thanks, man. Tell him we appreciate it."

"Will do. Can I get y'all anything else?"

"I'm good." Raven turned toward me. "Do you want any dessert?"

Only if it's you.

I let out a small giggle and they both gave me a weird look. "I think that will be it for now." The waiter loaded up his arms with the dirty plates and scurried toward the kitchen.

"I hear you talk a lot about your mom, but I've never heard you mention anything about your dad."

"Oh, yeah, um..." Raven rolled his shoulders a few times and took a deep breath.

I sensed that I'd crossed the yellow caution tape and needed to take several steps back. "I'm sorry. You don't have to answer that question."

"It's cool. You've shared your issues with me, it's only fair I do the same." He stalled for a moment and then said, "I've never talked about my dad because I don't know who he is."

"Oh." My heart dropped to my stomach. I wanted to tell him how horrible it must have been not to know his dad, but I didn't. "I'm so sorry."

His gaze traveled to the table and he picked at the edge of his napkin, shredding it in the process. He inhaled a deep breath and then released it in a slow, steady stream. The emotion was building like a sturdy brick wall, and I waited, as he struggled to tear through it. I almost told him never mind, but he spoke again. "I'm the result of a gang rape."

I covered my mouth and I wanted to punch myself in the face for asking. "Oh, Raven, I-I don't know what to say." My insides twisted at the revelation and I couldn't imagine growing up knowing that.

"It's okay." He looked up momentarily. "There's nothing you can say that will change the fact." His mouth twitched to the side and his shoulders caved. He appeared a bit relieved, like sharing his secret with me had removed some of the bricks in his way. "It's was tough growing up... knowing that my mom really didn't want me. She thought about aborting me," he snickered, "even tried to, but I guess God had bigger plans for me, because here I am."

He held out his arms, and I wanted to leap across the table and hug him tightly. Take away the hurt and pain etched deep into his eyes. Let him know how wonderful and special he really was and to ignore or refuse to accept anything different. Tears gushed from my eyes as I placed my hand on top of his and squeezed his fingers.

"You're right, Raven. God does have bigger plans for you. And don't you ever forget it."

"Don't cry." He reached across the table and wiped away my tears. "Especially for me."

"I'm sorry. It's just that... I feel your pain. I really do. I know you've been through a lot and although I don't know if the rumors are true—"

"They are. It's no secret. I've had a drug problem, off and on, for a few years."

I swallowed the thick lump in my throat. "But you are so talented, Raven. Don't throw it away for a good high or buzz."

"Sometimes it's easier said than done." He wadded up the napkin and tossed it aside. Was that how he felt about his life? Like it was a piece of a paper that wasn't worth anything? Did his mother care about him or bother to show him any love?

"I'm sure it is." I grabbed his other hand. "Do you remember when we sang *Lean on Me* that day at my dorm?"

"Yeah, why?" He cocked his head to the side.

"If you're ever feeling that down..." I paused, searching for the right words, "to the point where you feel you have to resort to the unthinkable, I want you to call me. I'll be there for you."

"Lexi," he said, as he shook his head, "I don't expect you to help me with my problems."

"Look, Raven, I know we haven't known each other that long, but I won't allow you to destroy your life when I know there is something great and big planned for you."

"Thanks, but the truth is—I don't know what I'm doing with my life. Sure, I have dreams of going to the pros, but that's what they are — dreams. I'm just taking everything day by day. If I make it, great. If I don't, it's no big deal." He relaxed against his seat nonchalantly.

I gripped his hands tighter. "You will make it to the pros. I know you will. You have a special talent and when you're on that field, it comes to life. So, if you need someone to help you battle those demons, I'll be there for you. I swear on my life, Raven Davenport, I will be there for you."

Σ

Chapter 2

"So what do you want to do next?" Raven turned on the car as I fastened my seat belt.

My body knew what it wanted to do, but I reminded myself to take things slow. "I don't know. There are so many things I haven't done."

Raven's head turned quickly in my direction. "I think you need to make a list."

"A list?"

"Yeah, you know, like the top ten or twenty things you want to do before you graduate."

I giggled. "You know, that sounds like a great idea."

"And you can already mark one of them off." He grinned.

I shot him a questioning gaze. "I can?"

"Yeah, you said you've never had a beer and we already took care of that."

"Oh yeah." I smiled as I recalled that day in the stadium suite. It was one of the best moments we'd shared. "I've always wanted to sneak into some place while it was closed, so I guess I can check that one off, too." I wiggled in my seat, trying to contain my excitement. This was beginning to sound like a fun challenge. Especially, since it was with Raven.

"See, you already have two down." He put the car in reverse. "I know one more you can check off tonight." He stretched his arm across the seat, resting it behind me. My checks burned as his stare turned knowing.

I know several I could mark off by midnight if you'd let me.

"Really? What's that?"

"A party."

I pressed my lips together, trying to hide the huge smile dying to escape from them. "Let's go."

Raven headed toward the university and turned on a street a few blocks from my dorm. He parked on the grass near the front of the house after one of his fraternity brothers directed him to a spot saved especially for him. I guess being the star quarterback had its perks.

"Are you sure I'm okay dressed like this?" I looked down at his jersey I still had on from the game.

"You bet you are. In fact, no one will mess with you, because they'll know you belong to me."

My hand stopped on the door handle. "Belong?" Even though the idea of being with Raven thrilled me, I wasn't so sure that I wanted to belong to anyone. Not yet.

"I'm sorry." An apologetic look softened his eyes. "That came out wrong. I guess what I was trying to say was, guys will know you are with me and won't try to hit on you."

I pushed the door open, relieved at his explanation. "Okay, I think I can handle that."

Music blared from the house, reminding me of a movie Delaney and I watched a while back. Empty beer bottles and red plastic cups cluttered the yard and it was only nine o' clock. I couldn't imagine what the place would look like by midnight. Several people hung around the porch, talking and drinking. Some were dancing and it was hard not to join in with the beat of the music. I took a deep breath and climbed the steps. If this party was anything like the one in the movie, either I was going to love it, or I would be ready to get the hell out within the first ten minutes.

"Relax. Just stay next to me and you'll be safe." Raven grabbed my hand and I clasped my fingers tightly around his as we walked inside. We entered the living area and several people did a double take.

"Hey, man, what's up?" Raven greeted a couple of guys standing by the pool table.

I looked around, wondering if Delaney was there with Shelby or anyone else. "Whose place is this?"

"One of my fraternity brothers lives here with several guys," Raven answered as he shook hands with a few more guys.

"It's a nice house." I noted the dark mahogany staircase and bookshelves in the craftsman style home. The floor squeaked as we walked through the great room and it reminded me of Collin's parents' house. I sighed and fought to push those memories out of my head.

"Yeah, but after tonight, it'll look like shit," Raven said as he continued to guide us through the house.

"Lexi!" Delaney scurried toward me and I was a bit relieved that she was there. "You made it."

"Yep, I'm here." I shot a quick glance toward Raven and he smiled.

"I can't believe it!" She flung her arms around me and a strong whiff of liquor hit me. "We're going to party all night long," she hollered in my ear and I quickly jerked my head away to avoid hearing loss.

"Damn, did you down a whole bottle or what?" I hugged her quickly before pushing her away.

"Uh, no." She rolled her eyes. "Just took a few shots. C'mon. You have to try this."

Grasping my hand, she pulled me away from Raven's side. "I'll be right back."

"I'm going to see who's here and then I'll come find you. Flip your phone to vibrate in case I can't find you," Raven said as he headed off in the opposite direction.

I reached in my back pocket for my cell phone and switched it to vibrate as Delaney dragged me into the kitchen.

Several people gathered around the center island as they chanted, "Abby... Go, Abby." I stood on the tips of my toes, trying to get a better look, but I couldn't see over the hordes of people surrounding her. Delaney squeezed through the people, pulling me along behind her. My stare immediately drew to the long, slender legs sitting on a stool. Legs that belonged to one of the Silicone Triplets.

Great.

The brunette's long fingernails curved around a small glass that she held up to her mouth. She lowered the glass for a quick second, as though hesitant to take the shot, and caught my gaze. A snarky grin spread across her lips and she rolled her eyes at me. Abby tilted her head back and downed the reddish-brown liquid in one gulp. Everyone clapped and screamed as she held up her hands in victory.

"Shit! That was hot." She fanned her mouth as she placed the glass on the counter. "Give me another one."

"You have to do one." Delaney pushed me toward the bar.

"What?" I tried not to shove the guy standing in front of me but plowed right into him as she yanked me forward. "Sorry," I apologized as I pushed past him. "Laney, I don't know if that's a good idea. Maybe I should start slow. Like with a beer."

"Don't be a puss." She wiggled us through the people until we had front row access. "I'll do one with you." Delaney danced to the beat of the music as she kept a watchful eye on Abby.

"Go right ahead." Abby stepped aside as she gave both of us a once over. Delaney huffed and waved her off with a dismissive hand.

"Delaney!" someone called out. We turned, as Shelby danced her way toward us.

"I wanna do one," she yelled in a singsong voice. Pushing through the crowd, she made her way to the island. When she saw me, she gave me a big smile and threw her arms around. "Hey, um, don't tell me...Lexi." A mixture of beer and cinnamon fanned over my face and I had to hold my breath so I wouldn't puke all over her.

"Hey, Shelby," I said with a restrained voice. Between the pre-party back at the stadium and the house party, I was certain they had drank their share of whatever they came across.

A short, thin guy wearing a white T-shirt with a Kappa Sig logo on the pocket manned several bottles of liquor. He turned over three glasses and filled each one of them. "Bottoms up, girls."

"Can I drink it slowly?" I pulled the glass toward me, unsure if I really wanted to drink it.

He laughed. "I don't think you want to drink this stuff slowly. Unless you enjoy your tongue burning like it's on fire."

Delaney tossed her long, dark curls over her shoulder. "Just swallow it all at once and you'll be fine. I promise."

I eyed her, not believing one word she said. But I was there to have a good time. Straightening, I picked up the glass and brought it to my lips. A hint of cinnamon layered with a strong infusion of alcohol infiltrated my nose. When the crowd around us started clapping and egging us to take the shots, I forgot all about how it would feel once it hit my tongue.

"Wait! Wait!" Shelby yelled. "On the count of three, okay?"

Delaney and I nodded. The crowd started the countdown. "One. Two. Three!"

I titled my head back as I dumped the ounce of liquor in my mouth. A burning sensation scorched my tongue as the warm liquid slid down my throat. "Ugh! What the hell was that?"

"A Fireball. Haven't you tried one before?" the bartender asked, giving me a weird look.

All eyes navigated toward me and I shrugged.

"She just transferred here from St. Mary's. Ya know, the Catholic university down in San Antonio," Delaney told the group of people gawking at me.

"Yeah, I was studying to be a nun, but it didn't work out so well," I quickly blurted, not wanting to look like a prude.

"Oh." The group all nodded and I wanted to laugh at how pathetic my excuse sounded.

"Do you want to do another one?" The bartender held up the bottle in his hand.

"No, that's okay." I retreated. "I better start slow."

"One more! One more!" the crowd yelled, but I ignored them, determined to do things on my own accord.

"C'mon, Lexi!" Delaney called, but I continued pushing through the crowd.

"Don't back out now," Shelby added. "This party is just gettin' started."

I held my hand up in the air and waved bye to them. Shoving past a few people, I finally broke free, but not without stumbling.

"Whoa. You alright?" Raven reached forward and caught me before my face met the floor.

"Yeah, I just—um." The words died in my throat as he pulled me close to him. He wrapped his arms tightly around my waist and I tensed. I silently took in a deep breath and relaxed against his strong, muscular chest.

I could definitely get use to this.

"What's Shelby complaining about now?" Raven's scent swept over me and my knees weakened once more. I stared deeply into his eyes and was instantly pulled in to his trap. My mind drifted as I became infatuated with the curve of his full lips, and I imagined them kissing me until I couldn't breathe.

Raven tilted his head from side to the side, breaking my hypnosis. "How many shots did you do?"

"Just one." I smiled. "Now I can check that off my list."

"Good. But what did you take?"

"A Fireball." I straightened, proud that I had done it.

He gave a slight nod of approval. "I'm glad you only did one. That shit's like sixty-six proof, it'll knock you on your ass."

"Is it stronger than tequila?" I placed my hand on his chest and it took all my strength not to rub the hard muscles under my fingers.

"Depends on the tequila. Cheap tequila isn't as strong, but a good bottle is about eighty proof." Raven sounded like he was a pro when it came to liquor and I couldn't help but wonder what else he specialized in when it came to his reputation.

"I guess a Fireball was a good choice to start with."

"We'll see." He had a sheepish grin on his face. "Just wait awhile before you do another one, okay?"

I nodded and relaxed even more. The liquor was taking effect quickly and I liked how it brought out a different, flirtatious and daring side of me.

"Hey, have you seen Shelby?" A guy with short, blond hair placed a hand on Raven's shoulder.

"Yeah," he said, as he pointed toward the kitchen, "she's over there doing shots."

"Aw, hell." The guy shook his head and his eyes narrowed.

"Hey, Josh." Raven grabbed his arm before he took off. "I'd like for you to meet Lexi."

Josh stopped and turned toward me. "Lexi? The tutor?"

"Yes, the tutor." I shook his hand and a little happiness filtered through me, knowing that Raven had talked about me to his friends.

"Nice to meet you, Lexi. I'm Josh Marshall."

Raven wrapped an arm around his shoulder. "This guy here is not only my teammate, but also my best friend."

"And don't forget roommate."

"Oh, yeah. That, too."

"Let's go dance!" Delaney crashed into us, flailing her arms in the air, and shaking her body wildly.

"Damn, girl. Take it easy on the shots. We're going to be carrying you out of here if you don't stop," Josh said.

Delaney threw her head back as a laugh bellowed from her. "I can hang with you guys. Trust me." Her eyes drooped. I'd never seen Delaney act so carefree.

"Yeah, yeah, whatever." Josh waved her off. "Where's Shelby?"

"Right here." Shelby shimmed up next to him, rubbing him up and down like he was a pole she was ready to swing on.

"And how many have you done?"

Shelby hiccupped and then giggled. "Enough to make this one wild night." She winked at him. He pulled her into his arms and kissed her deeply, as if they were alone.

"Damn, go back to the apartment." Raven pushed them aside and they stumbled out the front door, lip-locked the entire way.

"C'mon. I wanna dance." Delaney gyrated to the beat of the music and I couldn't help dancing along with her. Latching on to my hand, she pulled me to the great room where the music blared. I gripped Raven's hand and brought him with us.

"No, that's alright," he protested, but didn't stop me from leading him toward the makeshift dance floor.

The floor shook beneath our feet as the lyrics to *Moves Like Jagger* filled the air. We huddled in a group, dancing like we were trying out for a music video. Delaney sang, and I didn't have the heart to tell her to stop, even though she sounded horrible. Raven laughed as Delaney sang with her eyes closed and I shook my head at her silly impersonation.

It didn't take long for the cute guy with spikey blond hair that we'd seen after the game to make his appearance. With fine moves, he worked his way across the dance floor until he was dancing behind her. Delaney turned when he neared the side of her face. I waited for her to push him away, but instead, she started moving against him.

I looked away, not wanting to know what she would do next. Did my brother know she was here? Not wanting to get involved with their complicated relationship, I turned my focus to Raven.

His skin shimmered under the array of disco lights flashing across the room, mesmerizing me. Our eyes locked and he grabbed my hands, raising them high above our heads.

His body rocked against mine and my body claimed his instantly, moving in perfect sync.

Oh dear God.

The friction of his body against mine caused my breath to hitch in my throat. The room spun to the point where I thought I would faint. The movements from his hips told me that if I would've asked him to go home with me, he would've cradled me in his arms like a football and sprinted to his car. I sucked in a deep breath, filling my lungs because I refused to pass out. The experience was too damn good to miss.

He pulled me closer, rubbing his cheek along the side of my face. A half-strangled cry escaped from my throat and I was glad the music covered my yelp.

When he serenaded me, my heart totally freaked out. The entire room froze as Raven lured me in, one line at a time. The lyrics described our situation perfectly. I was broken and scared, ready for him to make me believe that he had that key.

I was definitely a member of The Raven's trap. No questions asked. We exchanged another silent understanding, like the day outside the library, and I had to remind myself that handing over my virginity might end it all. Ignoring the warning, I decided to tease him. Lacing my fingers around his neck, I sang in his ear, telling him that I wanted him to take control. I was ready for him to own me tonight. I was ready for him to rub me right from head to toe. But dare I share my secret and tell him I was a virgin?

Raven dug his fingers into my hair and his full lips covered mine. My stomach tensed and then relaxed. The room spun around us and I responded fervently, moving my lips against his and sliding my tongue into his mouth. He tasted like beer and gum, but I didn't care. I could have kissed him until my lips turned blue and even then, I'm sure they would have to bury me with my lips puckered.

Maybe I was ready to hand over my virginity. Tonight.

Σ

Chapter 3

The night ended too soon thanks to Delaney. I knew she had taken too many of those burning shots. I was glad it was her instead of me, even though I was the one that was supposed to be having a great time, since it was my first party. In all honesty, other than the Silicone Triplets showing up, the night had been exciting and thrilling. Being with Raven was unexplainably incredible.

"Laney, why are you crying?" She had one arm hooked around me and the other one around Raven. Her feet dragged as we stumbled across the grass to Raven's car.

"Why?" She sobbed and moaned. "Why doesn't he want to talk to me?"

"I've got her, just open the door." Raven handed me the keys as he held on to Delaney. I unlocked the car and then pushed the seat forward. "You better not throw up in my car," Raven told her, as I helped him lay her in the backseat. "That's all I'm asking."

"I'm not going to throw up." Delaney's words slurred from her mouth as she wiped away her tears. "I never throw up."

"Maybe we should put her in the front?" I moved my hair away from my face and took a deep breath. "Just in case she has to puke."

"It's only a few blocks. Hopefully she'll be alright."

"Okay."

Raven waited for me to get in the car before he shut the door. The kind gesture reminded me of the sweet things Collin would do for me, and I shook my head, determined to stop thinking about the past. I turned around to check on Delaney and saw that she held her phone close to her chest.

"Why won't he text me back?" she whined.

Raven started the car and with the help of one of his frat buddies, backed out onto the street. Cars lined both sides of the road and it was a narrow squeeze all the way to the dorm.

"Darn. Is the whole school at the party?"

"That's nothing." Raven motioned with his hand. "I think we only had about half the crowd we normally have."

"Seriously?" I looked down both sides of a street we passed and saw the never-ending line of cars parked everywhere. There wasn't an open spot for blocks.

"Yeah. I think students are still out of town for the Thanksgiving holiday."

"Wow. I can't even imagine a party with more people."

"What the hell is she crying about?" Raven ran a hand down his face and I could tell Delaney's complaining was wearing on him as well.

I turned around to face her. "Delaney, what's wrong?"

She held up her phone. "He doesn't want to talk to me. Ever."

I grabbed the phone from her hand. Luke's name appeared at the top of her text messages. Not wanting to get in the middle of their spat, I handed the phone back to her, refusing to read the messages.

"She's fighting with my brother," I sighed.

"Call him for me," she begged.

"No." I adjusted the seat belt and turned to face the front. "I'm not getting in the middle of this."

"But you have to tell him that I didn't do anything wrong."

"Why does he think you've done something wrong?" I tried to keep my voice steady and calm, but irritation seeped through.

She continued to cry like a two year old not getting her way. "Because he saw the pics I posted on Facebook and he thinks I hooked up with that guy."

"With Matt?" Raven shot me a questioning gaze.

"Who's Matt?" I pulled out my phone and hit the Facebook app. I quickly typed in her profile name and went to her page. Several pictures were posted, including ones with her and me. "Is this who you're talking about?" I showed her a picture of the cute blond guy with spikey hair that was freaking her on the dance floor.

"Yes. I knew I shouldn't have posted it." She wiped her eyes and let out a huge hiccup.

Raven pulled up to the dorm and parked in the loading zone. "Can I see?"

I handed him my phone. "That's my friend, Matt Russell." He scrolled through a few of the pictures. "Hey, look at us." Raven pointed to a picture of him and me, cheek to cheek. The guy had the face of a model with a square jaw, straight-line nose, and stark white teeth. He really was out of my league.

"Let me see that." I slipped the phone from his hand and stared at the cute pose of us together. "Aww. I want that pic."

He leaned closer to me and I wanted to snuggle up to him. "Tag me because I want it, too."

"How do you do that?" He looked at me like I was crazy. "Sorry, I'm not on Facebook that often."

"Oh." He leaned over me and touched the screen. "Just tap on the picture and it will take you to another screen. See that thing that looks like a price tag at the bottom?"

"Yes."

"Hit that and then tap the picture again." A box appeared with several people's names listed. "Now you can type our names."

"That's easy." I typed in my name and then Raven's.

Before I could check to see if the pictures posted to our pages, Delaney yelled, "Open the door. I'm gonna hurl."

We threw our doors open and Raven pulled her from the back seat quicker than catching a forty-yard pass. He held her as she purged the contents of her stomach all over the sidewalk. I felt bad for her and knew it was going to be a long night. After Delaney was done puking, Raven picked her up in his arms. I was slightly jealous that she was the one being carried instead of me. But after seeing how sick she got, I was fine walking into my dorm room.

"Are you sure they won't tow your car?" I pulled the keys from the ignition.

"Just make sure you turn on the hazard lights." He looked over his shoulder as he headed up the front stairs.

I reached into the car, hit the hazard button on top of the steering wheel, and then shut the door. I pressed the alarm button as I dashed up the walkway. With haste, I removed the access badge from my pocket and scanned it. The back door to Carter Hall unlocked and I held the door open for Raven. We quickly rounded the corner and waited for the elevator. Several people passed by us, doing a double take at Delaney lying limp in Raven's arms.

"She's going to hate tomorrow." Raven looked down at her while I brushed the strands of hair away from her face.

"Better her than me." I raised my brows.

"I'm sure you'll have your turn one day," he said as the elevator doors opened.

I hit the button for the sixth floor and leaned against the wall. "I don't think that's something I want on my list."

"Oh, come on," he laughed, "everyone experiences drinking too much and paying for it."

I shook my head. "Doesn't mean I have to."

The elevator doors opened and he shifted Delaney, holding her closer to his body.

"Is she heavy?" I walked quickly down the hall toward our suite.

"Anyone that's passed out is heavy," he grunted. "It's dead weight." I now understood what Luke said about my ass being heavy when he carried me up the stairs after my mimosa incident.

As soon as I opened the door, Delaney's cell phone rang. I glanced at it and saw Luke's picture flash across the screen.

"Ugh," I moaned, trying to decide if I should answer it or not. "Lay her on the bed." I pushed the door to her room open and stepped back.

"Hello?"

"Who's this?" Anger laced his voice and I held the phone away from my ear.

"It's your sister," I snapped, feeling a little irritated by the situation.

"Where's Delaney?"

"Passed out. Drunk." I motioned for Raven to help me pull off Delaney's boots.

"Oh shit."

After we pulled off her boots, she popped up from the bed. "I need to throw up." She motioned to the bathroom and Raven quickly picked her up. I pointed to the door across from her bed and he shot through it. A few seconds later, I heard her heaving and hurling. I stepped into the living room so I could talk to Luke.

"I take that back. She's in the bathroom throwing up again."

"Great." Heaviness filled his voice and I knew that wasn't the first time she had drank too much. "Where the hell were y'all?"

I pulled a bottle water from the mini frig. "At a party." I unscrewed the lid and then chugged down half the bottle. Why the heck did alcohol make you so thirsty?

"A party? Where? With who?"

I paced the small hallway back and forth, trying to keep calm. Luke didn't have to drill me about where I'd been or whom I'd been with. It was none of his damn business.

"A Kappa Sig party, why?" I said, as if it were no big deal.

"Were you drinking, too?"

I huffed, feeling more frustrated by the minute. "What does it matter? Why don't you get your ass over here and take care of her. She's the one that's drunk. Not me."

"You know what, you're right. Fuck it. You take care of her."

Before I could respond, he hung up the phone. I squeezed the phone in my hand to prevent a scream from escaping. Luke knew how to make me so frustrated at times. Even though he'd said the breakup was between Collin and me, he had grown colder toward me. The bond we once shared as twins didn't exist anymore and maybe it was all because I had hurt his friend.

I set Delaney's phone on her nightstand and went into the bathroom. Raven sat on the edge of the tub, holding Delaney by the hair as her head hung over the toilet.

"Sorry. It was my brother." I opened one of her drawers and took out a hair band. "I asked him to come and take care of her but he got mad and hung up."

"It's okay." Raven let go of her hair when I wrapped my fingers around the muddled strands.

"He doesn't want to help me?" Delaney slurred her words together as she tried to help me pull her hair up.

I filled a cup with water. "Here, rinse your mouth." She took the cup and attempted to take a sip but spilled half of it on her in the process. Instead of getting mad, I grabbed a hand towel and wiped her face.

"I think I've got this." I smiled at Raven.

"Are you sure?" He had his forearms pressed against his thighs as he leaned over. His eyes watched me intently and I took a quick peek in the mirror to make sure I looked somewhat decent. Thankfully, I didn't look anything like Delaney.

"I think I can manage, unless I have to carry her to the bed." I knelt beside her to make sure she was somewhat coherent. "Besides, you look tired... you've had a long day."

"I feel tired." Raven glanced at a big white watch he wore around his wrist. "Damn, it's only twelve-thirty. I can usually hang longer than this, but I really took a beating on that field today."

"I understand," I reassured him, even though I didn't want him to go. Aside from Luke, Raven was the first guy I'd had in our suite. Collin really didn't count since he refused to step foot in my room, claiming it was better if he stayed in the living room.

"I'm sorry... I ruined your night," Delaney mumbled. Then she said something else that I couldn't understand.

"I don't think I drank enough." He stretched and stood.

I let out a slight laugh. "What?"

He towered over me and the proximity of my face to his waist made my body flush with heat. I slowly leaned back, taking in his well-defined legs, not to mention the huge bulge below the hem of his shirt.

Stop staring!

"If I only have a few beers, I get really relaxed instead of a buzz. I think that's what happened tonight."

I got up from the floor, making sure Delaney had a tight grip around the toilet. "Oh, I see. I'm sorry you didn't drink more."

He cupped my face with his hand. Warmth spread up my neck and zing of desire hit every nerve ending. "Don't be sorry. I wanted to make sure I remembered this night with you."

Melt my heart, why don't you?

"It was my decision to not get wasted."

I soaked up every one of his words. I was on toxic overload and loving every minute of it. "In that case, thank you."

He winked and then kissed my forehead, both cheeks, and my nose. I froze, unable to handle the soft, tender pecks he adorned me with. I was shell-shocked and he hadn't even swapped spit with me.

"I'll call you tomorrow."

I nodded, completely breathless, not to mention, speechless. A multitude of emotions flooded me when he positioned his hands on my hips. He pulled me closer to him and I felt every lump and bulge that carved his lower body. My hands rested on his chest and my fingers splayed across his pecs. Flashes of what he looked like without a shirt on inundated me. Just as we were about to kiss again, Delaney started hurling. So much for a hot kiss goodnight.

"Hey, you awake?" Several knocks sounded at my door.

I shifted and stretched. "Yeah, just waking up." I yawned. "What times is it?"

Reaching for my phone, I tried to focus on the display.

"I don't know. I think it's a little after eleven." Luke walked into my room and sat down on the edge of my bed. He had shown up about thirty minutes after Raven left. I was grateful because Delaney passed out an hour later and he had to carry her to the bed. I would've had to leave her on the bathroom floor.

"Thanks for coming over." I laid my phone on my bed.

He shrugged his shoulders. "I'm used to it."

I sat up and ran my hands through my matted hair. "What do you mean, you're used to it?"

He cast me a dubious stare. "This isn't the first time she's done this shit."

"Um, I know she's my roommate and friend, but I've never partied with her. In fact, I've never seen her or heard her puking because she drank too much."

"Yeah, I guess you haven't." Luke leaned back against the bed. "She usually comes home with me or goes to Jordan's when she's that messed up."

I stalled for a moment, realizing that I really didn't know Delaney like I thought I did. She really had been living a life that I didn't know much about. And apparently, Luke had been a part of it more than I knew.

"Is that why you didn't want me to know you two had been hooking up?"

"What?" His head turned quickly in my direction. "No, that's not why."

"Then why didn't you want me to know?" I readjusted the pillow behind me. "It doesn't bother me that you're with her."

"I thought it would piss you off if you found out about us." He traced a fleur de lis pattern on my bedspread. "Besides, Delaney is complicated. I'm not sure what kind of relationship we have."

"More than friends?" I hinted, knowing about the time he came over here.

"Yeah, something like that." He rose up and then ran his hand through his messy hair. "By the way, sorry I hung up on you."

I shifted, leaning over on my left forearm. "I thought maybe you were mad at me because of Collin."

"I told you I didn't want any part of that." He crossed his arms and laid them against his chest. "That's between the two of you."

The sudden urge to ask how Collin was doing played on the edge of my tongue. Even though I was glad we were broken up, I still cared about him. I'd known him for way too long and getting over him completely would take some time.

"I know, but you've been acting shitty toward me lately so I figured it was because of the breakup."

Luke stood and I could tell he didn't want to have this conversation with me. "Look, I care about you, Sis. I really do. But what you do with your life is really none of my business. You're a grown woman and you need to make decisions for yourself. Just like I do. So, if you don't want to marry Collin, then that's your choice." He placed his hands on his hips. "Collin's my friend, but I'm not going to tell you to marry him if you don't love him."

"Mom and Dad thought they could."

He smirked. "Don't get me started on Mom and Dad." Luke apparently still had mommy and daddy issues like I did.

"You don't have to say that twice."

"Do me a favor. Tell Delaney I went home to shower. I don't want to wake her because she needs all the sleep she can get. I know she has tests to study for today."

I nodded and threw back the covers. "I'll tell her. I need to shower, too. I have two finals on Friday and if I don't get my butt busy, I might fail them."

"See ya later." Luke walked out of my room and I heard the front door shut.

As I walked to my dresser, I heard my phone chime. I crawled across the bed and grabbed it. Turning it over, I saw that it was a text from Raven. A smile crept over my face.

Raven: Are you awake?

Me: Barely.

Raven: Did you stay up all night with Delaney?

Me: No. My brother showed up a little while after you left. Thank God.

Raven: He's a good guy.

Me: Do you know my brother?

It had never occurred to me that Raven might actually know Luke.

Raven: I don't think so. I just meant he was a good guy to take care of his girl.

Me: Oh.

A slight flutter swirled around in my stomach. Would Raven be willing to take care of me like he did Delaney? He barely knew her, yet he stayed with me to help her.

Raven: How many finals do you have?

Me: Four. Two this Friday, one on Tuesday, and one on Thursday of next week.

Raven: Are you ready?

Me: No. I haven't really given school enough attention the last month.

Raven: Me either.

So, I wasn't the only one. Did I have anything to do with his lack of dedication?

Raven: Could I ask for a favor?

Me: Of course.

Raven: I know you have to study, but I really need your help with a paper.

Me: Sounds serious.

Raven: Haha. It is. I could fail.

Me: I guess I better help you.

Raven: I promise you won't regret it.

I bit my lip and sucked in a deep breath. Raven knew exactly how to tease me. I didn't know how much longer I'd be able to resist him, but then again, I didn't want to. I rested against the pillow, eager to see where our conversation was going.

Me: When and where?

Raven: Damn, you're easy.

Me: Crap. I forgot I'm talking to 'The Raven'. Maybe tomorrow.

Raven: Don't make me beg.

Me: Maybe I want you to.

I wanted to call him and continue the conversation, but I figured writing it was easier than saying it. At least, for me. I was new at this and I didn't want to sound like a rambling idiot or mess up our connection.

Raven: I've never had to beg a woman for anything.

Me: There's always a first.

I waited for his next message to appear but my phone rang instead and a picture of Raven and me appeared on the screen. The one Delaney had taken of us last night that I saved in his profile. I guess I'd be continuing this conversation instead of typing it. I cleared my froggy throat and answered the phone, putting on the best sexy voice I had.

"Hey."

"Hey." I could hear him breathing steadily through the phone. Had I worked him up or got him excited? "So, you want me to beg?"

Oh shit!

He didn't have to beg me, but I at least needed to pose a challenge for him. If I agreed, then I'd just be another one of his hoes. That was the last thing I wanted to be to Raven.

"Well, I do have a lot of studying to do," I stated matter of fact. A sigh escaped from his mouth and I knew he was dying to see me. "You know I could call Dr. Philips and ask him if Kyler could help you."

"But I don't want Kyler or anyone else to help me."

"Oh, well, then I guess you'll—"

"No, Lexi, that won't work." His voice wrapped around my name and I loved it. "Because I want you. Only you."

Every happy endorphin released, making my entire body ache in a way that I wasn't used to. I was definitely ready for whatever he had to offer. I was completely lost in his trap and loving every minute of it. "Are you sure?"

"Definitely."

Σ

Chapter 4

Raven and I decided to meet in the student union. I think we both knew that my dorm room would be too tempting, his apartment too dangerous, and the study rooms in my dormitory pointless, especially since a small sofa was in there. We sat in the dining area of Chick-Fil-A, even though it was closed.

"Thanks," I said as he handed me tall cup of coffee. I wasn't much of a coffee drinker, but after last night, I really needed the caffeine to get through the day of non-stop studying.

"You're welcome."

"Are those any good?" I asked, pointing to the silver can of Red Bull he held.

"I guess." He popped the top and took a drink. "They seem to keep me awake and give me a boost of energy." His tongue darted out, licking his lips and circling three times while looking at me.

"Stop." I kicked him under the table.

"What?" He held up his hands in surrender.

"You're staring at me again." I glared at him, wishing I could sit next to him and cuddle up to his chest while I gazed into his hypnotic eyes. "I can't study if you keep looking at me like that."

A sly grin formed on one side of his lips. "And how's that?"

"Um, like... well—"

"The Raven is in the house!" A group of guys trampled in, tossing a football between them.

They exchanged their typical teammate greeting that included fist bumps, pats on the back, and even slamming their chest into each other. There were no low 'T' problems within this group of guys.

"Hey, Lexi, did you have a good time last night?" Josh spun the ball in his hand with a flick of his wrist.

"Yeah." I shrugged. "I guess."

"Your friend Delaney sure had a good time," he snickered.

"Don't remind me." I sunk down in my chair, slightly embarrassed by her behavior. She had made a total ass of herself, dancing on top of the counters and tables with Matt. I was all for having fun, but not at the cost of being sick all night long. When I left my dorm, she was still lying in bed.

"How's Shelby?" Raven sat down in the booth. "She was pretty wiped out last night, too."

Josh shook his head. "Hung over and crying for me to go take care of her."

With a roll of his eyes, Raven said, "These girls, they think they can hang with the big dogs, but they can't."

"Tell me about it." Josh continued tossing the football.

"We'll be outside." One of the other two football players informed Josh and Raven.

Josh nodded. "C'mon, let's go throw a couple of passes."

Raven looked at me and then back at Josh as if he wanted my approval.

"Go ahead. I don't mind." I adjusted the book in front of me. "I'll be here studying."

"Are you sure?"

I nodded. "Yes. Go."

"We'll be on the lawn." He unzipped his backpack and started to gather his books and papers.

"It's okay. You can leave your stuff here."

"Thanks." He smiled at me as he placed the contents in his bag. "I'm just going to play for a while... ya know, get the blood flowing. I'll study better."

"That's fine." Through the windows, I watched as he exited the student union. I turned around in my seat, my eyes following him up the hill to the campus commons area. I considered moving to the other side of the booth so that I could watch him play, but I knew he'd be a permanent distraction. And since I really did want to pass my classes, I fought the temptation by pulling my headphones on and pulling my book close.

Thirty minutes later, my phone chimed. A message from Delaney flashed on the screen.

I swiped the screen and put in my passcode.

Delaney: Where are you?

Me: At the student union studying. Did you get my message about Luke?

Delaney: Yeah, thanks. Sorry about last night. Thanks for taking care of me.

Me: No problem. Is Luke still mad at you?

Delaney: A little.

Me: Hopefully he'll get over it soon.

Delaney: Thankfully, your brother doesn't stay mad very long. Not like Collin.

I stared at the message for a moment. Why did she have to bring him up?

Delaney: Sorry. My bad. I'm still not thinking very clearly. I'll be over there in a minute.

Me: Okay.

I set my phone on the table, trying not to think of the last spat Collin and I had and how long it took him to get over it. And it was over the same thing — alcohol. But I was nothing compared to Delaney. How would Collin have reacted if I had been that drunk? It wouldn't have been pretty, that's for sure.

I turned around for a quick peek. From afar, I saw Raven still playing football. At least with him playing, I was able to study. With him sitting across from me, I couldn't think or focus. At least not on my school work.

I drank the last of my coffee and picked up my phone again. I scrolled through the pictures I had downloaded to my phone from Delaney's Facebook page. When I came to the picture of Raven and me, I examined it carefully.

Was this too good to be true? Did Raven really like me enough to want to be with me, and only me? Even though he'd told me I was upgrade from the Silicone Triplets and Macy, and I knew I was from an intellectual and moral standpoint, it was obvious I couldn't even compare to them when it came to their looks. I was like Ugly Betty and they were prime candidates for American's Next Top Model.

"How many times are you going to look at that picture?"

"What?" I quickly pulled my phone to my chest. "I was just checking to see how I looked... next to him."

Delaney smirked. "Yeah, whatever." She sat her camera on the table and slid into the booth.

"Sorry. I can't help it." I held my phone a few inches from me. "He's so pretty to look at it." I pawed at my phone like I was petting him. The Raven's trap was sickening. Like a fever that wouldn't break, giving you hot and cold chills at the same time. I only hoped the contagious epidemic stopped with me.

"Let me see." She took the phone from my hand. "Mmm. He sure is." She handed the phone to me and slumped across the table. "Oh God. Why did you let me drink so much last night?" she moaned.

I laughed. "Are you asking God or me?"

She peeked through the strands of hair hanging in her face. "Uh, you."

My hand hit the table and it shook. She cringed as if her head had just bounced against a brick wall. "I tried to stop you, but you said you were going to party until the sun came up."

"Punch me next time I say that." She closed her eyes and moaned.

"The sad thing is you didn't even make it to one in the morning. Your head was hanging over the toilet by twelve-thirty."

With a hand held up, she said, "Please don't remind me."

"Sorry. Hey, what's the camera for?" I gathered the strap that was hanging off the table. She'd die if her camera fell on the floor. Her parents had paid nearly a thousand dollars for it and she made sure to take extra care of it.

"I have a project that's due next Tuesday. I'm so screwed."

Tucking my phone in my backpack, I asked, "What's it about?"

She ran her fingers along the pages of my textbook. "I have to put together a life story using the elements of photography. I have a hodgepodge of pictures but I can't seem to pull it together."

"I'm sure it will come to you. You're great with telling stories through pictures."

"I know." Her head lifted. "The problem is I have no idea whose story to tell. I'm sure as hell not telling mine. It's all effed up, if you know what I mean. Besides, it's not like I have some great success to talk about."

"Don't look at me." I brushed my hair away from my face. "Mine's not any better."

"I need like this awesome person. You know, someone who's been through hell and back."

I tapped my finger to my lips. "Why don't you ask Luke? My mom has tons of pictures from childhood."

"I already did." Her shoulders dropped. "He said no. He didn't want anyone getting in his business."

"That sounds like my brother."

"Oh, hell no!" Delaney's eyes widened. "Are those the bitches from the game?"

I whipped around to see the Silicone Triplets hovering around Raven. "What are they doing?" I stood, trying to get a better view.

"You need to get out there. Like now." Delaney put the strap of her camera around her neck and hooked her backpack over her arm.

I wasted no time shoving my stuff into my backpack. Grabbing my and Raven's bag, I headed out the door, following Delaney. The weight of both backpacks pulled me down, but I hauled my heavy ass up the hill as fast I could. Despite the cool air, I was sweating like I just ran a 5K. I really needed to get in shape. Raven gave me the perfect excuse.

He caught my gaze when we were about twenty yards apart. The relieved expression on his face told me he was glad to see me. The Silicone Triplets were laughing and hanging on his body. I was ready to rip them off. I didn't want their toxic hands all over him. Hell, I hadn't even had the chance to do that yet. I'd never been the jealous type, but every muscle in my body tensed and I prayed for restraint.

Several of the guys continued playing football while Raven attempted to ward off his fan-girls that looked like they were ready to pounce and suck his blood. Hunger circled in their eyes and I wondered if they were half-vamp and working for Victoria from *Twilight*. The girl with the long, brown, wavy hair held a marker in her hand and I could tell she was asking him to sign something. Without any shame, she lifted up her shirt, exposing her chest to him. Raven's eyes went wide. Super wide.

"Aw hell, if it isn't the Silicone Triplets." Delaney shouldered past the girls. "Why the pouty faces? Did you get too much Botox in your lips?"

"Shut up." One of the girls snarled at Delaney.

Dumping our bags on the ground, I prepared to take off my shirt. "Hey, can I get my breast signed, too?" I wasn't afraid to show him that I was ready to play with the big girls, even though I had no intention of exposing my breasts in front of them. The embarrassment would have been torture since I was barely a C cup and she had to be a D or larger. Compared to her, I looked like I had on a training bra. I seriously needed to go shopping for some prettier under clothes.

"Hey, now." Raven quickly wrapped his fingers around my hands, preventing me from taking off my shirt. "This isn't a topless show."

The girl huffed and then pulled down her shirt. "She had to ruin it for us."

"Calm down, Abby. If you want, I can sign your T-shirt or backpack."

Great, he knows her.

Before I could get mad, Raven wrapped his arm around me. A tingle of excitement hit my toes. He wasn't afraid to show these bloodsuckers that he preferred me over them. That had to mean something, didn't it?

Feeling the rise of bravery filter through my blood, I cocked a brow and let out a sneering smile. I was The Raven's main catch now. But... for how long? This was definitely new to me since I'd never had to fight for Collin. The rivalry tainted my blood and I kind of liked the challenge. The only question was, would I have to keep fighting for him? Did I want to?

"I guess." She rolled her eyes.

Raven took the marker from her hand and she stuck out her chest, shaking her boobs at him. I wanted to laugh, but refrained. Was she really that desperate for his attention?

With a quick flick of his wrist, Raven signed his name across the left shoulder of her shirt. The other two girls quickly wiggled their way closer toward him and he signed theirs as well.

"Maybe next time you can sign my ass when we're alone." Abby eased the marker from his fingers.

"Um... I don't think so." He took my hand and started to lead us away.

The three girls laced their arms around each other. "Oh, come on, Raven. You didn't fight us last time. In fact, I recall you handling all three of us just fine."

Raven's jaw protruded and his nostril's flared. He sucked in a deep breath. "Whatever."

"Come on, let's go," Abby said. "He wants to play with Suzy Homemaker."

The comment irked me. Maybe because I knew that was what my parents were grooming me for — at least when I was engaged to Collin. I had to remind myself that that description no longer fit me. I might have looked homely and innocent, but deep down, my alter ego was dying to be unleashed.

"Sorry you had to hear that." Raven pivoted me so we faced each other. I watched over his shoulder as the Silicone Triplets trotted off. I hated that Raven had slept with so many girls. It definitely complicated things between us. Was I even good enough for him? Was I that stupid to think he wanted to be with me?

I stared at the ground. "Look, Raven. I'm no match when it comes to those girls. I'm still—" I stalled. I hadn't told him I was a virgin, but I was willing to bet he already figured that out from last night.

"You don't need to compete with them, I already told you that." He kissed me softly on the lips and my anger and frustration evaporated. "You're exactly what I want and need."

Oh God, you're killing me.

Pressing my lips together, I savored his kiss that lingered on me. "And you're all that I want." I breathed out a quick breath and pressed my lips to his. Raven's arms encapsulated me and I grabbed a fistful of his shirt in my hands. Now I was the one ready to pounce on him.

"Raven, come on. Are you going to kiss her all day or are we going to finish playing? I got finals to study for," Josh yelled from across the lawn.

Raven's lips parted from mine and I nipped at his bottom lip. "Do me a favor?" he asked, with a playful grin.

"What's that?" I released my grip from his shirt and smoothed out the wrinkles.

"Save it for later?" He winked at me and I froze. "Okay?"

I nodded. "You're damn right I will."

"Come on, play with us." He looked at me and then motioned to Delaney who sat on the sidewalk, messing with her camera.

"What?" I shook my head. "I can't play with you guys, you'll freaking clobber me. Besides, I have absolutely no coordination when it comes to sports."

"What's up?" Delaney rocked on the back of her heels, showing a little too much excitement.

"Play some football with us." Raven held up his hand and Josh threw it to him. A whoosh sound flew by me and I blinked as Raven caught the ball effortlessly.

Delaney shook her head. "Um, that's okay. After last night, I don't think I could handle running. By the way," she rested her hand on his arm, "thanks for helping Lexi take of me. I shouldn't have drank so much." Her hand lingered on his arm, but I knew she flirted with everyone, so I tried not to think anything of it.

"Don't worry about it." Raven lifted his arm to throw the ball and Delaney's hand dropped. "We've all been there a time or two." Raven looked over his shoulder at me. "Are you ready for some football?"

"Oh, come on Laney. You can't leave me out here with these guys," I pleaded with her, clutching on to both of her arms.

"I'm sorry, Lexi, but I really need to get busy with this life story project or—"

"Oh my God! I have a great idea."

I let go of her arms. "Hey, Raven?"

"Yeah?" He caught the ball again and then held it in his hand.

"Delaney has to tell someone's life story through pictures for a project." Delaney shook her head and her eyes widened. "Do you think you'd want to help her out?" I smiled at him and batted my eyelashes repeatedly.

"What exactly do I have to do?" He turned in her direction.

She crossed her arms over her body in a coy manner. "I just need to take some photos of you, candid ones, which will tell your life story. And maybe get some of your past pictures as well."

"That's easy. The media's always taking pictures of me and my mom has a crap load of them since my childhood."

"Really?" Delaney's blue eyes brightened. "You'd really let me tell your story?"

Raven shrugged. "It's not like it's a big secret or anything. People know more about me then I probably do."

"Thanks, Raven. I appreciate it." She started to walk off and then stopped. "When do you think I can get some of those pictures from your mom? My project is due next Tuesday."

Raven reached into his back pocket and pulled out his phone. "I'll call her now."

Delaney extended a hand. "Oh, I didn't mean for you to ask her right now."

Walking off, Raven ignored her comment. He began speaking with his mom, so I turned away, not wanting to seem nosey.

"Can you believe he's going to let me tell his story?" Delaney whispered in my ear.

"I know. But you better be on your best behavior." I eyed her.

"What?" Her head jolted back. "That's your guy, not mine. Besides, I just plan on hanging out with you two and taking some pics, if that's okay?"

Rave stepped between us. "She said yes, but on one condition."

"What's that?" I asked.

Raven smiled at me. "We come over tonight for dinner."

I tried to conceal the smile, but it was useless. "Great."

"But first, I want to teach you how to catch and throw a ball." Raven reached over and gathered me in his arms.

"What? No," I protested as he lifted me off the ground. My arms flailed about, trying to break free from his grip.

He pitched me over his shoulder and carried me toward the center of the commons area. "Raven! Put me down!"

"Josh. Toss us the ball. I want to show her how to catch," he yelled as he placed me on my feet.

"Raven, I'm telling you... I can't catch a ball," I begged but his smile only deepened.

I looked around for Delaney, finding her walking toward us, taking pictures. I held my arm out, desperate for her to help me. She raised her head from behind the camera and shot me a thumbs up.

Raven laced his hand around my arm and drew it in. His big, strong arms surrounded me and his face rested against mine. "Bend your knees slightly and get ready to catch the ball when Josh throws it to us." His intoxicating scent made it difficult to concentrate. I sucked in a deep breath, trying to clear my airway.

About thirty yards away, Josh prepared to throw the ball. "Go easy," Raven reminded him.

Josh extended his arm back and released the ball. In slow motion, the brown leather spun in the air directly toward me. Raven held on to my hands, drawing my arms in as the ball flew straight toward me. In the blink of an eye, the ball hit me square in the chest. I coughed as it took the little air I had left in my lungs. I looked down to see to the ball, clutched between my hands.

"I did it!" I held the ball up in the air for everyone to see. "I caught the ball." A few passers-by had stopped to watch the guys play and clapped when I bragged about my victory.

Raven straightened. "See, you can do it." He patted me on the back and my body lunged forward. "Sorry."

I pulled my hair back into a ponytail. "Remember, I'm not one of the boys." I raised the sleeves of my fleece shirt, ready to try again.

"Alright, now I want you to throw the ball to Josh."

Over the next thirty or so minutes, Raven showed me some of the basics of football. There was something about him that made me want to try my very best. He didn't treat me like I was an idiotic girl that had no clue when it came to sports or a loser without coordination, but rather someone who had never been shown or taught how to catch or throw a ball. Instead of making fun of me or tearing me down, he built me up. Just like I did when I taught him how to become a better writer.

With every throw and catch, I continued to gain more confidence. By the end, I was running alongside him, trying to catch a ball that Josh had thrown.

"Come on, Lexi! Reach for it!" Raven yelled as I held my hands up high above my head.

With one quick movement, Raven jumped behind me and caught the ball with one hand, tackling me in the process. We tumbled to the ground. The cold ground seeped through the back of my clothes while the front of me felt like an oven simmering on high.

My lungs heaved for air as Raven lay partially on top of me. "Are you trying to kill me?"

"No, just having fun with you." He propped himself up on his forearms, allowing me to take a breath. "I told you that I wanted to have fun with you, remember?" His brows raised and my heart fluttered.

If this was having fun, then I wanted more of it.

"Yeah, I remember." I stared deep into his eyes.

"So, do you want to have some wild, wild fun with me?"

"More than you'll ever know."

"Good, because I'm just getting started on that list of yours."

"But I haven't even made it." My hands rose to his face and I drew my lips closer to his.

"That's okay, we'll make it together." His warm breath spread across my face and my eyes struggled to stay open.

"That sounds like a great idea. I guess I can check this off."

"A game of football?" He stalled a few inches over my lips.

I shrugged. "Not just a football game, but a football game with The Raven."

He lips spread into a full grin. "I'll play with you anytime, Lexi."

I started laughing. "I'm going to be so sore tomorrow, I won't be able to walk."

Raven snickered. "Damn, baby. And I haven't done half of the stuff I'm dying to do to you."

A whimper escaped my throat. He was making me lose my heart and mind all at the same time. He was driving me insane and quickly becoming part of my every thought. I was pretty sure I was going to fail all of my classes. His mouth met mine and my eyes fluttered to a close. I heard Delaney snap a picture of us and I knew I was right where I wanted to be, in *The Raven's trap.*

Σ

Chapter 5

I grabbed my purse and then stuck my head in the doorway to Delaney's room. "Raven is downstairs. Are you ready?"

She slipped on her shoes. "Yep, let's go." Hooking her backpack over her shoulder, she followed me out the door. I was a little excited to meet Raven's mom and brothers. I couldn't help but wonder what he had told them about me, if anything at all.

I locked the door behind us. "Hey, did you tell Luke where you were going?"

"No." She adjusted her backpack. "I haven't talked with him since earlier. He was studying. Why?"

"I was just wondering if he knew anything about me and Raven."

She gave me one of her looks, but I didn't elaborate. "I haven't mentioned anything to him. But if he saw the pics of me with Matt on Facebook, then I'm sure he saw you two together."

"Hmm, I didn't think about that." Had Luke saw them but just avoided the situation since he didn't want to get in the middle of my recent split with Collin? "He didn't ask me or comment that he saw them when we talked earlier this morning."

"Are you afraid he'll tell Collin?"

The doors to the elevator opened and we stepped in. Resting my head against the wall, I sighed. "I don't know." I looked at her and she raised a brow. "I just don't want Collin to find out... I mean, I'm sure he will eventually."

"What if he already knows?"

My head jolted. "Do you know something I don't?"

"No." She raised her hands in surrender. "I swear I don't."

The elevator opened and we exited. "You'd tell me if you did, right?"

"I swear. I..." she hesitated for a moment before continuing. "I've only seen him a few times since you broke up with him."

I blocked the door leading outside as I waited for her to finish. "And?"

"He just seemed kind of sad, that's all."

"Oh." A little piece of my heart stirred. I hated not knowing how he truly felt, if the end of our relationship had a significant bearing on him or if he was glad I had called things off. But I refused to call him. If he couldn't speak up when he had the chance, then it was clear to me that he didn't love me enough to get married. If he did, he would have already called me by now.

I sighed heavily and pushed the door open. Leaving him was for the best. At least, I hoped it was the right decision.

We walked down the steps to Raven's car and got in.

"I love your Challenger," Delaney said as she got in the back.

"Thanks." Raven smiled at me as I sat in the front seat and goose bumps formed from my head to my toes. I wondered how he afforded such a nice car, but I refrained from asking. When he shared some of his dreams with me at the stadium suite, he insinuated that his mother struggled financially. My curiosity peeked, but I withheld my questions.

Raven revved the engine and raced down the narrow drive and onto the main street. A chill set in as the sun disappeared behind the skyline and I shivered. Winter was quickly approaching, but in Texas it could be icing one day and sunny and warm the next.

"Cold?"

"Yeah, a little."

Raven turned up the heat, but instead of returning his hand to the steering wheel, he reached for mine. I interlaced my fingers with his and the warmth from his palm thawed mine instantly. It felt good to feel his affection for me and I relished every tender moment of it.

"Hey, did your mom want us to bring anything?" I asked as we passed a grocery store.

Raven shrugged. "I don't know. I didn't think to ask."

"We should probably bring a dessert or something." I pointed behind me, indicating for him to turn the car around.

"Yeah, I think we should." Delaney leaned between the two front seats.

"Okay." Raven made a U-turn at the next light and pulled into the parking lot.

I opened the door and Delaney and I got out of the car. "We'll be right back."

"I got this." Delaney urged me to get back in the car.

"Are you sure?" I gave her a confused look.

"Yeah." She winked, but I wasn't sure what she was trying to tell me. "Is apple pie and vanilla ice cream okay?"

"I guess." I turned to Raven as I got back in the car.

"Yeah, that's fine." Raven reached in his pocket. "Here's a twenty." He waved a crisp bill in front of me. I took the money and handed it to her.

"That's okay. I'm the one who asked for this favor, I can at least bring something."

"Okay," Raven responded and I handed him back the bill.

I closed the door. "Thanks for agreeing to help Delaney."

He flipped through the radio and I could tell he was avoiding my comment. The muscles in hand tensed and his jaw jutted out.

"Raven."

"Huh?"

"You don't have to do this, you know." I placed my hand on his arm. "She'll understand."

He stopped flipping stations and *Boom Clap* started playing over the radio. He turned toward me and I shifted closer to him. His jaw relaxed and he let out a full breath. "I'm not going to lie to you, this project of hers will stir up some past hurts."

"I'm sorry. I shouldn't have offered for you to help her. It really wasn't my place." Even though I knew bits and pieces about him, I realized that his story wasn't a lighthearted one. He had some serious baggage and I felt guilty for placing him in that position.

He looked down and picked at the leather that wrapped around the gearshift. "But that's just it. I do want to do this. I've been holding it all in, maybe this will help me." He glanced at me and I saw the hurt embedded deep in his eyes. "Like bring some closure or serve as therapy."

"I'm definitely no therapist," I cupped his face with my hand, "but like I told you, I'm here for you."

"I don't know what it is, but when I'm with you, I feel like I can conquer the world, like I can defeat any obstacle that I encounter. You've been more than a tutor to me, you know that?"

I inclined my head. "Damn, Raven, you make me sound like I'm your heroine or something."

"That's because you are. Being around you does something to me. I want to be good... do everything right." In a gentle motion, he pulled my hand away and raised it to his lips, giving me a tender kiss. His eyes meet mine and for a moment, we simply stared at each other.

"My world is so much better with you in it, Lexi."

I took in several deep breaths, trying to calm my racing heart. Raven definitely knew how to make me feel like I was the queen of his trap. I didn't mind because it was a kingdom I wanted to be a part of. "When I'm with you, I feel so safe. I know there's nothing in this world that I can't face." I covered my mouth, hiding a snicker. "I do have to admit something, though."

"What's that?"

"When I'm around you, I want to be bad." I traced a finger down his chest, not afraid to show him how I really felt. "A very bad and crazy girl."

His eyes drilled in to me and in an instant, Raven captured my lips with his. Our breathing became rapid as our kiss intensified. It was as though we couldn't get enough of each other. His sex appeal was more than I could handle and I was ready to tell him to take me right there. My hands spread across his chest and I squeezed his shoulders tightly. Without notice, his hands flew to my waist and he pulled me closer to him. I started to cross over the console when I remembered Delaney was in the store. I pulled back slowly, letting out a slight moan.

"Sorry." I licked my lips, savoring his sinful taste.

He didn't move, keeping his position like he was ready to take me at my command. "Remember what I told you. You don't ever have to apologize to me for anything you do."

I straightened my shirt, trying to regain my composure. "You also said that you wouldn't do anything unless I asked you to. Is that still true?"

"Yes," he whispered. "Because when it comes to you, Lexi, I don't want to screw things up. The last thing I want you to think is that you're just another girl to me, because you're not." His eyes appraised me with finite detail. "You're so much more."

I felt the boom of my heart as he dressed me up with his luring words. Raven knew how to deliver the reassurance I needed to hear and within them, I sensed his sincerity. "Good, because I want to be so much more."

"So, you're not keeping count of why you shouldn't be with me?"

I had to stop and think for a moment. "Oh, you mean the fifteen reasons I gathered?"

"Yes. Are you still keeping count?"

I shook my head. "No. I'm actually thinking of all the reasons I should be with you."

He smiled. "I was hoping you were going to say that because all I know is that together we will stand tall, but apart we will fall."

"Oh my God." I snickered. "Is that another one of those sayings you've heard?"

"I don't know. Maybe." He nuzzled my ear and my body hummed in delight. "I just like the way it sounds."

Just as he was about to kiss me again, Delaney knocked on the window.

I opened the door and leaned forward so she could crawl in the back.

"Damn, were y'all making out or what? The windows are all fogged up and it's hot as hell in here," Delaney huffed.

My cheeks flushed with heat, but I didn't say a word.

"Sorry," Raven commented before cracking the window and turning the defrost on.

We passed several neighborhoods before slowing to a small wooden frame house. A single car driveway led to the house and Raven parked in the street. Cream-colored paint matched the reddish brick along with the black shutters and the front door. "It's not much, but my mom makes the best of it."

"I think it's charming." I opened the door and got out of the car.

Delaney handed me the bag with the pie and ice cream. I moved the seat forward and she crawled out of the back. "Oh, it is cute. I like it." She pulled up her jeans and huffed as though it was a chore to wiggle her way out of the vehicle.

"Thanks." Raven took the dessert from my hands and led us to the door. He knocked and opened the door. "We're here."

The smell of home cooked food wafted through the air and my stomach growled. We entered the living room consumed by a large, overstuffed, black leather sectional and a huge flat screen TV. Trophies were stacked from the floor to the ceiling on bookcases, along with pictures of Raven and his brothers, leaving no wall bare. The accomplishments between him and his brothers were shown with great pride.

Raven's two brothers were sitting on the couch, playing a video game. The older one gave a slight nod to us while the younger jumped at the sight of Raven.

"Raven! You're home." The young kid high-fived Raven while revealing a mouth full of braces and rubber bands. "Great game! You kicked their butts."

"Thanks, Ashton." Raven rubbed his head. "I'd like you to meet some of my friends. This is Lexi and Delaney."

"Nice to meet you, Ashton," I said, shaking his hand.

"You kind of resemble your brother." Delaney smiled at him and waved.

"Hey, Trey, put the game on pause for a minute," Raven told his other brother.

Out of the corner of my eye, I saw a tall, slender woman with bleach blonde hair and fair skin come around the corner. She wiped her hands on a dishtowel and then swung it over her shoulder. "Hi. I'm Trish Williams, Raven's mom." She had a strong Louisiana accent that fit her perfectly.

"It's a pleasure to meet you, Ms. Williams." I shook her hand and immediately noticed the resemblance between her and Raven from the shape of their eyes to their big smile. She appeared to be in her forties, but the wrinkles around her eyes showed the stress she'd endured through the years.

"Please, call me Trish."

"Thanks for inviting us to dinner, Trish. A home cooked meal is always nice." Delaney gave her a slight hug as if she knew her. I tossed the idea out because I knew that was just how Delaney was — everyone she met was automatically her friend.

"Sure. I'm glad you guys could break away from studying." She leaned toward Raven and he wrapped an arm around her, giving her a hug. "How was Thanksgiving? Your granny sure missed you."

"Okay. Josh's family made a great dinner." He leaned forward and kissed on her on the forehead. "But not as good as yours."

"I brought some leftovers home so you can take a plate back to your apartment." She squeezed him tighter. "I'm so proud of you. You played like a champ. We all watched the game. Your aunts and uncles, too." She looked over her shoulder. "Trey, where are your manners?"

"Huh?" Trey looked up for a quick second before placing the game on hold.

"Get over here now," she scolded.

Trey rose from the couch and slowly made his way toward us. "Hey, what's up?" he mumbled, nodding slightly

"Hi, I'm Lexi." I shook his limp hand. "And this is my friend, Delaney."

"How's it going?" She shook his hand and gave him a big smile.

A timid smile formed across his face but he didn't say anything. He casually walked back to the couch and plopped down, grabbing the remote for his game. Like Raven, I could tell there was more to his story.

"We brought dessert. Apple pie and ice cream." Delaney pointed at the bag in Raven's hand.

"Thank you." Raven handed his mom the sack. "You girls want to help me in the kitchen?"

"Sure." Delaney and I followed her into the kitchen.

"I'll be playing a game with my brothers." Raven touched the tips of my fingers while winking at me.

"Okay." I held on to him, keeping a steady gaze as I walked toward the kitchen until the space separated us. I was pathetic. And no matter how hard I tried to fight the feeling, I couldn't. He was like a drug that I wanted more of. Being around Raven was exhilarating and I wanted to spend every passing minute with him.

Black appliances and bright red decorations gave life to the slightly outdated kitchen. It was apparent that Raven's mom took pride in her small home, giving it a warm, homely touch with each item she had hung.

"If you girls would set the table, that would be a big help." She pointed to one of the cabinets.

"Of course." I opened the cabinet, removed a stack of crimson ceramic plates, and handed them to Delaney. We continued removing the dishes, glasses, and eating utensils from the cabinets and drawers and then worked on setting the table in the kitchen.

"Raven tells me you've been helping him with his writing." Trish glanced at me as she placed rolls on a tray.

"Yes, that's right. I work in the writing lab and Raven was assigned to me. I'm an English major studying to be a teacher, so I enjoy tutoring people." I stopped, momentarily thinking about what I had just told her. Aside from the slight lie about still working in the writing lab, I contemplated if I really wanted to be a teacher. Growing up, I always liked helping people and teaching others came naturally. As I recalled that Collin and my parents planned for me to homeschool our children, I began to have second thoughts about being a teacher.

"That's great. No wonder he's doing so well." She smiled at me.

"He's been working really hard." I wanted to reassure her that I wasn't writing his papers for him.

"Thank you for helping. Writing has never been a favorite subject for Raven." She tossed the empty plastic wrapper in the trash. "So, you two are roommates?"

"Yes." Delaney filled each glass with ice and then handed them to me to pour the tea. "We've been rooming together since last year."

"How nice. Are you studying to be journalist or something?" Trish removed a roast from the oven and placed it on top of the stove. Then, she placed the tray of rolls on the rack and closed the oven door.

"No, I'm actually working toward being a professional photographer." Delaney closed the freezer door.

Looking over her shoulder, Trish replied, "Okay, that make sense. Why you needed old pictures of Raven, that is."

"I really appreciate it. I had no idea who to base my project on until he agreed," Delaney said. "Do you mind if I take candid pictures of everyone today?" She picked up her camera case sitting on the hutch.

"No, not at all." Trish gave a slight pose and I could immediately tell that she was fun to be around. Unlike my mom.

"You didn't have to make us dinner, but we appreciate it." I leaned against a chair, unsure of what to do next.

Trish waved, holding a carving fork in one hand a knife in the other. "It was no trouble. These boys were complaining that they didn't want any more turkey leftovers. Besides, I really wanted Raven to eat a nice, home cooked meal since he didn't get to go to New Orleans with us for Thanksgiving."

"It's very thoughtful of you," Delaney added.

"To be honest, Raven's never brought home any girls from college. So when he told me he had a friend that wanted to tell his life story and needed pictures, I figured it was the least I could do. Then when he said he wanted me to meet the girl that had helped him improve his writing, I knew I had to make a nice meal."

My stomached fluttered at the revelation that Raven had at least told his mom something about me. "Thanks, Trish."

"Do you need help with anything else?" Delaney glanced around the kitchen.

"The rolls will be ready in a few minutes. Can you tell the boys to wash up so we can eat?" She smiled and then returned to her task of cutting the roast.

"Sure, no problem." Delaney and I walked to the living room where Raven and his brother's stared intently at the TV screen, ranting and cheering as they played Madden NFL, one of my brother's favorite video games.

"Time to eat," I announced. They nodded but kept playing. I shot Delaney a questioning look.

Delaney placed her hands on her hips. "Your mom said to go wash your hands. Now." They all turned to look at her before scurrying to place the game on pause.

"Why do they jump when you tell them to do something and do nothing when I asked?" I smirked.

Raven leaned forward and kissed me on the forehead. "You just need to add a little oomph to the request. That's all."

I rolled my eyes and made a mental note to mimic her if the opportunity presented itself again.

We sat around the small kitchen table, elbow to elbow, enjoying the savory pot roast, mashed potatoes, and corn that Trish cooked for us. Trey eventually warmed up and told us how proud he was of Raven and how he hoped to follow his brother's path and play for a major university. Ashton treated us as if we were his sisters, joking with us constantly. His laugh was contagious. Raven beamed with pride. I knew he cared for his brothers and truly wanted the best for them.

"Trey, Ashton, do me a favor and clear the table while I get the pictures," Trish instructed her younger sons to help.

"Can I help with anything?" I started to stand.

Trish motioned for us to stay seated. "No, you girls have done enough. The boys can wash the dishes."

"Who wants dessert?" Raven looked at each of us.

"I'll take a slice with ice cream," I told him.

"Do you want your pie hot?" Raven cocked a brow and his words teased me in all the right places.

I cleared my throat, but before I could respond, Delaney spoke up. "Of course she does. Who wouldn't? And make mine hot, too."

"You've got it." Raven turned around and walked toward the refrigerator. His hips swayed to the left and then to right, and I swore I saw his butt cheeks tense and then release under his jeans.

Holy crap! Why is he teasing me in front of everyone?

I inhaled a silent breath, trying to calm the tension building quickly as Delaney nudged me under the table. I didn't know how much longer I could handle his flirting. Every part of me screamed his name and he hadn't even touched me. The guy was blessed with sex appeal and I was ready to take our relationship to the next level. Whatever that was.

Raven returned with our apple pie alamode, followed by his mom with several picture storage boxes covered in different colors.

"Can I help you, Mom?" Raven asked before he sat.

"Nope, I've got it." Trish made a few more trips before placing the last box on the table. She blew her bangs away from her face and sat in front of us. "Do you want to see pictures of Raven from birth until now?" She moved around the boxes, reading a label on each of them.

"Yes, please. Pictures from pivotal moments in his life would be awesome." Delaney moved closer, eager to see them. I did the same.

Trish thumbed through several pictures from one box and then laid them on the table. "Here are a few from when he was born."

"Wow, you were a big baby." Delaney picked up the picture and showed me.

"How much did you weigh?" I eased the photo from her hand.

Raven turned toward his mom. "Like ten pounds, right?"

She nodded. "He was nine pounds, seven ounces, and twenty-three inches long." Her voice cracked and tears formed in her eyes. "Born at five fifty-five in the morning on September twenty-ninth."

Before Raven picked us up, I asked him if he was okay with Delaney telling his life story. He reassured me he was and I suggested that we tell Delaney that he didn't know who his father was. Then maybe he could let his mom know that he disclosed how he was conceived, just to make it easier on everyone. He agreed and said that he'd tell his mom. Before we left, I told Delaney that vital piece of information. It wasn't easy repeating it and she felt horrible for him.

"Don't cry, Mom. It's okay." Raven wrapped an arm around Trish. She cradled his face and kissed him on the cheek. Delaney snapped a pic. It was touching to see how close they were after everything they had endured over the years. No one should have to endure such pain and tragedy.

"Do you mind if I borrow this?" Delaney pointed to the picture in my hand.

"That's fine." Trish wiped her eyes and Raven released his arm from her. She continued searching through the boxes, pulling out several pictures in the process. She showed us several shots of Raven playing peewee and little league football, followed by middle school and then high school. She had so many photos of him winning district and state championships.

It was obvious as to why he was a strong contender for a pro football contract.

Like a proud mom, she took us to the living room and showed us all the trophies he'd won over the years. Raven tried not to boast about his winnings, but eagerly told us about each of them. Happiness flickered within his eyes and it was obvious how much he enjoyed playing football. He had worked hard his entire life and I really hoped he landed with a good team. He truly deserved it.

"It hasn't been easy. Raven's had some tough times, but he's pulled through every time." Trish patted her son on the back while giving him a meek smile. "Isn't that right?" I wasn't expecting Raven's mom to be supportive or loving toward him, but she showed just the opposite.

Raven shuffled his feet and crossed his arms. "Yeah." He stared at the floor and for the first time, I saw the regret and condemnation etched deep in his face. Raven might have pulled through the tough times, but he hadn't learned how to forgive himself.

Delaney took a couple of shots of the trophies before we returned to the kitchen.

"Who's this with your boys?" Delaney pointed to a tall, dark man leaning against a car with the boys standing in front of him.

Trish took the picture from Delaney. "Oh, that's Trey's dad." She shook her head and a twisted expression formed on her face. "You don't want that picture. Believe me. He's a no good, lazy, lying, cheating piece of shit."

"Mom." Raven motioned with his head toward the living room where Trey and Ashton were.

"What? Trey knows it. He can't stand him either." Trish didn't hold back when revealing her family issues to us. "I'm sorry, girls. We're not the Cleavers and I won't pretend to be."

"It's okay. My family's not perfect either. Even though they pretend to be." I tried to ease the thick tension in the room.

"No family is perfect." Delaney shuffled through a couple of photos scattered on the table and made a stack. "My parents were killed when I was little and I was put up for adoption. I didn't have the best childhood, but I'm trying to make the most of my life now. Which isn't much." She took a deep breath and her eyes watered. Delaney never talked much about her past and she still had quite a few demons she was battling. She blinked rapidly, trying to keep the tears at bay.

Trish wiped her eyes. It seemed that our confessions were helping her. "My parents try to rule my life," I added quickly, trying to take the pressure off Delaney. "I was homeschooled and sheltered from almost everything. I always did everything they asked of me." I sucked in a quick breath. "It wasn't until recently that I decided I needed to live my life for me. I was tired of living to please them," I openly admitted.

"See? We don't come from picture perfect families either. And we aren't here to judge." Delaney smiled at Trish.

"Thanks. I appreciate that...it's just been tough. Not only for Raven, but all of us. Especially after Ashton's dad died... I haven't got back on track with life." She sniffed and wiped her eyes again, smearing mascara in the process. "You know what I mean?"

My heart ached for her. Raven had never mentioned anything about his stepdad dying. "I'm so sorry for your loss. How long ago did he pass?"

"Two years ago. He had an accident at work." She sighed. "I'm still fighting with those bastards. They claimed he didn't have an insurance policy and worker's comp barely covered the medical bills and his funeral."

"Oh my God. I'm so sorry." Delaney's voice shook and I could tell she was on the verge of tears again.

I swallowed hard, trying to fight back my own tears. "If there is anything we can do for you, please let us know."

Trish grabbed a napkin from the table and blew her nose. "Thank you, girls. I appreciate that." Turning toward me, she said, "Just keep an eye on this one. He's trying hard to get his shit together." She gave him a disapproving look and Raven's eyes darted to the floor once again. "I know you're too good for him, but he probably needs that." She pointed a finger at Raven. "And you better treat her right, not like all those other skanks. You hear me?"

Raven nodded but didn't make eye contact. "Yes, ma'am." The shame his mother placed on him was more than enough. I now understood what he meant when he said he wanted be good and make things right in his life. I eased back in my chair, thinking about everything his mom had said. What exactly had Raven told her about us? She made it seem like we were together or dating. If we were, that was news to me.

Σ

Chapter 6

Raven remained somewhat silent on the way back to the dorm. I figured it was what his mom had said. We hadn't discussed where we were headed or what we wanted from our relationship. Probably because it was too soon. Instead of asking, I kept to myself and allowed him to work out his own demons.

"I'll give you a call later." Raven leaned forward and kissed me on the cheek. My eyes closed and for a moment, I swore it was Collin kissing me. Did he not want to kiss me on the lips anymore? Were we headed down that same road? I just left an empty and emotionless guy; the last thing I wanted was another one.

"Okay. I'll be studying." I opened the door and grabbed my purse, keeping my eyes away from him. If I looked at him, I wasn't sure what I'd do — jump him or cry and beg him to kiss me.

"Thanks again, Raven," Delaney said. "I'm going to scan these photos and then I'll give them back to you so you can return them to your mom."

"Yeah, no problem." He casually looked over his shoulder, acknowledging Delaney.

We got out of the car and I closed the door. He drove off slowly and something told me that things between us were not the same.

"Wow. That's one messed up story." Delaney opened the door to the building and I trudged in behind her.

"Yeah," I muttered.

"After hearing all of that, I need to read one of your romance books." She removed the strap of her camera from her neck. "Then again, I'm sure this project will have a happy ending." She gave me a slight nudge.

"Yeah, I guess."

"What's wrong?" she asked as I hit the button for the elevator.

"I don't know. He's acting kind of distant."

"Distant?"

"Yeah." I stepped into the elevator and Delaney followed behind me. "Didn't you notice he didn't even bother to kiss me on the lips?"

"Now that you mention it, yes. Maybe the pictures just brought back a lot of bad memories." Delaney waved a manila folder that encased pieces of Raven's life. The good and bad.

Delaney had a point. "You know, I didn't think of that." I leaned against the wall for support and sighed. As the elevator rose, the lightness in my stomach pressed hard against my diaphragm, causing my breaths to become shallower. "But I think it was what his mom said."

"About you being too good for him?"

I nodded.

"Maybe so, but quit worrying and give the guy a break." The elevator doors opened and she laced her arm through mine. "I know he's crazy about you."

"You really think so?" I leaned my head against hers.

"I've got the pictures to prove it." She held up her camera and smiled.

She might have seen something between us, but I recognized the negative vibe in the car and what lurked in the depths of his eyes. Something had definitely changed.

My intuition proved to be right. The entire week passed and I had only heard from Raven a few times, one of them being a request to review his term paper. When I had finished my edits, I asked if he wanted to meet in person to talk about them, but he said he'd let me know if he had questions. Unfortunately, he never asked to see me.

I tried to remind myself that we were friends who happened to share a few moments of fun, but the kisses he left on me told my body something else. My heart had even felt it. But other than telling me he wanted to have fun with me, Raven hadn't made me any promises. So why was I missing him so much?

"I'm headed to the library to meet Luke." Delaney popped her head in my room.

I glanced up from my laptop. "Okay."

"Is everything okay?" Delaney resituated her backpack.

"Yeah, I guess." I reminded the ache coming from the center of my chest to stop bothering me and just let me be.

"You still haven't heard from Raven?"

I pretended to be typing even though none of the letters formed any words. Raven was totally distracting my mind. How could a guy have that effect on me? Especially when we had only kissed. "No, but it's probably because he's studying for exams," I said, using first excuse that popped up my mind.

"Exactly. So stop obsessing over it. But if you need an excuse to call him, I think I can help you." She placed a manila folder on my desk.

"What's that?"

"The pictures I borrowed from his mom." She winked and my fingers stopped. "Tell him I put the pics on a CD as well. It's in there."

Picking up the folder, I smiled. "Okay, I will."

"See you later." Her voice lilted as she spun on her heels and left our suite.

Opening the folder, I removed a few pictures. I shuffled through them and stopped on a picture of Raven kneeling in the center of a football field. In one hand, he held his helmet, and in the other, a football. His face looked a few years younger and his body leaner but still muscular. He had that same charming smile and that enticing sparkle in his eyes that woke every nerve ending in my body.

Damn I miss those eyes on me.

Not caring if I seemed like the desperate girl, because in all honesty, I probably was, I picked up my phone and typed out a message.

Me: Are you busy?

I stared at the screen for a while, waiting for him to text me. Checking the time, I saw that it was only eight-thirty. He couldn't be asleep. I had a final the next day, but I didn't care because I wanted to see him.

Thirty minutes later, he replied.

Raven: Yeah, studying. What's up?

What's up? Seriously? What happened to all the flirting and dying to see me? His flirtatious swagger had completely evaporated into the abyss.

Me: I've got the pictures Delaney borrowed from your mom. She even scanned them on a CD.

I added that extra tidbit of information, hoping that would urge him to want to meet me.

Raven: Okay. I can get them from you later.

Crap! So much for that idea.

Me: No problem.

The screen remained blank and I waited to see if he would tell me anything else. More time passed and nothing. After checking my stupid phone every few minutes for over an hour, I finally turned it over and returned my focus to the paper I was trying to write. It took me four hours to type two pages. I was screwed. I'd never finish the paper in time.

I heard the door unlock and Delaney shuffle into the suite. A loud thump sounded, telling me she had dumped her backpack in the doorway of her room.

"Are you still up?" She popped the top on a can of Coke Zero, her favorite, and took a sip.

I rubbed my eyes and then blinked a few times. "Yeah, I can't seem to finish this paper."

"Let me guess," she sat on the edge of my bed, "thinking about Raven?"

Swiveling around in my chair, I sighed. "Unfortunately, yes."

She took a few more sips. "Did you tell him you had his pictures?"

"Yep. He said he'd get them later."

A frown formed across her face and her eyes narrowed. Then, like a light turning on, her eyes widened and smile crept over her face. "I've got a great idea." She whipped out her phone and started texting a message.

"Who are you texting?" I eyed her suspiciously.

"Raven."

In one quick leap, I lunged for her phone. "No. Don't."

"Don't worry." She pulled her hand out of my reach and held the can of soda up with the other, as if it were some type of defense tool. "This isn't about you."

I tried to grab her phone one more time, but she crawled backward onto my bed. "Please don't," I pleaded, but she ignored me.

"But I have the perfect idea." She shot me an evil grin and then tucked her phone in her back pocket. "I need a few more pictures of Raven before next Tuesday. If he agrees, you can come with me."

It might have been a good strategy to see him, but the last thing I wanted was to force him to see me. If he wanted to be with me, he would tell me. His text proved that he didn't. It was simple. Raven was no longer interested in me and I wasn't completely sure why. That part sucked the most. My shoulders slumped and I plopped down beside her on my bed. "Delaney, if you have to trick him to see me, then forget it."

"Maybe he just needs a little nudge." A few minutes later, a sound came from Delaney's phone.

"That's not your text message tone." I looked over her shoulder. "Unless you changed it."

"It's not. It's my Facebook messenger." She hit the app on her phone.

"Why are you messaging Raven through Facebook?"

She arched a brow and it was like I was having one of my mom's blonde moments. "Because I don't have his phone number."

"Well, I can give it—"

"That's okay. I don't need it." Her eyes focused on the screen. "He says he'll meet me tomorrow at the stadium at noon."

"What? Let me see that." I yanked the phone from her hand, scanning the messages.

Delaney: Hey, Raven, I really need a few more shots of you to finish my project. Can I take some of you in your football uniform at the stadium?

Raven: Sure. How about noon tomorrow?

"I don't care." I handed the phone back to her. "You can go take pictures of him. I'm not coming."

"Yeah, that's what you said last time." Her disdaining stare irked me. Probably because I knew it was what I wanted to do. I watched her prance out of my room and shut the door behind her. Why was she always right?

After Delaney left my room, I got the sudden urge to write the best damn paper ever. The words flowed from my brain and poured onto the paper until I finished at three-thirty in the morning. Supporting statements and arguments were like words to songs, each of them deep and meaningful beyond my understanding. I reasoned with myself that I didn't want any excuse to not go with Delaney tomorrow. Funny how some things will motivate you.

"Are you coming?" Delaney stood in my doorway, checking the functions on her camera.

I stuffed one of my books in my backpack for my final test I had the following Tuesday, even though I knew it was pointless because I'd be staring at Raven the entire photo shoot. I needed a practical decoy and a book was perfect.

"I wouldn't miss it." I swung my backpack over my shoulder.

She smiled. "Good."

I followed her out the door. "Did he mention anything about me to you?"

"No," she said in a low tone. "But I also didn't mention anything either, so quit reading into things."

I held on to the straps of my backpack as reality continued to remind me that Raven and I were only a dream.

A fantasy.

As much as I wanted to be in his league of hot bitches, I wasn't. I may have been smarter and more talented than most of them, but not when it came to doing what he wanted most — sex. It was something I had only read about in romance books and dreamed about with him. I had to be kidding myself to think he'd want to be with me.

"He has no idea I'm coming with you." I blew out a stressed breath. "Does he?"

Recalling what he said, I reminded myself I could change. I would change. If that's what it took to be with him, I'd do it.

After all, I didn't like the old Lexi Thompson. I needed to release the ego dying to come out.

"Relax. I'm sure he'll be glad to see you." We crossed the street and headed toward the stadium. The wind had a chilly breeze, but the sun kept it tolerable, at least for a southern girl.

"So, how are things between you and Luke?" I was eager to take the focus off me.

Delaney's face scrunched in confusion. "Oh, I don't know. One minute we're okay and the next he's all pissy with me. I have no idea what the hell he wants."

"Why are guys so wishy-washy?" I sighed and then stopped at the guard booth outside of the stadium. I peeked through the window, but the guard that was there last time was nowhere to be seen. I shrugged. "I guess we can enter."

We walked down the hill until we came to the main gate. I pulled on it, but it didn't open.

"Great." Delaney pulled her phone from her backpack and sent Raven a text through Facebook.

Lexi: I'm here at the front gate but can't get in.

It took a few minutes before he responded. I glanced over her shoulder as we read the message.

Raven: I'll send someone to let you on the field.

"Okay, we have to wait."

I slid my backpack off my shoulder and sat on a ledge. Delaney dropped her phone in her bag and then sat next to me.

"How did you two get in last time you were here?"

Damn, did she have to bring that up?

As much as I didn't want to recall my last time with Raven, it definitely took my heart to a place that made me feel all warm and fuzzy inside. It was a good time, a memorable one that I'd never forget.

"We snuck in through a side gate." I pointed to my right.

"Seriously?" Delaney followed my hand. "And you didn't get caught?"

"Nope." I inhaled deeply as I battled with the side of my brain telling me to get up and leave. That I was stupid for coming here with her. That I had no business trying to capture Raven's attention.

"Maybe they let y'all in because of Raven." Delaney got up and stepped up to the gate, pressing her head against the thick, black bars.

"No, I don't think so. We pretty much went in without authorization. Aside from the guard knowing, we had to be careful that we didn't get caught."

"I guess you got lucky."

I kicked a few small pebbles, making them fly across the sidewalk. "I guess so." The question was, had my luck run out? Was I that lucky girl that got a chance to be with the star football player, only to never been seen with him again?

"Sorry you had to wait." A short guy appeared wearing a white PHU polo shirt and khakis. He punched a code in the keypad on the opposite side of the gate and it opened.

"It's okay." Delaney smiled at him and I followed her.

"Raven will be on the field in a few minutes." We trekked behind him, going down a few stairs until we were in front of another gate that led directly to the field. With a key, he unlocked it and pushed it opened for us. "When you're done, wait here and I'll let you out."

I nodded and Delaney responded, "Okay."

The guy turned and walked down a path toward the locker room area, disappearing behind a set of double doors.

"I'm going to wait in the bleachers, okay?" I pointed to the right.

"Are you sure you don't want to come on the field with me?"

"I think it's best if I stay here." I took a few steps back.

Delaney shrugged. "If you say so."

She walked through the gate and it closed behind her. I sat on the metal bleachers and immediately was glad the sun was shining brightly. A cool breeze wisped around the stadium and I shuddered.

If only Raven were here to wrap his arms around me.

No matter what I did, I couldn't stop thinking about him. I really missed him. I sighed and hoped that being there wouldn't make him mad. That was the last thing I wanted, but I had to make an effort. I'd give him one last chance and after that, I was done. I refused to chase him, especially if he didn't want to be with me.

I watched Delaney walk to the center of the twenty-yard line and set her bag on the ground. Hopefully her idea would work and he'd call me to come to the field. Unzipping my backpack, I pulled out my book and flipped it to the last chapter I had been reviewing. I stared at the page, but I didn't read one word. All I could think about was Raven. I pulled the book closer to me, trying to focus, and started at the beginning of the chapter for the third time.

Out of the corner of my eye, I saw Raven walk on to the field fully dressed in his football uniform. My heart rate picked up at the sight of him, but I forced myself to stay calm. The guy that opened the gate for us followed behind him, lugging a cart of footballs. Raven immediately acknowledged Delaney and then caught my gaze. I released a gentle smile, unsure of how I should greet him. What I really wanted to do was rush the field and jump into his arms. He raised his head slightly as though noting my presence, but didn't smile or wave. The fluttering in my heart seized and my lungs deflated as I let out a huge sigh.

Maybe this was a bad idea after all.

I leaned against the hard metal bleacher behind me and crossed my arms, soothing myself once again the best way I knew how. What had happened to all the excitement between us? The special attraction that neither of us could deny? I knew mine still existed for him, but what happened to the feelings he had for me? Had my innocence scared him off?

Snubbing my mom's voice in my head that continuously reminded me that Collin was the one I should be with, I picked up my book. I ran my hand over the page and then slammed it shut. As I started to place it in my backpack, another voice filtered through my muddled mind.

Don't leave.

I stopped and opened the book. If I left, I'd never know if he was glad to see me. If I stayed, I could wait until Delaney was done taking pictures and go talk to him. This was my chance to ask him what was going on in person. Of course, he could lie to me or avoid the question, but I had to ask. I wanted to know what had changed over the past week to make him standoffish. He owed me an explanation.

Over the next hour, I kept one eye on my book and the other on Raven. Delaney took several shots of him throwing and catching the football, running on and off the field, and different poses that made it difficult for me to stay seated, much less read or study. Why was he so damn sexy? Every ripple, bulge, and muscle seemed to call to me, despite his refusal to look at me. I buried my face in my hands. I was such a hot mess.

How the hell did I get like this?

I was supposed to be smarter, not to mention more discerning, when it came to guys like this. I knew better. I blamed my lack of experience and my sheltered life for it, because I had no other way of explaining it myself.

The Raven's trap was an addiction that I couldn't get out of my head, my mouth, off my skin, or stay away from. I was in too deep to walk away.

I wanted him.

I needed him.

I had to have him.

Shit! This totally sucks.

"Thanks, Raven. I'll let you know when I have everything done." Delaney's voice echoed in the distance.

I quickly glanced up, just as Raven walked off the field. He didn't bother to say bye to me. All hope for us vanished in a second and I felt so stupid for going there. Delaney looked at me with a heartfelt expression, even though it wasn't her fault. She had tried and I had attempted, for the second time, to see him. I had failed once again. For whatever reason, Raven was no longer interested in me.

Grabbing my things, I headed toward the gate when Raven turned around. Our gazes caught and I saw a look of regret cross his face. I continued weaving through the bleachers until I stood at the gate leading to the field. The guy that had been helping Raven pushed it open for Delaney and started to shut it when Raven spoke up.

"Lexi, can I talk to you for a moment?"

The sound of my name rolling off his tongue always sent my body into a frenzy, but this time it was so aloof that I knew what he had to say wouldn't be good.

"Do you want me to wait for you?" Delaney glanced at Raven and then at me.

"No, that's okay. I'll see you at the suite."

She gave me a quick nod and then leaned forward, whispering, "Go easy on him."

My head retracted, somewhat taken back by her comment. I mean, whose side was she on? The guy stepped back and allowed me on the field before disappearing with Delaney.

"Is everything okay?" I tried to feign ignorance. He pursed his lips together and his eyes narrowed. He had seen right through my little act but it was worth the try.

"Let's sit down." He pointed to the bleachers.

We walked through the small gate and sat on the nearest bench. Sitting next to him dressed in his protective gear and huge shoulder pads, I felt so small. Fragile. Docile. I reminded myself that I was no longer that person. Things had changed and I was slowly changing, too.

"I'm sorry that I came." I shrugged off my backpack and set it in front of me.

He sighed and then said, "I'm not upset because you came with Delaney, if that's what you're thinking. It's just that..." He held his helmet between his massive hands and I imagined me between them. Feeling their warmth and soothing touch. His thumbs stretched across the front mask area and he fiddled with the sun visor, flipping it up and down. The helmet was covered in reptile markings with a dragon sketched on the side. The purple paint shimmered under the bright sunlight and it really was beautiful. Just like him.

"What?" I leaned forward, trying to catch his gaze, but he refused to look at me.

"Lexi, I... I really like you. I do." His head lowered and my heart sank.

Even though I had a feeling he was going to tell me he didn't want to see me anymore, I had hoped I was wrong. I took a deep breath and in one breath, said, "Let me guess. You don't want to see me anymore." My chest squeezed and my stomach did a somersault. I had said it, even though I didn't want to.

"I'm not good for you, Lexi." He slowly turned his head in my direction.

"Don't say that. You're a great person, Raven." I pressed my lips together and blinked a few times, feeling the onset of tears. Why was I on the verge of crying? I may have liked Raven, but I didn't love him. Or did I?

"It's the truth and you know it. You deserve to be with a guy that has his shit together and isn't a total screw up like me." He set his helmet on the bleacher.

I knew at that moment that my intuition was completely on target. What had sparked the change in the way he was acting toward me had everything to do with what his mother had said the other day.

"But you're not a screw up Raven. Can't you see that?" I pivoted my body and grabbed his arms, turning him to face me. "You're a great guy and an awesome football player, with a great future ahead of you."

"Lexi, my family isn't like your family. We're all effed up." His eyes darted to the side and then back at me, pain circling around them. I knew this was hurting him, just as much as it was hurting me.

"I'm not here to judge you, Raven. I know you've had it rough and you deserve to have someone that will be there for you. Encourage you. Support you." I wrapped my hands around his. "I want to be that person."

He pulled back, forcing me to let go of his hands. "I wish you could be, but it's better that you aren't. You're too good for me."

My body slumped forward, but I straightened, forcing myself to get through to him. "I'm sorry that you think that I'm Miss Goody Two-Shoes, but I've got news for you. I'm not as innocent as you think."

"Oh, come on." Raven shot me a disdaining look. "Who are we kidding? You had never drank a beer or took a shot of liquor until you met me."

"That was my choice. I didn't have to drink the things you offered me, but I did because I wanted to," I assured him.

He cupped his hands around my face and I relaxed into them. It took all my effort to keep my eyes from closing. It was so easy to get lost in his trap. The trap I loved being a prisoner to. "I'll destroy you, Lexi. Trust me."

I titled my head back. "No, you won't. Because I won't let that happen to either of us."

"Lexi, my problems stem deeper than you can imagine. All of the forces of nature couldn't keep me from doing some of things I know I'm not supposed to do. I'll just pull you down with me and I can't do that to you." He stared deep into my eyes and I waited eagerly to see if the connection we once had would take over and make all of this better somehow. But it didn't.

In that moment, my heart broke all over again. How had I fallen for him so quickly?

"Please, Lexi." He rested his forehead against mine, but his hands drifted away from my face. "Don't make this harder for us. Just go back to your fiancé."

"What?" I jerked my head away and sucked in a deep breath, pissed that he had the nerve to tell me to go back to a guy that he knew nothing about.

"You heard me, Collin is waiting for you."

"How do you know that?" I pressed him hard for an answer but he didn't say anything. "What exactly did Delaney tell you?"

"Not much... really. But I know who Collin is—"

"You know Collin Norris? Personally?" I snapped. Every word he spoke reminded me of something my parents would have said. The last thing I needed was another person telling me what to do.

"Well, not personally, but I know of him." His forehead creased and his eyes narrowed. This might have been hard for him, but he hadn't even considered what it was doing to me. He had assumed he knew what was best for me. Why was he making this so hard on both of us when he didn't have to? "He's a good guy. His dad's a preacher and he's the one you should be with, not me."

I shot up. "Oh my God! You know nothing about him, yet you're ready to dump me at his doorstep. I guess you really don't care about me or what makes me happy because it sure isn't Collin."

"Lexi, please." Raven took my hand and urged me to sit. "Calm down."

My eyes watered and I quickly wiped away the tears. Didn't he know I wanted to be with him, not Collin? Pushing all fear aside, I placed my hand on his cheek. I had to tell him.

"It's you who makes me happy. It's you who makes my heart beat wildly. It's you who has showed me more affection than Collin ever had in the four years we were together. You've given me more attention than anyone ever has. Attention that I need and want. Raven, I want to be with you. Is that such a bad thing?"

"It is when you're a guy like me." His eyes closed for a moment and he inhaled deeply. "I'm sorry, Lexi, but I can't see you anymore." He picked up his helmet. "You're better off without me." Without saying anything else, he stood and stepped off the bleachers. I watched as he walked through the small gate and onto the field.

I didn't know what to think about what had just happened, except that I had to prove that I wasn't the same Lexi Thompson he had met that day in the writing lab. I refused to be the innocent and sweet Lexi. If all the hoes at PHU had a chance, then I sure as hell did. All I had to do was show him.

Σ

Chapter 7

"Get up, it's already eight." I nudged Delaney and she moaned.

"I'm tired... go away." She covered her head with a pillow and turned in the opposite direction, facing the wall.

"You owe me." I pulled the pillow away from her and she tried to stop me, but I yanked it from her limp hands.

She continued mumbling incoherent words so I flipped on the light. "Lex, turn that damn light off."

"Not until you get up." I swirled the drink in my hand close to her ear. "Can you hear that?"

"Hear what?"

"The sound of paradise calling your name."

She slowly turned her head and blinked a few times, trying to focus on the cup in my hand. "What are you drinking?"

I took a sip and smiled. "Something called a Tropical Dream." I stared at the pale blue drink, determined not to let what had happened between Raven and me turn my mood sour. "I hope you don't mind, I took your Malibu Rum and Blue Curacao."

"Let me taste it." Delaney eased up from the bed and took the cup from my hand. "Damn, that's good. Where did you get the recipe?"

"Google." I winked and took the cup from her. "You want me to make you one?" Grabbing the remote to her small portable speaker, I turned it on and hit her 'favorites' playlist. A fast beat played and I started gyrating to the music.

"I hadn't planned on drinking tonight. In fact, I was going to pack so I could go home tomorrow." She picked up her phone from the bedside table and started scrolling through it.

I lowered the music a little and then opened her closet door. "You can pack later. Tonight you're going to a party with me."

"A party?" She sounded surprised, as if parties were news to her. "What party?"

Skimming through her clothes, I pulled out a short black mini skirt and held it up to my waist. It was shorter than what I typically wore and I knew it would attract lots of attention. Did I want that kind of attention? "There's a big end of the semester party at the Sigma Chi house and we're going." I shoved the micro skirt back into her closet.

"Whoa. Wait a minute. How did you find out about that party?" She threw off the covers.

"I was snooping around on Facebook and saw a post," I said, matter of fact.

"I don't know, Lexi. Things got pretty crazy the last time I went to their end of year party in the spring. I don't think it's a good idea if I go."

I turned around, ignoring her pitiful excuse. "Since when did that stop you?"

Springing from her bed, she said, "Since I made a complete ass of myself and since your brother asked me to stop partying so hard."

Dying to know what she did, I asked the obvious. "What the hell did you do?"

"You don't want to know." She shouldered past me. "Your brother will be pissed if I go."

"Don't tell him." I reached in her closet and pulled an off-the-shoulder blue sweater. "Can I borrow this? It will look great with my black skinny jeans."

"Um, yeah. I guess." She ran her hands through her long, matted hair. "Wait a minute, you want me to lie to your brother?"

I shrugged. "I didn't say lie. I just said not to tell him."

She cocked a brow. "What did you do with my roommate?"

I laughed and did a little dance move. "Meet the new Lexi Thompson."

She rolled her eyes at me. "Don't tell me you want to go just to get Raven's attention."

I had spent the last few days trying to convince myself to move on and that I'd have one less problem without him. But no matter how hard I tried, I couldn't stop thinking about him.

I needed him.

I wanted him in my life.

Everything he told me was one-hundred percent true. I was better off with Collin. But he wasn't the one for me. Raven was the one I wanted. And the one I couldn't have.

"Come on, Laney. You said we needed to make the most of this year since we're seniors." I crossed my arms and pouted. "What happened to my roommate?"

She took another drink from my cup. "His name is Luke Thompson and I'm totally obsessed with him."

"Okay, whatever." I sighed. "But this one time, I need you. I can't go to that party by myself and I don't have anyone to go with me."

"Call Shelby, I'm sure she's going with Josh."

I shook my head. "Bad idea. I don't want Raven to know that I'm going."

Delaney opened her dresser draw and rummaged through it, pulling out a thong and bra. "What's your plan?"

"Plan?"

"Yeah, your trap to get him back?" She swung her panties around her finger. "Because you're going to have to work it, girl."

"I don't know." I pulled half my hair up and gave her a sexy pose. "Seduce him?"

Laughing, she shook her head. "You and every other girl will be doing the same thing. Trust me, I've seen it."

"Okay, then tell me what I need to do."

With her head hanging down, she shuffled to the bathroom. "But I don't want to go."

"Laney, please," I begged.

It took several more tries to finally convince her to go to the party with me. I was determined to do what I had set out to do. Enjoy my senior year, with or without Raven. My plan would be to show him that I wasn't the sweet, innocent Lexi that he knew. I honestly had no idea if he would even be at this party, but I had to take the chance.

We arrived to the party around nine-thirty and my head felt light as every muscle relaxed. Delaney and I had already had a few Tropical Dreams and I was ready for a shot or two. I didn't want to get stupid drunk like Delaney had the last time we went out, but I wanted the college experience that was promised to me when I entered my freshman year. I had been waiting four years to have a good time.

I nearly tripped as I walked up the stairs but managed to catch myself before face planting.

"Damn, are you already drunk?" Delaney grabbed my elbow and helped me steady my balance.

"No, it's these stupid heels you told me to wear."

"Shit. I guess I should have given you lessons first."

I pulled down my skirt and focused on placing one foot in front of the other. We walked up the steps and entered into the loudest and wildest party I'd ever seen. The house reeked of beer, liquor, and cigarettes. Several people stood in a circle with their mouths wrapped around a tube attached to a huge funnel, fed by a guy that was pouring pitcher after picture of beer. They guzzled it down like they were dying from thirst. A girl motioned for us to join them in the race, but I shook my head no and urged Delaney forward.

In the living room, there was a DJ with his computer and disco ball that flashed a rainbow of colors around the room. The music was loud and people were pressed up against each other, grinding and humping. Two girls were sprawled on the couch, going at it like they were the only ones in the room. Sweat, funk, and body fluids floated in the air and it made me want to puke.

"Okay, this is pretty crazy."

"Told ya." Delaney rolled her eyes and I could see the regret laying within them.

We walked through the kitchen to the backyard where there was a huge kiddie pool filled with blue Jell-O. Two topless girls were smearing it all over each other like sun-tanning lotion. A group of guys cheered them on as one girl rubbed it all over the other girl's nipple and sucked it off. As we walked past them, the girl licking and suckling winked at me and ran her tongue over her lips. I froze. What she trying to hit on me? Never had I seen anything like this. I was appalled, to say the least.

"Oh my God." I pulled Delaney back and whispered in her ear. "Did you see what that chick just did to me?"

"No, what happened?"

"I think she likes me."

Delaney burst out in laughter. "Everyone here will like you. Trust me."

"Let's go inside. I'm freezing." I shuddered and wrapped my arms around myself. "I can't believe I let you talk me into wearing this." I straightened the off-the-shoulder purple dress I had on. Delaney wouldn't let me wear the sweater I wanted to borrow from her. She said that I'd look like a prude in it. Noting all the girls dressed in micro mini skirts and dresses, she was right. They were dressed for a mid-summer party, minus the pool.

"Oh shit." Delaney scurried behind me. "Hide me."

"Why?"

"Matt is here. I don't want him to see me."

I put my hands on my hips in an attempt to block her behind me. She pushed me, moving us through the hordes of people. "If I fall, it's totally you're fault." My ankles wobbled as I tried to balance myself on the three-inch platforms. I made a mental note to practice walking in heels more often.

"Stop griping. They make your legs look sexy."

We stopped in the kitchen where a guy was pouring liquor into the mouths of all those that had lined up. Everyone was yelling and shouting that they wanted to be next. And so did I.

"Come on, I want what he's giving out." I pulled on Delaney's arm, making her stand.

"Are you sure?"

I wiped the sweat from my palm and sucked in a deep breath. "Yes."

"Are you sure you won't be regretting it tomorrow?"

Winking, I eased behind a group of girls. "No regrets." With an accidental bump, one of the girls turned around. "Oh, sorry."

"Hey, you're, um..."

"Lexi. And you're Amber, right?"

"Yep." She adjusted the tight bun on her head. "Hey, Delaney, didn't see you."

"Hey, Amber. Where's Shelby."

"Somebody say my name?" Shelby danced her way toward us.

"Hey, girl, let's do a shot." She flung her arms around me and breathed her tainted breath all over my face. "Whoa. Are you sure you need another one?"

She flashed a lopsided smile. "I'm just getting started."

"Where's Josh?" I looked around. If he was here, so was Raven.

"He's over there somewhere." She motioned with hand. "Where's Raven?"

Delaney looked at me and then back at her. Maybe Raven wasn't with Josh after all. "Um... I don't know."

She pouted. "Don't tell me he already dumped you."

Her comment hit me square in the chest and I tried to ignore the wrenching pain tugging at my heart. "Well, umm—"

"Who wants one?" A guy sat on the bar, yelling as he held a bottle in each hand. "Line up girls!" He motioned for Amber, Shelby, Delaney, and me to sit. I eagerly approached the square bar chair and sat, pressing my back against the edge.

Another guy handed me a lemon and then sprinkled a heap of salt between the webbing of my thumb and index finger.

"What's this for?" I looked at Shelby and she smiled.

"First you lick the salt." Shelby's long, pink tongue scraped the salt off her hand and I copied her movements with my own.

"Heads back, girls," the guy with the bottles instructed as he kept one thumb on the spout of the liquor bottles.

"Woo hoo!" Shelby yelled and wiggled in her chair.

"Let's do this!" I screamed and relaxed my head against the cold marble. The guy moved down the line, pouring a shot full of liquor into each of our mouths. Cold liquid filled my mouth and I raised my head, swallowing it in one gulp. The feeling of fire shot down my esophagus and I yelled, "What the hell was that?"

"Lemon. Suck on your lemon." Shelby shoved the slice of fruit in her mouth. I followed, sucking on the tart and sour lemon, trying to mask the horrible taste that filled my mouth.

"Otro! Otro!" a group of Hispanic guys started chanting and I shook my head.

"Hell no. If I take another one, I'll probably vomit." I turned away from the guy ready to fill my mouth again.

"Only one?" A cute guy with thick, brown hair that swept to the side stood in front of me. He studied me purposefully, his gazed traveled from my head to my toes, and I tingled all over.

"Yes, just one." I pulled on the hem of my dress, hoping I hadn't flashed him.

"What's your name?" He had a cute Texas twang and I couldn't help but notice his tight shirt squeezing his biceps. Was he a football player? He seemed a little bit smaller than most of the guys on the team.

"Lexi." I smiled and he smiled back. Maybe I needed to forget about guys that played sports. My stats weren't looking too good in that area.

"Don't tell me that was the first time you took a tequila shot."

"That was tequila?" I looked over my shoulder, trying to catch a better glimpse of the liquor bottles in the guy's hand.

"Damn, woman," he laughed, lifting a huge glass mug to his lips. "Where did you say you were from?"

"I didn't." I hopped off the bar stool and just as I walked past him, he turned around.

"Sorry. I didn't mean to offend you." He held out his hand. "I'm Brian. Brian Levinson."

"Nice to meet you, Brian." I shook his hand and noted the way his fingers caressed my skin. They were callused along the palm but warm and gentle at the same time.

"I think you did the right thing."

I eyed him for a moment, trying to place his sincerity or lack thereof. "I did?"

"Yeah, if you're not used to taking tequila shots, then you don't want to do one shot after another."

Giggling, I tucked my hair behind my ear. The alcohol kept my blood nice and warm and I liked how it soothed my nerves. Maybe being single wasn't so bad after all. The taste of freedom had me begging for more. "Why? You think I'll get drunk and pass out?"

"Lexi, let's go." Delaney grabbed my hand and tried to pull me away.

"I'll be over there in a minute." I pulled back, making her release my hand. Brian was damn cute and had one heck of a body. But he was nothing compared to Raven. I sighed internally, wishing I could get him out of my mind. She eyed me for a moment and when I didn't budge, she walked off with Shelby and Amber.

"That or it could make your clothes fall off." He winked and took another swig of his beer.

"What?" I was a little surprised by his comment. Although I wasn't that experienced when it came to guys, I knew he was flirting with me. Hard. And, I liked it.

"Haven't you heard that song...*Tequila Makes Her Clothes Fall Off?*"

I shook my head. "Um, no."

He shrugged. "It's an old country song."

"Oh." I made a mental note to look it up. "I don't listen to country that often."

He took another sip and said, "Can I get you something to drink?"

"Umm..." I looked around for Delaney, wishing I had gone with her. Recalling what she had said about taking drinks from people I didn't know, I knew I had to tell him no. I clasped my hands together as the jitters set in, looking for the nearest exit. The kitchen was jammed packed and he closed in on my personal space. "Well, that's okay. I—"

"Relax. I won't slip you anything, if that's what you're thinkin'."

Could I really trust a guy I didn't even know? He seemed really nice and against my better judgment, I allowed my shoulders to relax. "Okay. I was drinking Malibu earlier."

"I think I know where some is." He grabbed my hand and I flinched. I almost pulled away but reminded myself that he was just being friendly. I had no reason to panic or get overly excited. He snaked through the crowd of people and led me further into the kitchen.

Opening a few cabinets, he rummaged through them. The sleeve of his shirt inched up, revealing a blue shield with a cross in the middle, with the Greek letters of Sigma and Chi underneath. His muscles flexed and the letters danced, and I rolled my fingers against my leg as if I were playing the piano. I was eager to strum them against his skin and trace the outline of his tattoo. I shook my head, trying to ward off the alcohol that fought to take control. I had to calm down, or I could end up in deep shit by the end of the night.

"Do you live here?"

"Huh?" He turned around. "Sorry, can't hear you over the music."

"I said do you live here?"

"Found it." He pulled out that white, familiar bottle. "Yeah, this is our frat house."

"Oh, I see." I watched as he opened a two-liter bottle of Coke and poured some in a red plastic cup. Then he added a capful of Malibu and topped it off with ice.

"See. No drugs." He handed me the cup and I took it from him.

"Thanks."

"So, do you go to PHU?" He leaned against the counter and I noted his tight jeans and cowboy boots. Cowboys had never really caught my attention, but this one was damn hot.

"Yes, I'm a senior."

"Really?" His head retracted. "How come I've never seen you around?"

I shrugged. "I guess because I was one of those girls that focused on her school work."

"Oh, I see. And what kind of girl are you now?"

Holding on to my lower lip, I contemplated how to respond. Brian was definitely hitting on me. "One that wants to have a good time." My answer escaped from my mouth with ease.

His baby blue eyes lit up and my warning light came on. I ignored it, my curiosity getting the best of me. I was a free woman and I wasn't doing anything wrong, right?

"Well, I can sure show you a good time." He leaned closer to me and whispered in my ear, "If you'll let me."

Oh hell.

"Do you want to dance?" I took a sip of my drink and felt myself melting away with all that it promised.

"Sure." He grabbed my hand and led us to the living room.

It was still crammed with sweaty people dancing, but I managed to spot Delaney dancing with Amber and Shelby. I dragged Brian to where they were and started gyrating my hips to the beat. He had a quirky bounce when he moved, but I didn't mind. I was eager to have a good time and get to know him.

"Lexi!" Delaney shrieked as she threw her arm around me. "Selfie time." She snapped a shot of us and continued taking pictures with everyone. I quickly reminded her not to post them on Facebook. She assured me that she wouldn't.

"Where's Luke?" I hadn't thought to ask what she had told my brother.

Moving to the beat of the music, she shrugged. "He totally thinks I'm home with my parents."

"I know he's you're brother, but what a dumb ass." Shelby leaned between us and Delaney snapped another picture. "Like this girl would miss this party."

"Leave Luke alone," Delaney pouted. "He's my dumb ass."

I shook my head, feeling somewhat bad that I had asked Delaney to lie to my brother. It was my fault that she was there. I just hoped he didn't find out.

One hour and two more drinks later, Brian and I were still hanging out. I made a conscious effort to pace myself. I didn't want to get stupid drunk like Delaney had, but I also wanted to party. So far, the end of my fall semester didn't seem that bad. Determined to make the most of it, I contemplated how far I would allow things to go between Brian and me.

Brian chatted about his family's real estate business and I tried my best to act interested. The more he talked, the more I realized I had nothing in common with him. But I didn't care. I was there to have a good time and if Brian was willing to show me that, I'd take it.

As I feigned an attentive laugh, I noticed Raven sitting on stool surrounded by a mob of women. I elbowed Delaney but she was too busy chatting with a group of people. They were laughing and flirting with him. If I had to guess, he had probably drenched his body in his trap-catching cologne. The more I tried not to stare, the more I did. I wanted to be the one that was flirting with him, not them.

"Excuse me, Brian. I need to go the bathroom."

"Yeah, sure. It's down the hall and on the right." He pointed me in the right direction.

"Come with me." I grabbed Delaney and pulled her through the crowd, trying to keep a low profile. The last thing I wanted was Raven to see us.

"Is everything okay?"

"Raven's here."

"Where?"

"Over there." I pointed, keeping my finger close to me. "Who the hell are all those women around him? They don't even look like they're in college." I eased around the post in the hallway, trying to catch a better glimpse of the sex-starved banshees parading themselves around him.

"That's because they probably aren't." Delaney yanked on my hand. "Come on, I have to pee and the line is probably long."

"Go ahead." I pushed her hand away. "I want to hear what they're saying. I'll be there in a minute."

"Fine." She trotted off and I moved closer, eager to listen in on their conversation. He had a big smile on his face and that familiar rush hit my veins. Clenching my teeth tightly, I forced my mind to forget all the good times I had had with him. But like a magnet, he tugged me in his direction.

Shit, I was still a victim in his trap!

But it was a trap I didn't mind wrapping myself in.

"Iris. I can't do that." He grinned and gave a slight shake of his head.

"Oh yes, you can," she said with a Spanish accent as she flipped her long, black hair.

Bitch, I huffed under my breath as I anticipated his reply.

"Well, if you can't do that with her, then what about me?" I rose on the tips of my toes, trying to catch a better glimpse. A lady with blondish-red hair pawed at Raven's chest.

Those damn women have no shame.

"How about you just take all of us?" A girl with short, dark hair adjusted her boobs and I nearly choked on my gum.

"I've never had five women in one night." Raven pressed his hands against his thighs and leaned forward. "But I can try."

"Hell, baby, you don't have to do anything. We'll do all the work for you. All you need to do is just lay there," the next woman said, eyeing him like she was ready to attack him.

I covered my face with my hands and then ran my fingers through my hair. Why did I fall for him? Raven was right, he wasn't good for me. He spelled disaster, but that only made me want to be with him. I tucked my hair behind my ears and inhaled deeply. I had to get my shit together. I took off down the hall toward the bathroom. Delaney was next in line and I cut in front of her.

"So, what happened?"

"Those damn women are like freaking vampires." I seethed. "Ready to suck his blood."

"I doubt they want to suck his blood." Delaney snickered. "More like his dick."

I squeezed by eyes shut, trying to crush the visual. Raven was not right for me. I didn't want a guy that had threesomes, let alone fivesomes. I wanted a guy that showed me attention and showered me with affection. I thought Raven was that guy. Apparently, he wasn't. But I wanted him to be.

Badly.

"Shit, I need another drink."

"Here, drink this." Delaney shoved her cup in my hand and I downed it.

"Holy shit, that was strong. What was that?"

Delaney shrugged. "Hell if I know."

After a quick bathroom trip, we returned to the living room. I made a conscious effort to ignore Raven and his tramps. I was there to have a good time and I wouldn't allow him to ruin it for me. He didn't want to be with me. It sucked, but I had to move on with my life.

The room tilted but I managed to maintain my footing, claiming the floor with each step I took. Shelby and Amber danced on top of a coffee table, motioning for us to join them. Enjoying the effects of the alcohol, I joined them. Shelby handed me her drink and I down it, tossing the cup behind me. I froze when she embraced me from behind. After several awkward seconds, I surrendered my better judgment and moved with her. She ground against me, running her hands over my body. I had never dirty danced with a girl before — or a guy, for that matter — but I kind of liked it. It made me feel sexy, promiscuous, and daring. Brian spotted me and entered the freak show.

I felt so brave, so free. I shimmied against his body, sliding up and down his taut form to the beat of the music. He turned me around and pressed his hips to mine, humping me from behind. My heart beat faster and I realized that he had actually turned me on, and I liked it. I rubbed my butt against his crotch, and I thrilled at the telltale hardness through his jeans. At that point, there was no holding back, and I added a little twerking action. He immediately grasped and squeezed my thighs, inching up my dress.

As I danced without shame to the beat of music, it dawned on me that I definitely had one less problem without Raven, just like the song said. But as Brian ran his hands over me, I wished Raven had felt me up instead. I reminded myself that I was the wiser one, but it was no use. No matter how much I wanted to hate him, I couldn't.

I wanted him.

I had to have him.

And I was willing to forget about everything to be with him.

At that very moment, Raven looked up and caught my gaze. I froze with my arms in mid-air, while Brian continued to grind on me. In one swift move, Raven pushed through his groupies and headed toward me. Before I could react, Raven grabbed and pulled me off the table.

"Put me down!" I kicked and screamed.

"Hey!" Brian yelled. He jumped off the table and started in my direction, but he stopped when he did a double take. I guess he didn't want to mess with Raven. I'm not sure many guys were willing to take on the PHU's star quarterback, unless they enjoyed death threats.

"Stop, Lexi!" Hoisting me over his shoulder, he carried me outside, barreling through the groves of drunkards. People yelled and chanted, as if Raven had selected his prized possession for the night. The old Lexi would have died at the prospect of what the crowd might have been thinking, but part of me wanted every girl in that party to know that he was taking me home.

"Put me down, Raven." I pounded his back, trying to wiggle free from his binding grip.

He darted out the front door and flew down the steps, without stopping. Once outside, he set me on the front lawn. I stumbled back, hitting a tree. "What the hell is wrong with you?" he huffed, trying to catch his breath.

"What the hell is wrong with you?" Despite the cold air, my blood boiled. "I was dancing. Is that a crime?"

He blinked his eyes a few times, obviously having difficulty processing what I had said. "You were practically having sex with that guy."

"What?" I gasped, clutching my hand to my chest. "No, I wasn't." My head began to spin and I suddenly felt the alcohol take over with a vengeance.

"I was watching you the whole time. I saw what you were doing with him."

"You were watching me?" I tried to focus on him but my eyes were dancing all over the place, making it difficult to see straight.

He took a step back and stared at the ground for a moment. "Why are you here, Lexi? You shouldn't be at this party." His eyes narrowed and I struggled to stand.

Everything turned around me, spinning in slow motion. I leaned against the tree for support and tried to focus on Raven. "Why not? I'm a student at this school. Not like those hoes that were all over you." I pointed to the house and nearly tipped over, catching myself before he could intervene.

"Shit." He kicked the dirt. "You're fucking drunk."

"And?" I smiled, realizing that I could mark one thing off my list. "Besides, what do you care?"

"This isn't you, Lexi." He took a step closer and I pressed up against the tree. The air suddenly turned hot and my cheeks flushed. "I know you, you're not acting like yourself."

"Whatever. Now, if you'll excuse me. There's a party that's waiting on me." I placed my hand on his chest and tried to push him out of the way, but he wrapped his hand around my wrist and pulled me into him. My chest slammed against his and even though my body liked it, I fought it.

"Let me go, Raven," I snapped.

"No." He scooped me up in his arms and I was defenseless once again. "I'm taking you home. Now."

Σ

Chapter 8

I started to protest but stopped when I realized how much I missed being in Raven's arms. He delivered a comfort and security that warmed every part of me and fastened every loose end. The more I told myself not to fall for it, the harder I fell. Every force of nature led my heart straight to his and I hoped he wouldn't destroy it like he said he would.

"You can put me down," I said, gazing up at him. "I promise I'll let you take me home." I mean, how lucky could I get? Raven wanted to take me home. Every woman at that party would have died for the opportunity, why fight it?

"Are you sure you're not going to run off?" He stopped in the middle of the street. His eyes drilled into mine and excitement shot through my veins. I wanted to kiss him so bad. Make him regret that he said he couldn't be with me. But I was afraid of how he might react. Restraining myself, I nodded. Slowly, he lowered me to my feet but kept me enveloped in his arms. "Can you walk?"

My heart felt like it was stuck on a spinning ride while my brain demanded it to stop. The conflicting war within me made it hard to concentrate. Being drunk wasn't as fun as I thought it would be. I had gone past my limit and I hoped I wouldn't pay for it later.

I tilted my head to the side and gave him an impish grin. "As long as you help me."

With one arm wrapped tightly around me, he led us down the street to his car. He opened the door and helped me get in. I rested my head against the seat and closed my eyes. My ears were ringing and my heart was going ninety miles an hour.

"Are you okay?"

"I think so," I mumbled. "Everything is spinning."

"Please don't puke in my car, that's all I ask." He started the engine and I opened my eyes to see him pulling onto the main road. "I think we should get you something to eat."

"Why?" I turned to look at him. I blinked slowly, trying to process what was happening, but my mind only focused on one thing.

Raven.

Even though it was cold outside, he had on a short-sleeve shirt and my eyes fixated on the way his muscles tensed. He was so pretty. Too pretty for me. I had to be the luckiest girl in the world.

"The grease will help absorb the alcohol." He turned at the intersection and pulled into the parking lot of Whataburger.

"Okay, whatever you say," I mumbled, staring out the window in a partially incoherent daze. Christmas lights twinkled against the windowpanes of the restaurant. Fake snow dotted the corners of the windows with shiny tinsel in purple and white strung along them.

"Do you want cheese on your burger?"

"Yeah and a Dr. Pepper." I rarely drank sodas but since I had already had a few tonight, I figured what was one more?

He handed me the bag of food and the greasy smell filtered through my airways, making my stomach growl. Grease had never smelled so good. By the time we got to my dorm, I had almost finished my French fries.

"Cool. There's a spot right there." Raven sped forward, claiming a parking space across the street from the commons area, which I was glad for. I wasn't sure I could walk very far without busting my butt. He parked the car and I quickly took off Delaney's platform heels. I was smart enough to know that I'd end up with either a twisted ankle or scraped knees. I got out of the car and shivered when the cold air hit me.

"Cold?" he asked as he shut the door for me.

I nodded. He reached in the backseat and grabbed his jacket. He put it on me and I immediately snuggled in the familiar scent. Raven smelled so good. Too good. He held me close as I stumbled toward Charter Hall, praying I didn't fall down. The brisk air blew against us and he drew me closer. Raven was like a huge stuffed teddy bear that I was dying to take to bed with me.

We entered through the back door since it was after curfew and my heart immediately started racing. I knew Raven was acting out of concern for me, but a part of me couldn't help but wonder what might happen. Luckily, the elevator doors were open. We slipped in without anyone seeing us. The ride seemed to take forever and the movement upward made my stomach feel funky.

The doors opened and we got off. As we walked down the hall, we passed a few girls and they eyed me. I started feeling slut-shamed and retreated like a turtle into Raven's jacket, hoping they didn't think I was another one of his hoes. Then I reminded myself that I wasn't. If I were, we would have been in my dorm room the first day we met.

"Do you know them?" He eyed me and I suddenly became self-conscious over how I was reacting.

"Unfortunately, yes." I relaxed, allowing his jacket to fall past my shoulders. "Do you?"

"Fortunately, no." Relief flowed over me as he looked back and shook his head. "But I have to know something." Our eyes met and a familiar energy pulsed through me, warding off my buzz. "Are you embarrassed to be seen with me?"

"No, it's just that..." I tried to think of what to say but no words formed.

Stupid liquor.

"You don't want Collin to find out." His eyes dropped and I saw a sadness that wasn't there before.

"What?" I struggled to unzip my wristlet, thankful that I had thought to take my keys in case Delaney and I were separated. "No, he's history. Trust me."

"Let me help you." Raven took my hand and worked the leather strap off my wrist, removing it in a slow and deliberate motion as his fingers brushed over my skin. Every stroke drove me crazy and I couldn't help wanting to feel his hands all over me. Chills shot up my arms and down my spine. Could I get Raven to stay the night with me?

"You know any other girl would die to be seen with me," he said, unzipping my little purse.

I bit my lower lip and sucked in a deep breath. "Who says I'm not dying right now?"

He grinned and his eyes flashed that enticing sparkle like that day at the stadium. At that point, I knew I was in trouble. It would take more than the forces of nature to stop me from attacking him. All I had to do was get him in my room.

Raven unlocked the door and then pushed it open. "After you."

I walked into my dorm room, but it didn't look like my place. For a moment, I thought I was walking into his lair. The Raven's trap. Though I had no idea what it looked like, I was sure it wasn't decorated in pink pillows with a black fleur de lis on the wall and ornate mirrors. In a matter of seconds, I lost all confidence.

He shut the door and locked it. My heart rate kicked up a notch and I found myself confused over what I should do. I had no idea when it came to sex. Then again, did he want to have sex with me? My mind spun out of control, tossing different ideas around like it was a political debate and I was the candidate trying to defend my position. But what position did I have? Clearly not the upper hand since I had no clue when it came to sex.

Damn it! Why didn't I ask Delaney or reread my books?

I tried to recall how the girl seduced the guy in the latest romance book I had read. All I could remember was Kyler and Syd were in a vacation home in the mountains, trapped by a horrific snowstorm. I tried to remember the details of how they ended up sleeping with one another, but the only thing that came to memory was they were stuck without electricity and little food.

Curse you alcohol.

"Are you going to stand there or eat?"

"Huh?" I turned around as he took a bite of his burger. "Yeah, I guess I should eat." Hopefully he was right about the grease absorbing some of the alcohol. I tossed Delaney's heels to the floor and shucked of his jacket.

Unwrapping my cheeseburger, I consciously sat at the opposite end of the couch, as if he had some kind of disease or sickness that I didn't want to catch. Then, it hit me. What if he had herpes or AIDS? I knew he had been with tons of girls. The last thing I wanted was to catch something from him.

I sat in silence, eating my burger and conjuring horrible imagery. I had to give my mind a standing ovation; it sure knew how to kill the mood. One minute, I was dying to have sex with him. The next, I was freaking out about catching something from him. I was one screwed up girl.

"Why are you so quiet?" Raven wadded up the wrapper to his burger and tossed it in the bag.

"Just thinking," I blurted before taking a big drink of my soda. I had so many off-limits questions for him. Questions I knew I shouldn't ask, but things I had to know.

"About what?"

Tossing out everything my mom taught me about being prim and proper, I asked, "What's with you? I mean, why do you insist on being with so many girls?"

His eyes widened and he let out a slight laugh. I knew my question had surprised him and if we ended up together tomorrow, I could always blame the alcohol.

"And don't tell me it's because you're a guy." I pivoted in his direction.

He clasped his hands together and drew in a deep breath. "You really want to know?"

I nodded as I continued sucking on the straw, drawing the last of the soda from the cup.

"I guess I like sex."

On second thought, maybe I didn't want to know.

"That's such a guy response." I set my drink on the coffee table, grabbed the last two fries from the sack, and chewed on them, nearly eating my fingers in the process.

He shrugged and turned his body in my direction. "Well, I promised I'd be honest with you. Now you know."

And my knowing made me even more curious. "Yeah, but aren't you scared you'll catch something?"

His head jolted back and he seemed somewhat surprised by my question. "No, not really. I practice safe sex, Lexi. Don't you?"

"Um..." My heart leaped from my chest to my throat as I struggled to breathe. Raven wanted to know if I practiced safe sex. Because he did. That meant he was more than likely disease free. It'd be safe to sleep with him. But should I tell him the truth? That I was a virgin?

"I suppose I would, if I were having sex."

That wasn't so hard.

I exhaled and rested against the pillows.

His lips parted and he looked like he was holding back a laugh. A tinge of fury hit my blood. Was he making fun of me?

"I forgot I'm talking to an English major."

I stared at him in confusion. "What's that supposed to mean?"

"I guess I should have asked, when you have sex, Lexi, do you or your partner use a condom?"

Oh crap, he really didn't get it.

I pressed my lips together, trying to think of the best way to phrase it. The phrase repeated over and over in my head, but I couldn't bring myself to say it out loud. I had to tell him. Or did I? Unsure of where our conversation was headed, I made the decision to confess. Besides, if we did have sex, he would know.

"No," I straightened as best as I could with the heaviness of the alcohol setting in, "because I've never had sex."

"Ahh, okay." He blinked a few times and shifted his weight.

"Surprise," I said with a meek smile.

"Yeah, I wasn't expecting that. I mean, I knew you were a good girl, I just figured you'd had sex with your fiancé."

"Ex," I reminded him. "He wanted to wait until marriage, I didn't."

"Are you saying you wanted to have sex with him?" His voice wrapped around me and a thrill that I couldn't explain hit my veins. The room began to narrow and I focused on him.

Only him.

Somehow, I managed to speak.

"Yes, but he refused to break his vow."

"That's one committed guy." He brought his hands to his thighs and rubbed them a few times against his jeans. He kept his gaze fixed on the floor instead of me. Had my confession been too much? Did I blow my chance to be with him? Maybe I shouldn't have told him.

"Yeah, but it sucked. I had no idea if he even loved me, because he never showed me." I went in for a quick recovery, hoping that my confession touched some part of him.

Raven moved closer toward me, as if my comment did mean something to him. "I'm sorry. I mean, that must have been hard for you." He held up his hand. "Assuming that you were attracted to him and cared for him."

"Of course I was and it hurt. All I knew was that I couldn't marry him, not without knowing whether he truly loved me or not." I tucked my hair behind my ear, feeling another flash of heat hit my face. "I'm better off finding someone who's not afraid to show me how they feel about me."

"Yes, you are, Lexi, and you should save yourself for the right person." He looked at his watched. "It's late and I better go."

On impulse, I jumped to my feet. I wasn't ready for him to leave. I looked at him and the front door. I didn't know if I should try to kiss him or beg him to stay. How the hell would I convince him to stay? Pounce on him like a puma does her prey? Suddenly, the urge to pee hit me and I couldn't hold it.

"Don't leave yet." I motioned for him to stay put. "I need to—" I motioned toward the bathroom and bolted through my bedroom door and into the bathroom. I sat on the toilet and released a portion of the alcohol I had consumed. It was amazing how adrenaline sobered my body. I flushed the toilet and stood in front of the mirror, washing my hands. I wanted to splash cold water on my face, but I knew I'd ruin what little makeup I had on. I fanned myself as I brushed the tangles out of my hair. I took out my makeup bag and quickly refreshed my blush and lip-gloss. I was a drunk, hot mess.

Raven's hot mess, once again.

I proceeded to open the door, but stopped. What was I going to say? What was I going to do? I paced the small area, feeling all of the familiar sensations in all the right places, like I did when he was having phone sex in the writing lab. My ears continued to ring and my heart beat wildly, gearing up for the sex-a-thon.

Smoothing the wrinkles out of my dress, I opened the door. I reared to the left, bumping into the doorframe when I saw

Raven sitting on the edge of my bed. He had the covers pulled back and my bedside lamp on. The glow reflecting on his face made his light brown skin shimmer a golden color. He was god-like. Eros himself was in my room.

Holy shit.

His hands were clasped together, as if he were patiently waiting for me. He looked up and our eyes met. The glint in his hazel eyes reeled me in and I was one-hundred-percent his victim. All sense of rhyme or reason left me. If he wanted me, I'd let him have me. Whether it was part of me or all of me, just as long as I got to experience him.

"Are you okay?" He stood and walked toward me. My eyes fixed on him and nothing else.

"Y-es." I tried to catch my breath but couldn't seem to inhale deep enough. "I just had to pee. A lot." Once the words left my mouth, I wanted to punch myself. That comment wasn't going to turn him on.

"Oh." He had a quirky expression and I knew I was blowing it. "Then why aren't you ready for bed?"

My legs went limp and I pressed up against the wall. Raven wanted to have sex with me.

Holy shit!

What was I supposed to do? Take off my clothes? I had kind of hoped he would have wanted to do the undressing, but maybe he just liked to get to it, not waste any time. What the hell did I know?

"I, um...I couldn't get my dress off." I had no idea what to say. I still felt drunk, but more coherent than when we left the party. Was this really happening, or was I passed out in the back of his car, dreaming the entire damn thing? I forced my head back and when my head hit the door, I knew it was happening. I was really going to lose my virginity tonight.

He stared at me, as though committing every part of my face into his memory. I tried to focus but my eyes darted all over the place, taking in every part of him. From his head to his toes. If I weren't careful, I'd pass out from Raven overload.

"Do you need help?" He rested his hands on my waist and I flinched. It felt like it had been an eternity since he had touched me, even though he had just carried me to his car.

"Uh huh," I managed to say.

He examined my dress for a moment and then gathered the hem in his hands. "Are you sure you want me to help you undress?"

I nodded, unable to verbally respond. Every muscle in my body went limp and I started leaning to the side.

"Whoa. You alright?" He pulled me against him and then returned his hands to my dress.

"No," I replied. I definitely wasn't alright. Raven was about to take off my dress and see me in my bra and panties. How in the hell could I be alright?

Don't pass out. Don't pass out. Don't throw up. Don't throw up.

The last thing I wanted to do was ruin this incredible moment. The anticipation was overwhelming and I rotated between deep and short, panting breaths. Raven began to lift my dress and then stopped around my hip area. "Are you going to get sick?"

I shook my head. "No. I'm good."

"Okay, just making sure you're not going to vomit all over me." His warm breath spread along my neck and my eyes fluttered close. I was ready for him to start kissing me. There was no way I was going to throw up.

"I won't, I promise."

Raven continued in his quest and I stiffened when he had my dress at my waist. Need and desire crashed into each other, revving up my hormones. I opened my eyes, taking in his massive chest. My fingers tingled, eager to rip off his shirt and feel his muscles under my touch. Not knowing what to do, I helped him pull off my dress, inching it over my breasts. In one quick sweep, he slipped the dress over my head and tossed it to the floor.

His eyes swept over me and I cringed inwardly. Was I sexy to him? How did I compare to the other girls he had? I wrapped my arms around me, covering my poochy midsection. I made a mental note to do crunches at least three times a week from now on.

"Let's get you to bed." He picked me up and carried me. My body formed to his and I never wanted him to let me go. I wrapped my arms around his neck and tried to control the tremors, but they were too strong. I was freaking out. Should I try to kiss him? Wait for him to kiss me? I had no idea what to do.

He laid me softly on the mattress and stared at me for a moment. "You are so beautiful."

"Thank you." I smiled; relieved that he thought I was pretty enough to be with him. Even though I knew I wasn't much compared to some of the girls he'd been with.

His body hovered over me and my heart walloped against my chest. The tension undulated within me and I wasn't sure how much more I could take before I passed out from lack of oxygen and too much alcohol. I inhaled his scent and it was too much for my senses to handle. My already foggy brain thickened and my lips quivered. My hands started to slip away as he rose, but I held on to him tightly. His huge biceps pressed against my hands and I squeezed tighter.

"Goodnight, Lexi." He leaned forward and kissed me on the lips. "Sweet dreams." The light turned off.

"What? No. Don't go." I bolted upright, reaching for him in the dark. My head collided with his face and he moaned.

"Oh, shit."

"I'm sorry." I turned on the light. "Are you okay?"

Raven held his nose and he squinted his eyes as though in pain. "Yeah, I'll be alright." His eyes watered and I could tell he was holding back the tears.

"Let me see." I urged him to sit down. I placed my hand on top of his and slowly pulled his hand away.

"Is it bleeding?" He tilted his head back and sniffed.

I checked his nose for any signs of blood. "No, it's not." I increased the space between us and took a deep breath. My shoulders slumped forward and I felt like an idiot. "I'm sorry. I shouldn't have done that. I just got confused."

"Confused about what?"

What an epic fail the night had been. One minute, I was freakin' a guy I barely knew, then I was swept off my feet by Raven, and then about to have sex with him, only to find out that I wasn't. My throat tightened and my eyes watered. Why the hell? Was I about to cry?

Stupid liquor.

"Why are you crying?"

I shook my head and wiped away the tears. "It's nothing."

His brows knitted in concentration and he leaned closer toward me. "Don't lie." His alluring stare made me nervous, but in a good way. My lips quivered as I watched him speak. "What's bothering you?"

Pressing my lips together, I withheld the sobs threatening to escape. What the hell was wrong with me?

"Tell me, Lexi. Please."

I threw my hands up in the air. "I thought you wanted to have sex with me," I blurted in one breath.

Raven sighed heavily. "Shit. I'm sorry."

I shook my head. "It's my fault, I'm still buzzing."

"Lexi, you don't—"

"No, I totally misread you. It's just that when you asked me why I was still dressed, I assumed you wanted to have sex."

"Damn, Lexi, you're making this so hard for me." His voice broke and a shimmer glinted in his eyes. The muscles in his neck tightened and I could tell he was holding in his own emotions.

"I was stupid for thinking that you did. I mean, you just told me the other day that you didn't want to be with me."

"Lexi, it's not that I don't want to be with you, because I do. I want that more than anything. It's just that..."

"It's okay, Raven, I get it. I'm not what you want."

"Hell, you're everything I want and more." He cupped my face with both his hands and using the pads of his thumbs, wiped away the tears streaming down my cheeks. My body was unraveling under his simple touch. I hated that he had that effect on me. I didn't want him to.

"But you said you didn't want to be with me."

"Just because I said I'm not good for you, doesn't mean that I don't want to be with you."

My head spun. Between the liquor and the conversation, I was struggling to understand what he was telling me. Did he want to be with me or not? "I'm so confused, Raven."

"It's really not that complicated." He inclined his head and I followed his movement. "You see, because not only do I want to be with you, but I also want to make love to your body until you can't stand it. Until your begging for me to stop."

"What?" I muttered, more confused than before.

Did I hear him correctly?

"But not like this. Not while you've been drinking." He stroked his fingers against my cheek and my body shivered against his touch. Hot and cold clashed inside of me and my stomach took flight. My entire body soared to an unbelievable height. Never had I experienced so much affection and attention without even a kiss. Raven wanted to be with me. He also wanted to have sex with me. But I was too damn drunk to do it.

Shit!

I couldn't breathe.

Couldn't think.

Couldn't function.

"Raven, stay with me... please," I said, looking deeply in to his eyes. "I don't want to be alone."

"If I stay with you that could be dangerous."

"I like dangerous." I bit down on my lower lip, trying to contain the surge of emotions flowing through me. It took all my strength not to pull him in bed with me.

"No, you like stupid and that's me."

I let out a soft laugh. "You're not stupid, Raven."

"Well, I'm stupid, crazy for you."

"Will you show me just how crazy you are for me?"

He kneaded his fingers through my hair and rested his head against mine. The exchange of energy between us was practically unbearable. Never had I encountered a connection like this before. Especially not with Collin. My soul called out to Raven's, dying to be connected with the piece that had been missing. Raven held a piece of me that I couldn't function without. I needed him to be whole.

"I want to, Lexi, I really do. But I'm not taking your virginity, not like this." Placing a soft kiss on my lips, he said, "You deserve to feel every part of me. To remember every part of me."

$$\Sigma$$

Chapter 9

The next morning when I woke up, I couldn't help wondering if I had dreamed the entire thing. Had Raven really told me all of that or was I so drunk that I made it up? I grabbed my phone to check my messages. If things had took a turn for the better, then surely he had texted me. Staring at my phone, I saw several messages from Delaney.

Delaney: WTF? Did you take off with Raven?

Delaney: Are you okay?

Delaney: I'm on my way to the dorm. Hopefully you and Raven are screwing and that's why you're not responding.

A laugh escaped me. Oh how I wished that were true. But seeing the message did confirm one thing. Raven had definitely brought me home last night, which meant that I didn't dream everything that happened. I threw back the sheets and got out of bed. The dorm was quiet, so I figured Delaney was still asleep. I shuffled down the hall and approached her room.

The door was open, so I peeked in. "Delaney?"

I looked around, but she was nowhere to be found. Her bed was made, which was unusual, and everything was in the right place. Had someone abducted my roommate and cleaned her room in the process? In the distance, I heard my phone chime. Scurrying back to my room, I picked up my phone. I frowned when I saw that it was a text from Delaney instead of Raven.

Delaney: I didn't want to wake you, but I had to get going. I was supposed to be home last night.

Me: Let me guess, you don't want Luke to find out you went to that party?

Delaney: Yep and my parents just told me were going to Arizona for Christmas so I need to pack.

Me: Okay. I promise I won't say anything. Thanks for going with me.

Delaney: No problem. So, what happened? I expected to find Raven in your room or you with him.

I laid on my bed, reminiscing over our conversation. I licked my lips, recalling how he kissed me tenderly. How his body hovered over mind. Why was his touch so intoxicating? Butterflies fluttered in my stomach and I wanted more of it.

More of him.

Me: He brought me home, obviously. We kissed a little and he said that he really wanted to be with me.

Delaney: Aww. I'm so happy for you guys. Why did he leave?

Me: He said I was drunk and that he wouldn't take my virginity like that.

Delaney: My heart just melted. He's a keeper, girl!

Me: I know!

Delaney: Talk to you later. Have a Merry Christmas if I don't talk to you before then, but I'm sure we will. I'll be back for New Year's Eve and we'll party!

Me: Okay ☒

The second I pushed the send button, my screen switched to a picture of my mom. I hesitated to answer the call, but knew I couldn't avoid her.

Reluctantly, I hit the green button. "Good morning, Mom."

"Good morning? It's almost noon. Why didn't you answer last night?"

Um, because I was drunk and had a hot guy in my room.

"Sorry, I guess I didn't hear my phone ring."

"I left a message. Did you not get it?"

Holding the phone away from my face, I hit the recent tab and saw that I had a voicemail from her. "Stupid phone. I don't know why it didn't alert me," I stated, blaming my lack of responsibility on technology. She huffed over the phone and I knew she was frustrated with me. What else was new?

"I thought you and Luke were coming home last night."

"You did?" I paused for a moment, trying to recall my last conversation with her or Luke. "Sorry, I don't remember saying that we were. I had my last final yesterday, so I've been concentrating on school," I lied, because I'd really been thinking about Raven more than my tests.

"Oh, I see." Mom's voice instantly changed from accusatory to understanding. "Well, what time will you and Luke be home? I want to finish putting up the Christmas decorations and I need to get started on my shopping. I didn't get a chance when your aunt and uncle were in town..." Mom continued to ramble and I was glad that I didn't have another hangover. The greasy hamburger had worked wonders. I smiled, thinking about Raven again. He really did care for me.

"Lexi?" Mom interrupted my pleasant thoughts.

"Yeah?" I redirected my focus and rolled on to my stomach.

"What time can I expect you two?"

The irritation swelled inside of me. I really didn't want to go home, even if it was the holidays. Being around my mom was not fun or relaxing. I'd forgo the presents just to get her off my back.

"I don't know, let me call—" I stopped midsentence when my phone beeped. I pulled away, hoping it was Raven coming to my rescue. My head hit the mattress when I saw that it was Luke. "That's Luke calling. I'll talk to him and then I'll let you know when we're leaving."

"Okay, but don't be too late. The day is halfway gone and—"

"Gotta go, Mom." I hung up, not giving her a chance to say bye.

"Hey, I was just on the phone with Mom."

"Good. Now I don't have to call her back." Luke sounded relieved, but I knew I would take the brute of the nagging since my breakup with Collin was at the top of her conversation list. I just hoped she didn't have plans to try to get Collin and me back together. But something told me that would be her new quest.

"Yeah, yeah, whatever." I sighed. "She wants to know when we're coming home."

"Never," Luke snorted.

"I'd stay here at the dorms if they were keeping them open, but they aren't."

"Yeah, too bad for you. At least I can escape to my apartment."

I rolled off the bed and opened my closet door, pulling out my luggage. "Rub it in, why don't you."

"Well, you can always come over here."

Struggling with the straps, I gave a hard yank. "Um, no thanks. My luck, Collin would be there."

"Have you talked to him?" Luke's voice lowered and I listened in the background for Collin. Was he with him or had he already headed to his parents' house for the break?

"No," I quickly answered. "I don't plan to either. I'm done with him."

"Shit. Don't get so defensive."

"I'm not." Thumbing through my clothes, I pulled a few shirts and pants off the hangers and tossed them on my bed. "It's just that I don't have anything to talk to him about. Our relationship is over."

Luke stalled for a moment and I got the sense that he had talked to Collin. Part of me wanted to pry and ask out of curiosity and the general care I had for Collin, but another part of me didn't want to know. I made the decision to end it and I had moved on.

"Maybe you should give him a call. See how he's doing."

I grabbed another handful of clothes and flung them on the bed. Frustration tinged my blood. Why did my family insist on telling me what to do? "I'm guessing you talked to him, right?" I prodded. "Otherwise, why would you be telling me to call him?"

"Look, I told you I'd stay out of it and I meant it." I could hear the frustration building in his voice, too. "I really don't care if you call him or not. I just suggested it, that's all."

"Fine." I opened the drawer to my dresser, grabbed a handful of my panties, and tossed them in the suitcase.

"Fine." His voice was firm and deep. "What time will you be ready?"

Glancing around my room, I sighed. Clothes were strung along my bed and hangers were everywhere. "In a few hours. I need to finish packing and take a shower."

"Alright, I'm in no rush anyway." His voice shifted once again. I thought about asking him about Delaney, but figured he had already talked to her and it was best if I didn't get involved in their business. After I had forced her to go party with me last night, I didn't want to get her in trouble.

"I'll text you when I'm ready."

"Okay," Luke replied and hung up the phone.

For the next hour, I gathered everything I would need for the four-week holiday break. I was dreading every minute of it, wishing I didn't have to go home. I checked my phone several times, wondering why I hadn't heard from Raven. If last night's conversation had taken place, which I was pretty sure it had, why hadn't he called me? I checked the time once more. It was half past one and I knew he had to be awake. Why hadn't he called me? My fingers hovered over the keyboard and I clenched my teeth together. It took all my effort not to reach out to him, but I forced myself to be patient. To wait and let him call me. I didn't want to seem desperate, even though I was.

At two-thirty, I was beside myself. I messaged Delaney and she told me what I didn't want to hear — either be patient or call him. It wasn't the advice I wanted, but in reality, those were the only two choices I had. I opted for the toughest one and continued to wait. After getting dressed, I finally convinced myself that he wasn't going to call and I was so damn drunk that I must have dreamed the whole damn conversation.

Picking up my phone, I texted Luke.

Me: I'm ready when you are.

It took him a few minutes to respond.

Luke: I'll be there in about thirty minutes. Let Mom know.

Growling, I reluctantly typed out a message to our mother.

Me: We'll be home in an hour or so.

Mom: Please hurry. The news said a storm is coming in tonight. Snow and sleet. I want to get to the mall as soon as you get here. We can decorate tomorrow.

I thought about telling her that she didn't need me to go shopping, but I knew that would result in a phone call and I really didn't want to talk to her more than I had to. With indifference, I responded.

Me: Okay. We will be there soon.

Sitting on the edge of my bed, I stared at my phone as if that would do any good. No matter how hard I willed for a message or call from Raven, it didn't happen. I reached into my bag and took out my Kindle. I scrolled through several books I had last downloaded and settled on *Taking the Heat* by Samantha Long. I propped up against my bed to start reading, but no matter how hard I tried, I couldn't focus. My mind wouldn't stop thinking about Raven. Why hadn't he called me?

Feeling overly frustrated, I powered down my Kindle, grabbed my stuff, and headed downstairs. I refused to sit around in my room for one more minute. Raven's scent lingered in the air and it was driving me even more insane.

I rolled my luggage behind me and walked toward the one thing I knew would help, the piano. It had been weeks since I had played. A vivid memory crossed my mind and I recalled the last song I had played was with Raven.

Maybe this isn't such a good idea after all.

Pushing aside the memories, I sat my things along the wall and took a seat on the bench. People shuffled behind me, hauling their belongings out of the dorm, but I didn't let it stop me.

I lifted the fallboard and stretched my fingers across the keyboard. The cold, ivory keys felt good against my skin. The tips of my fingers hovered over the black and white keys and automatically started pushing them as if the song couldn't wait to be released from me. I played softly at first, then louder and stronger as I unleashed all the pent up anguish harboring around my heart. Why the hell were guys so damn confusing? Why couldn't they just face their emotions?

Tears filled my eyes, but I blinked them back. I had nothing to cry about. Just because Raven had told me he wanted to be with me and wanted to have sex with me, didn't mean he would.

I played the chords over and over again, whispering the lyrics to *Stay* by Rihanna under my breath. I truly didn't know what to think or how to feel about Raven and me. But there was something about him. Something about the way he made me feel. Something that I couldn't live without.

I closed my eyes as my fingers continued pressing the keys. The song fit Raven and me so perfectly. I hated it, but I couldn't stop playing it. It soothed me in a weird kind of way. I wished Raven could hear me playing it. Hear me saying how much I needed him and how much I couldn't stand being without him.

"It's not much of a life you're living." My breath faltered and my body stiffened. I knew I had to be dreaming again because Raven's voice was echoing in my ear. I opened my eyes and turned to see him standing behind me. How long had he been watching me? He stood with his jacket hanging off the tip of his finger, hitched over his shoulder. He had on a blue, striped shirt and faded jeans, paired with work-type boots. My eyes stayed glued to his sexy, model stance and I wondered what magazine cover he'd be on next. Raven was the best eye candy I had ever seen. The candy my body craved.

He laid his jacket on the floor and took a seat next to me. He continued singing and I had to take a deep breath to get my body moving again. I hit a few wrong keys, but kept playing. I couldn't believe that he was actually there. He stared intently at me and all sense of worry and sadness seemed to vanish in an instant. His presence had a way of doing that to me and no matter how hard I tried to warn myself to be cautious, my heart took full control of the situation. Every time.

Something told me the words he sang were exactly how he felt. That he couldn't live without me; that he wanted to stay with me. My heart soared to a new level of contentedness as our gazes connected. We began to sing, creating a lyrical dialogue that we were both too afraid to say out loud. Telling each other that the reason we held on was because we both needed the hole in our bodies gone. That we were both broken and we both needed saving. Even though we had no idea who was in need of it most.

We continued singing, not missing a beat until the song ended. Our eyes stayed fixed as we poured our hearts into each other. Our connection not only reunited us, but also took us a step deeper. I knew exactly how he felt and I was one-hundred percent sure he knew how I felt. We were the only people that could truly save each other.

"That was beautiful, Lexi." Raven tucked a stray strand of hair away from my face, reducing my body to a puddle of water.

I was a lost cause and totally consumed by The Raven's trap. But there was no one else I'd rather be imprisoned by.

"Thank you, but I messed up." I removed my hands from the keyboard and held them tightly in my lap. Every muscle twitched, eager to embrace him and never let go.

"It's okay. No one's perfect." He leaned closer to me and nudged me with his shoulder. "We all make mistakes. At least, I know I do."

I swallowed hard, trying to clear the knot in my throat. Why the hell was I so nervous? "I'm, um, no exception. I make mistakes just like you."

He cocked a brow. "Then that only means one thing."

"What's that?" My voice lifted in anticipation and my stomach twisted, hoping that he was about to tell me what I wanted to hear.

"We're good for each other."

Σ

Chapter 10

I smiled and my heart filled with an insurmountable amount of joy. Raven was confirming his decision to be with me. I pressed my lips together, trying to stop the trembling because I was on the verge of happy tears. But it was no use. One escaped and Raven caught it with the pad of his thumb.

"Lexi?" He cupped my face with his hands and I instantly lost myself even further.

Placing my hands on his chest, I responded, "Yes, Raven."

"Do you wanna hang out today?" His alluring eyes roamed my face as though committing every part of me into memory. "And every day after that?"

"More than you will ever know," I whispered against his lips.

His mouth parted and my eyes fluttered to a close. My heart did a happy dance as his lips pressed to mine. I spread my hands over his broad shoulders and pulled him into me. His familiar scent encamped me and I felt safe and somewhat whole again.

"Lexi?"

We stopped kissing and I jumped at the sound of my brother's voice.

"Luke. Hey. I, um..." I hopped off the piano bench and retrieved my phone from my back pocket. "I didn't realize you'd be here so soon." I glanced at the clock on my phone, but my mind couldn't piece together how much time had passed since I'd texted him.

"What's going on?" Luke looked at me and then at Raven. His eyes were as wide as saucers and his mouth was slightly agape.

Raven got up from the bench slowly and then stood beside me. He shoved one hand in his pant pocket and ran the other over his short hair. A perplexed expression formed on his face as his eyes darted back and forth between Luke and me.

"Hey, man...good to see you." Raven extended his hand and Luke hesitantly gripped it. Apparently, Raven knew my brother. "Lexi is your sister?"

"Yeah." Luke nodded.

"No shit." Raven's voice lilted.

They continued shaking hands as their stare deepened. I said a silent prayer that things weren't about to get ugly. "What are you doing with her?" Luke asked.

Adrenaline coursed through my veins. I felt like I had just been caught with my pants down even though I knew I had nothing to be nervous about. I was free to see whomever I wanted. The air thickened to the point I was barricaded between them, but refused to let the situation turn bad. "You two know each other?"

They both looked at me and finally stopped shaking hands as reality set in. "Yeah, we've known each other for a while." Luke shot me a quick gaze while keeping a watchful eye on Raven.

"I've trained with your brother several times." Raven's head bobbed back and forth, as he was working to put two and two together. "I can't believe Luke Thompson is your brother. You two look nothing alike."

"We're not identical, remember? And we have the same last name, so..."

"I know, but it just never occurred to me." The revelation left a star-struck expression on his face.

"Luke, can you give us a moment?" I motioned with my head toward Raven and waited to see how my brother would respond.

Luke raised his brows, shooting me a warning stare. His jaw worked from side to side and I knew he was holding back from telling me something. I couldn't blame him because I knew what he was thinking. What the hell was I doing with Raven Davenport?

"Yeah, I guess. I'll be waiting out in the car." He turned to Raven and said, "Give me a call. I have a new routine I'd like to show you."

Raven lifted his head with a slight nod. "Yeah, I'll reach out to you over the break."

"Do you want me to take something to the car?" Luke pointed to my bags along the wall.

"I've got it." Raven quickly darted over to them. Luke rolled his eyes and I returned the same warning stare he had given me.

"Whatever," Luke mumbled before walking outside.

I exhaled, glad that introduction was over with. I couldn't imagine how I would introduce him to my parents if that opportunity presented itself. I'm sure Luke had a thousand questions for me and was already on the phone with Delaney, trying to find out what she knew.

"I can't believe Luke is your brother."

"I can't believe you two know each other."

"Small world." Raven hitched a bag over his shoulder. "And you're right. You two look nothing alike." Raven gave me a thorough once over and my cheeks flushed with heat. I wrapped my arms around myself, suddenly feeling self-conscious.

Setting my bags down, he asked, "What's wrong?" He reached for my hands, pulling them away from my body. His fingers caressed my skin, giving me the warmth it had been crying out for. "Did I embarrass you?" One by one, he laced his fingers through mine and pulled me close. My body trembled and I took long, steady breaths, trying to ease back into my comfort zone. Raven knew how to get my blood flowing, not to mention a couple of other things, too.

I nodded and stared at the floor. His minty breath surrounded me and I gripped his hands tighter, using him for support. "Yeah, kind of."

"Well, get used to it." He nuzzled my neck and I about came undone. Chills dotted up my back and spread across my face. I bit my lower lip, trying to hold back my desire to jump into his arms. "Because I'm going to be doing a lot of staring." He nibbled on my ear and a moan escaped my throat. "And touching."

Oh, shit.

"Raven," I whispered in his ear, "why are you telling me this when you know I have to go?"

"That's just it, I don't want you to go."

I glanced at the girl behind the front desk. "But they are about to shut the dorms and my mom is waiting."

"I know." He rubbed his thumb along the top of my hand and I fidgeted, trying to fend off the need calling deep inside of me. "I was kind of hoping we'd hang out today."

"How will I get home? I don't have a car."

The green in his eyes flickered. "I can take you home later. If you want."

"Seriously?" I had to stop for a moment and think about what he said. I really wanted to go with him, but I knew my parents would flip. Then again, did I really care what they thought? I wasn't with Collin any longer.

"Yeah. Your parents live in Dallas, right?"

I nodded and then smiled. "I'll tell Luke."

Raven picked up my bags. "Let's go."

It took all of my effort not to run to Luke's car. I was sure that what I was experiencing is what most girls went through with their high school crush. At twenty years old, it was a little embarrassing, but I loved every minute of it.

Luke was leaning against his car, smoking a cigarette while texting. I knew he was chatting with Delaney. I made a mental note to message her and ask her what he wanted to know.

"I'll be right back." I lifted to the tips of my toes and planted a quick kiss on Raven's cheek. The cold wind whipped around me and I zipped up my jacket.

"Ready?" Luke tossed his cig to the side and started to round his car.

"I'm not going home," I blurted, wanting to get this over as quickly as possible. I hated to admit that I was terrified to tell my brother, but I think it was because I knew what he was going to tell me.

Luke stopped and pivoted on the heels of his Chucks. "You're going with him?"

I pulled at the edge of my knee-high boots, feeling my legs shake. I sucked at these situations. "Yes. He's going to take me home later." I gave a casual glance to Raven. Even though he was a few feet away, I knew he could hear our conversation.

"I promise I'll bring her home when ever she's ready," Raven quickly interjected.

Luke gave him a doubtful look and then opened the car door and got in. He shut the door and rolled down the window. "You tell Mom, I'm not going to."

I nodded, relieved that he wasn't going to give me a hard time like I thought he would.

"Lexi, I'm sure you already know this," a low chuckle escaped, "but Raven's probably not the best guy for you."

Throwing my hands up in the air, I wondered what Delaney had told him and what he knew about him. "Why does everyone keep telling me that?"

Luke's finger tightened around the steering wheel and his eyes narrowed. "Because it's the truth. Raven has some serious issues."

"I know." I huffed and then gripped the door between my hands. "And I'm trying to help him work through them."

"Oh, so now you're a shrink?" The cynicism wove through me, making me angrier by the minute.

"What? I'm no—" Luke started his car, drowning my words with the motor.

With his head cocked to the side, he said, "Look, I'm not here to tell you what to do. You're a grown woman and have to figure things out for yourself. All I'm saying is please be careful. If he tries to get you to use drugs, you better walk away."

"Don't worry, Luke, I'm not about to get involved with drugs."

"That's what you think." Luke shifted the car into drive.

"How can you say that?" I shook my head. "You know me better than that."

Luke glared at me and a wave of uneasiness washed over me. "No, I really don't. Not anymore."

My stomach dropped. Was my brother serious? I knew I had changed, but it was for the better. I was living my life for me instead of for our parents. I hadn't changed that much. I mean, sure, I'd been to a few parties and done a few shots, but I hadn't become some wild girl who had gone crazy. Or had I?

Before I could respond, Luke said, "Just call me if you need me."

"Thanks," I replied and then stepped back. I watched as he drove off and wondered if I was truly making a horrible mistake.

"Everything alright?" Raven asked as I bent down to pick up my purse.

"Yeah. We're good," I said in a low tone, trying to sort through the thousands of voices echoing in my head.

Why couldn't people just let me live my life?

"Your brother's a great baseball player and trainer."

"Thanks. I grew up watching him play." I walked next to him as we trekked down the sidewalk.

"Too bad he prefers to be a trainer," Raven commented. I knew if he had that tidbit of information, he knew my brother pretty well.

"I know. He plays to appease my parents." We crossed the street to the parking lot across from the dorms and near the stadium. Raven clicked the trunk and it popped open, then he lifted my bags and placed them inside.

"Sometimes we have to do things even though we don't want to."

I tossed in one of my bags. "True. But at what point do you finally say, 'I'm going to do what I want to do'?"

Raven closed the trunk and pressed his weight against it. He held that stance for a while as he contemplated my question. "I guess when you realize that it's not what you want or you just can't handle it anymore."

"Exactly."

Raven unlocked the doors and we got in the car. He turned up the heat and I placed my hands over the vents, wiggling my fingers. "Are you cold?"

"A little."

He took my hands in his and brought them to his lips. Warm air spread over my fingers as my breath stalled in my lungs. He did it repeatedly, causing more flesh bumps to raze my skin. In a slow and deliberate manner, he placed soft kisses on the top of my hand and then pressed his lips in a trail up my arm. I shivered internally as a rush of heat inundated me, causing a moan to escape from my throat.

"Better?" He glanced up and drew my face to his.

"Yes, much better." I shifted in my seat, trying to keep my body under control. Needless to say, I was quickly losing the battle. I was no match for The Raven's charm and affection. I was a glutton for his touch, but I was right where I wanted to be. It was all clear to me now. I knew the reason why I was ready to fall into him, despite my fear of being able to trust him. Raven awakened a piece of me that I never knew existed. For the first time, I truly felt alive.

"I promise you, it will only get better." He stared deeply into my eyes and kissed me softly on the lips.

My heart rate picked up and I couldn't help but feel excited. I hoped what he told me last night was true and that he wouldn't hold back because of my virgin status. "I'm holding you to that promise."

Raven pulled out of the parking lot and sped down the street. It was as though we didn't need a green light to go where we wanted. We could run all the red lights and let the road take us wherever. I had nothing to hold me back. Not Collin or my parents. It was up to Raven how far he wanted to take things with me, because I knew I was willing to go all the way.

We ended up in downtown Fort Worth. Thousands of tiny white lights twinkled in the trees, warming the cold December air and reminding us that Christmas was only a few weeks away. Large boxes wrapped in shiny red and gold paper lined the steps of the town hall and people stood near them, taking pictures. A tall, wooden nutcracker saluted us as we passed the stately steps of the courthouse and I was glad that he brought me there.

"This is so pretty." I peered out the front windshield.

"I heard there's an outdoor ice rink near the city Christmas tree. Do you want to go check it out?"

"Sure."

Raven parked nearby and we got out of the car. He slipped on his jacket, and then laced his fingers through mine. Knowing that he wasn't afraid to show his affection toward me made me smile. We walked along the sidewalk in perfect sync with each other as Christmas music played in the distance. People shuffled in and out of the trendy shops carrying shopping bags and the smell of fresh gingerbread filled the air. I loved Christmas time and spending it with Raven made it even more special.

"Have you ever been here before?"

"No, never. My family tends to hang out in the downtown Dallas and Northpark area. But I think I like it here better." A couple sat on a nearby bench, drinking coffee and laughing. "It feels quaint and friendly. Dallas has a pretentious crowd that can make you feel out of place, if you know what I mean."

"I know exactly what you mean. I've never hung out in Dallas, but we definitely had places like that back in Louisiana."

We crossed the street to the main area where a thirty-foot Christmas tree stood. Thousands of white lights, along with big, red balls and snowflakes, decorated the tree. Large, fake gingerbread houses and boxes wrapped like presents surrounded the stately Douglas fir. "It's so beautiful."

"Just like you." Raven squeezed me tighter.

I couldn't help but giggle. "Thank you." He totally knew how to push all of the right buttons. "Now, it feels like Christmas. Thank you for bringing me here."

He glanced at me. "Were you not in the Christmas spirit?"

Shaking my head, I responded, "Not really. Since I missed Thanksgiving dinner, it didn't seem like the holidays."

"And now it does?"

"Most definitely."

"Good." Raven smiled and placed a soft peck on my forehead. "So, is there anything on that list of yours that you'd like to do?"

"Um, well, I haven't thought much about that list to be honest with you." I didn't want to lie to him, so I told him the truth. Even though I had thought about him a lot, I hadn't given much attention to the list after he had told me that he couldn't be with me. "Besides, I thought you said we'd make it up as we went along." I elbowed him in the ribs.

"I did say that, didn't I?" An impish grin formed on his face and I couldn't help but wonder what was going through his head. "Hey, I have an idea. Have you ever been ice skating?" Raven turned to the large outdoor ice rink behind us.

The suggestion sounded fun but knowing my lack of coordination, I saw disaster spelled in big letters. Families and couples circled around the large rink while the less coordinated ones hovered in the center or along the walls. I knew I'd be the one stuck in the middle. "A long time ago."

"Then, let's do it." Raven urged me forward and I took a step back.

"Oh, I don't know." I tucked my hair behind my ear to keep it from whirling around my face. "I know I won't be able to balance myself."

"I promise I won't let you fall." He grabbed my hands and started taking slow strides backwards. "Come on, Lexi. You know you want to go skating with me." He winked, teasing me. "I won't take no for an answer."

"But I thought you said you wouldn't do anything unless I asked you to."

Raven stopped and took a step toward me. "I was referring to other things." He leaned closer and nuzzled me along my neck, making my body tense and then relax.

"Oh, okay. I'll have to remember that," I said, in between laughs, though I doubted that I would forget. If he gave me the chance, I'd be telling him all the things I wanted him to do to me.

"If you really don't want to, we don't have to." Raven stopped his contagious flirting, but it didn't help. I was already sucked in by his charm. Part of me wanted to let go and not worry about making a fool of myself, but the other part reminded me that it would be dangerous. That I could fall and hurt myself. The more I listened to that other part, the more I realized it was Collin's voice I heard.

Blinking a few times, I managed to turn off that nagging voice. "No. I want to. Let's have some fun."

"Seriously?"

"Yes, let do it."

"Cool. This is going to be fun." Raven led me toward the rink and my mind shifted between excitement and fear. I prayed that I wouldn't bust my butt and make an idiot of myself.

"I'm warning you now, I'm going to be like a newborn deer on the ice. Please don't let me get hurt."

"Don't worry, Lexi. I've been ice skating for years." His voice was full and resonant. It gave me a sense of comfort that established a new level of trust with him. Regardless, I was still weary as to how good he really was on the ice.

"Seriously? I mean, you don't look like the Disney on Ice type."

"Thanks," he snorted. "Actually, one my coaches in middle school said it taught great coordination, so I decided to give it a try and he was right. I've been skating ever since."

"I wish I would have gotten that advice when I was younger. You saw how horrible I was at playing football and that was on dry ground."

"You weren't that bad. Give yourself some credit."

We entered the park area and Raven stopped at a vendor outside the rental desk. "Do you have any gloves?"

Pulling the lining out of my coat pocket, I showed him they were empty. "No, why?"

"Because it would be a good idea to protect your hands." Raven picked out a cute pink and brown knitted cap with braids made out of yarn on each side and matching gloves. "Do you like these?"

I held them against my chocolate brown pea coat. "Yes, they're perfect." I reached in to my purse for my wallet, but Raven had already handed the lady some money before I could give her my card. "I can pay for them."

"Just consider them a gift from me." With ease and precision, he helped me slip on my gloves one at a time. He smiled and slightly adjusted the hat before tugging on the braids that hung down. "Damn, you look so sexy." Reaching in his back pocket, he pulled out his phone. "I think I need a picture."

"What?" I froze, shocked that he would want a picture of me. Regaining my senses, I ducked my head away from his phone. "No, I'm sure I look silly."

"No, you don't. Come on, baby, smile for me."

Baby? Oh my God!

A flush of heat consumed my cheeks and I couldn't help but smile for him. I was never one for pictures, aside from when Delaney took them, but Raven taking them of me, had me on a new edge of excitement. He totally had me eating out of his hands.

Damn, I wanted him so bad.

"Your turn," I said, reaching for his phone.

He pulled the phone from my reach. "You really don't want a picture of me."

"Oh, yes I do." I yanked my phone from purse and held it up. "Give me a sexy smile."

"Sexy?" He grinned and I captured a picture of him with his thumbs shoved in his pockets. His weight was shifted to the left and he held a sexy stance. I knew I'd be drooling all over my phone as I slept with it every night.

"Man, how did I get so lucky?" he said, appraising my picture on his phone.

"What?" I looked down at his phone, trying to determine what he saw in me.

"How did I get so lucky to be with a beautiful girl like you?"

"Oh, um, thanks." I bit on my lower lip, trying to build the courage to tell him how freaking hot I thought he was. Instead, my throat tightened and I struggled to speak. "I..."

He looked at me, staring deep into my eyes. "I never thought it would be you."

"What do you mean?" A sudden fear crept over me. Had he meant that in a good or bad way? Because no matter how hard I tried to convince myself that I was better than the girls he had been with, my mind had a hard time believing it.

"Being with you makes me feel like a completely different man."

"Umm, is that good or bad?"

"Definitely good." He winked. "Are you ready to have some more fun?" He took a knitted cap out of the pocket of his coat and placed it over his head.

"As long as it's with you." I pulled the cap over his eyes and laughed.

Lifting it, he said, "Just what I wanted to hear." He held out his phone. "But first, let's take a selfie." Raven wrapped his arm around me and pressed his cheek to mine. "Smile, beautiful." He held out his phone and snapped a picture of us making a silly face.

"Let me see." Raven brought our picture to the screen. We looked so happy together. I never imagined that he'd be the one I wanted. "Aw, we look so cute."

"I think I need to post that on Facebook." Butterflies swirled inside of me. If Raven was posting things about us, it was probably a good indication that he wanted everyone to know he was with me. I was pretty sure that was a sign that we were going to the next level.

He led us to the rental desk where we got our skates. After we changed our shoes and got a locker for my purse, he took me by the hand and led me to the ice. "Just practice balancing first, then we will work on taking strides along the ice."

"Okay." My legs wobbled and shook as we walked along the foam floor. If staying balanced on a thin piece of metal was this hard, I knew I was going to struggle once I got on the slippery surface. Raven stepped onto the ice without trouble. Holding on to the edge of the wall, I made my way into the rink.

"You alright?"

I nodded. My heart thumped and fear consumed me, but I knew Raven wouldn't let me get hurt. With him, I had nothing to worry about. "I just don't want to fall."

"Don't worry. I won't let you get hurt." He stood close to me, protecting me from the people that zipped past us. I gripped onto his hand like he was my lifeline.

I tightened my legs and straightened my back, demanding my body to balance itself on the slick block of ice underneath me. "I think I got it."

"Are you sure?"

"Yeah."

Raven let go of my hand, but remained next to me. "Try to glide by moving your feet forward, but don't pick them up."

"Okay." I did as he said, concentrating on my movement. Before I knew it, I was floating along the ice. We circled around the ring a few times, building my confidence. With each turn, my feet seemed to learn how to move along the ice and my legs stopped shaking, enabling me to balance myself.

He grinned and I saw the delight in his expression. "Lexi, you're ice skating."

I pressed my lips together, trying not to get overly excited. "Yeah, but if you take away the wall, I'll fall."

"Oh, I think you'll be fine." Raven eased my hand from the railing. I hesitated at first and then wrapped my fingers around his big, strong hand.

I looked around, taking note of all the people who skated around the rink like they were running on dry ground. "I don't think I'm ready."

"Sure you are." He took my other hand. "I promise I won't let you fall."

"Oh, Raven!" A high-pitched screech escaped from my throat as he guided me away from the edge. With one arm wrapped around me, we skated around the huge oval rink. The brisk air hit my face and filtered through my hair. I felt so free and being next to Raven made it more incredible. "This is so much fun!"

"Told ya!" He picked up the pace and we held hands, forming memories that I'd never forget. With each passing minute, I gained more trust along the slick surface, allowing him to drag me around and around. We formed a figure eight over and over again, until we wore a permanent number in the ice. Raven knew how to make me feel like I was the only girl in his world. I just hoped that I would be.

Maneuvering backwards, Raven glided us effortlessly along the ice to the center of the rink where we formed our own intimate circle. The lights from the trees flickered and the cold air surrounded us, but our warm breaths created a level of comfort that made my body forget all about the fear I had been experiencing. I was totally in The Raven's control.

"See, this isn't so bad, is it?" He cocked a brow.

"No, but only because I'm with you." I had envisioned what it would feel like to be surrounded by thick, strong arms for longer than ten seconds and it was absolutely divine. My body didn't know how to react and a war zone quickly erupted inside of me. One side told me to take things slow while the other encouraged me to go in for the kill. Everything was happening so fast and I absolutely had no idea what I was doing.

"I know we agreed to make your list as we go along, but I was actually thinking of all the places I'd like to take you." He pulled me closer and my head tilted back naturally as I gazed into his eyes. "All of the things we can do together." His hands dropped to my waist and my body tensed, soaking in every stare and touch.

"Oh, that's right. You said you couldn't wait to have more fun with me," I teased.

His hand splayed across my lower back and his magnetic touch seared my skin through the thick fabric of my coat. "Are you still game for that?" The warmth of his breath tickled my ear and neck causing goose bumps to raise along my arms.

I nodded because my brain was unable to formulate coherent words.

"I thought we could go back to my place tonight." He eyes captured mine and our lips neared. The small puffs of cold air that were escaping our mouths were quickly warming. "Unless you want me to take you home."

Home? Oh, hell no!

"No. I mean, yes." My fingers dropped to his hands, gripping them tightly. "Yes, I'd like to go to your apartment." I tried to downplay my eagerness, but lost the battle when I realized I was pulling him toward the exit gate. Raven knew how to propel my body to give in to every desire and need. But I didn't mind. In fact, I welcomed it.

"I guess you're ready to go." A grin spread from ear to ear as he moved forward.

"Oh, we can stay." I immediately stopped in my tracks, causing him to bump in to me. "I didn't mean we had to leave right now." My voice lilted as I stumbled back. My left skate went forward while my right skate went back, the slippery surface making it nearly impossible to stay upright.

"I've got you!" He grabbed my arms and pulled me into him. My feet wobbled as I fought for purchase on the ice.

Raven's body was like a well-built tank, standing firm on the slick surface. "You got it?" He held me tight and my legs slowly stopped.

"Thanks. I'm good." My hands rested against his puffed out chest and all I could think about was how much I wanted to see him shirtless. Would I get the chance tonight?

"So, are you ready to start working on eliminating more things on your list?" He cocked a brow and all self-control slipped away. My head tilted to the side and my lips aligned directly to his. His lips pursed together and I imagined them skimming over every inch of my body.

"The sooner, the better."

Σ

Chapter 11

I crossed the threshold of Raven's apartment, unsure of what to expect. Would tonight be the night I'd lose my virginity? Tremors shot through my legs, impairing my muscles and turning them into mush. If I didn't faint from the rush of excitement, it would be a miracle.

Raven flipped on a light. "Come on in." He set my bags on the floor and shut the door behind us. I jumped at the sound of the door meeting the frame, my senses heightened and over sensitive.

"Where do I put this?" I held out the large pizza box in question.

"Just set it on the coffee table." He motioned with his head. "We can watch a movie while we eat."

I quickly put the cardboard box on the wooden table and took a few steps back. Raven placed his hands on my shoulders and I whirled around. My breathing picked up and I struggled to keep up with the extra inhalation my lungs required.

"Relax. I was just taking your coat."

"Oh, yeah. Of course." I shucked my coat off and laid it on the chair, feeling like a complete idiot. I took several even breaths and managed to pull my brain back into function mode. "You have a nice place." My eyes scanned the miraculously kept apartment decorated in a browns, reds, and yellows. A leather-like sofa and loveseat surrounded a flat screen TV. In the kitchen, a tall dining table large enough to seat eight, dominated the small area. For two guys living there, it seemed professionally decorated and oddly clean — no funky smell or dirty clothes lingering. "Where's Josh?"

Raven walked to the kitchen and opened the refrigerator. I heard the sound of bottles clank against the counter and hoped he was getting me something to take the edge off. "He took Shelby home this morning."

"Oh." I rounded the couch and walked toward the kitchen. "Where's home?"

"Oklahoma City for her, Azle for him." He popped the tops off two beers and handed me one of them. "Cheers."

I tipped the neck of my bottle against his. "Cheers." My hand shook as I raised the glass to my lips. The liquid was icy cold, but it felt good funneling down my throat. I didn't want to get drunk like I had the night before, but I desperately needed some liquid courage. Especially if I was going to show him that I was more than ready to go all the way. Though, internally, I was scared as hell.

Would it hurt? Would I bleed? Would it be gross? Most of all, would I be able to please him? My mind was quickly spiraling into the fear zone and if I didn't stop it, I'd be running out of his apartment before I knew it.

I took a few more swallows, praying for some instant relief. Never had I been so nervous. Inhaling deeply, I managed to calm my erratic heart. "When will he be back?"

Raven lowered his beer bottle and licked his lips. My eyes focused on the movement of his tongue and every muscle in my body tensed. His lips moved and I knew he answered my question, but I didn't hear one word. I was too enamored by the wetness of his mouth.

"Huh?"

His eyes narrowed and a smile crept up over his face. "I said, probably the week after Christmas."

"Oh, wow. So are you just going to hang out here by yourself or go to your mom's house?" I quickly took another gulp, eager for the buzz to start. I shifted my weight from the left hip to the right, but couldn't seem to relax.

Come on alcohol start working!

"I'm not sure yet."

"Oh." I twirled a stand of my hair with my finger, around and around until I cut off the circulation. With my other hand, I gripped the cold bottle, trying to fizzle the intense flame burning inside of me. It was pointless. My body was aflame, burning with desire for Raven.

Approaching me, he placed his hands on my waist and pulled me close. His scent looped around me, unfettering the bundle of nerves inside of me while keeping me in a captive state. My mind numbed and only one command echoed inside of me.

Sex.

I wanted Raven more than I could ever imagine.

"Kind of depends on how things go tonight."

"Um, I—" My phone rang, cutting me off. I shuddered as I heard my mom's tone ring loudly. Her timing was impeccable. I got the eerie feeling that she knew I was up to something she wouldn't approve of.

"Is that your phone?" A questionable look crossed his face.

"Yeah, it's my mom." I retrieved it from my back pocket and showed him the screen with a picture of her.

"Darth Vader's theme song?" He let out a slight laugh.

Silencing the call, I replied, "Yes. My dad and I specifically coined that theme song as hers." I knew she was calling to find out when I was coming home, even though I had already texted her and told her I'd be home later. I prayed that Luke didn't tell them anything and quickly made a mental note to message Delaney as soon as I got a minute.

"That's hilarious. Do you like Star Wars?" His gaze transformed into one of curiosity.

"Yeah." I flipped my phone to silent and set it on the dining table. "I know, I sound like a geek, but my dad got me hooked on Star Wars and superhero stuff. That's how we connect."

"Seriously?" He smiled and I didn't know whether he was making fun of me or happy about what I had just revealed.

"Yeah, why?"

"I'm a huge comic book and Sci-Fi fan."

"Really?" I started laughing, amazed that we had one more thing in common.

With his hands on his hips, he said, "Well, I know what we're doing tomorrow."

Tomorrow? Yeah, baby!

"What's that?" I followed him into the living room, skipping along the way.

"We're going to the comic book store." He opened the media cabinet below the TV and took out a few movies.

"Sounds like fun. How did you get hooked on comic books?"

His smile turned downward and his stare drifted off behind me. "I used it as a way to escape. I'd pretend I was Spiderman or Batman and could take on all of the bad guys."

His voice was laced with pain and my heart ached for the past I knew very little about. I wanted to know about those deep, dark times but I knew right now wasn't the time. He'd tell me when he was ready. My phone vibrated against the table and we both automatically turned to look at it.

"Maybe you should talk to her." Raven kept glancing at the phone. "Let her know you're okay."

"I already told her I'd be home later tonight. I'll just send her another text." I quickly retrieved my phone and typed another message. "The truth is... she won't be happy if I tell her I'm with a guy."

"Oh, well the last thing I need is your parents accusing me of kidnapping or something." The thickness in is his voice told me he was concerned.

"Don't worry, I'd never let that happen." I wanted to assure him that being with me wasn't going to be a problem, even though my parents had no idea I was with him. "But you remember what I said about my parents being really strict, right?"

His eyes softened and his shoulders relaxed. "Yes, I recall."

I shoved my phone in my back pocket, grabbed my beer, and went straight to him. I placed a hand on his arm, trying to extinguish any thoughts that my parents didn't approve of him. Even though, deep down, I knew they would. "They would tell me to get my butt home right now, so it's better if I just tell them I'm staying with a girlfriend and that I'll be home later."

"Lying to your parents isn't good, Lexi." Raven's eyes bore into mine and for a second, I heard Collin's voice.

I shook the nagging sound out of my head and said, "I know. But trust me, I don't have any other choice."

"I get it." He gave me a meek smile. "So, what movie do you want to watch?" He held up a selection of Sci-Fi movies. "I'm sorry, I don't have any chic-flicks on hand."

Smiling, I pointed to *Man of Steel*.

"Superman it is." He winked and then loaded the disc into the player.

I lowered to the middle of the couch, unsure of where to sit. Stupid little thoughts taunted my mind and I fought to ignore them. With my knees pressed firmly together, I guzzled the beer like I hadn't drank in days.

"Pizza?" He flipped the cover back and the smell of fresh dough and pepperoni filled the air.

"Sure." I grabbed a piece and took bite. I wanted to chow down because I hadn't eaten anything since that morning, but I didn't want to have a huge carb belly in case things got a little heated later.

"Have you thought about anything you'd like to do?"

Have sex with you.

"Um, well... I'm not sure."

He took another bite of his pizza and swallowed. "What haven't you done?"

"Nothing." I took a small bite and chewed carefully. I'd read that eating slowly filled your stomach and I prayed it worked.

"Oh, come on. It can't be that bad."

"Trust me, it is." I covered my mouth, trying not to show him my food. "My parents didn't let us do much."

"That sucks." He grabbed another piece and shoved it in his mouth. "Name some things you've never done."

"Let's see..." I pressed a finger to my lip and my eyes traveled to the ceiling, "I've never been in a helicopter."

Raven hiked a shoulder. "Neither have I. Maybe that's something we can do together."

"Possibly."

"You don't want to?"

"I'm kind of scared of heights, to be honest."

"Oh, okay. We don't have to do that. I'm sure there's a crap load of other stuff we can do together."

I smiled, liking his suggestion. "I've never been to the beach. Luke has, though. He went with one of our cousins."

"Shut up." He gave me a weird look. "You've never been to the coast?" Getting up, he headed to the kitchen.

"Nope. Never. My mom has a phobia of the water. Her sister, my aunt Charlotte, almost drowned when they were little so she didn't allow us to go swimming."

"Damn." He returned with two beers. "Do you know how to swim?"

"Thanks," I said as I took the cold longneck from his hand. "I do. My dad convinced my mom that we all had to take swimming lessons to be on the safe side. She agreed and he took us." I took a quick drink. The liquid slid down my throat effortlessly and I began to relax.

"This spring break, we're going to change that." He winked at me. "We'll go down to South Padre Island and party our asses off."

Wiping my mouth, I tried to conceal the huge smile spreading across my face, but I couldn't hide my excitement. "You promise?"

"Hell yeah, baby. We're going."

I said a silent prayer, hoping I'd get to see that come true. We chatted through most of the movie, connecting further with every word we spoke. Raven was one of those people that you couldn't help but like.

After we finished eating, we both took off our shoes and relaxed against the overstuffed couch. The movie was more than halfway over, but since I had already seen it a few times with my dad, I didn't mind that I hadn't been paying much attention to it. I knew the best part was yet to come — Henry Cavill shirtless. The wind whistled outside and the windows rattled. A draft crept over me and I shuddered.

"Cold?"

"A little." I snuggled next to him, eager for him to hold me. Without warning, he got up and I frowned. What did I have to do to get a guy to hold me? I stopped the vicious thoughts when he picked up the flannel blanket folded over the edge of chair. Sitting down next to me, he draped it over us and then slipped his arm around me. His warm breath spilled over me and my body instantly warmed. He slipped the bottle from my hand and sat it on the table. "I think you've had enough. I don't want you drunk." He flashed me an enticing grin that sent my body into overdrive. A fire ignited in my belly and I knew it wasn't from the alcohol.

"Yeah, drunk is not good." I pressed my lips together and took a deep breath. "At least, not tonight."

His lips neared mine and I eagerly pressed a kiss to his soft mouth. Raven had the fullest lips I'd ever seen. Then again, he was only the second guy I'd ever kissed. Regardless, I loved his mouth and couldn't wait to savor it.

He kissed me gingerly at first and I followed his lead. Our tongues swept back and forth, twisting and turning in a slow ballad. He tasted like warm beer and dough, but I didn't care. His mouth was like an addiction mine refused to part with. Desire swept over me and I lost all self-constraint. I thrust my tongue deeper into his mouth and he responded favorably, pressing his chest against mine. I prayed he didn't feel the heaving of my breasts against him, but based on the hardness of my nipples, I was willing to bet he did.

My breathing quickened, but I managed to keep calm. He lowered me to the couch and the blanket slipped to the floor. I pivoted my body, aligning my hips with his. With our lips still joined to one another, he rocked his pelvis against me and I moaned into his mouth. Instinctively, my leg curled up and rubbed against him in slow, long movements. The friction of my jeans against him sent tiny shocks all over my lower body. His hand dropped to my thigh and he squeezed it tightly.

"You are so sexy," he whispered as his hand covered my breast.

A gasp escaped my throat and he caught it, filling my mouth with his tongue. I kissed him deep and hard, showing him just how much I wanted him. Tonight, I wanted him to take me to the other side. The side I'd been waiting to experience. The side that had been waiting for him to show my body what it wanted... what it needed.

Another whimper escaped my mouth when he suckled on the nape of my neck. Chills dotted my skin and I pressed into him more. It was like my body had an internal magnet that it was dying to connect to. My insides tingled like tiny electrically charged particles seeking the opposite end that only Raven could fit.

"Not as sexy as you." My hand trembled against his hard pecks and I tried to pace my actions. "You're like a Calvin Klein model supercharged on steroids."

"Whatever." A low laugh filtered through his lips. "I'm not like Superman."

"Oh, I'm sure you're ripped like him, if not more." I winked, stoking his ego. Honestly, I was dying to find out. It had to know.

"I promise you, I'm not." His lips pressed to mine repeatedly and I held on to each of them, not wanting him to stop.

"I don't believe you." My fingers twiddled with a button on his shirt, eager to unfasten all of them.

His head lifted and an enthralling smile settled over his lips. "Do you want me to show you?"

Hell yeah!

I nodded and bit my lower lip in anticipation. With one arm pressed against the couch, he slowly began to unbutton his shirt. His body hovered over mine and my body sank further into the couch. The wait was eating me alive. I had seen Collin without his shirt a few times, but I never had the pleasure of touching his bare chest. The tips of my fingers pulsated and it took everything in me to not reach out and rip his shirt off.

Damn, this is taking too long!

I grabbed a handful of his shirt and helped him pull his arms from the sleeves. "Desperate are we?" He laughed, but I didn't care.

To my disappointment, he wore a white T-shirt underneath. Even in a tight tee, he looked too damn hot. But I wanted to see his bare skin. Run my hands all over him. My palms landed on his chest and I inched his shirt upward. Rising to his knees, he said, "Easy now." His waggled his brows at me and I about came unglued. My body pulsed with an uncontrollable need that I was quickly falling victim to.

He curved his fingers around the hem of the shirt and raised it slowly over his chest, purposely teasing me. I liked it and wanted more of it. His huge biceps flexed and his stomach stretched as he peeled his shirt over his head. He rolled his shoulders and puffed out his chest. Ripples upon ripples covered his upper torso. He was perfection, as if Donatello had personally sculpted him. I couldn't even imagine what his lower body looked like.

The entire event happened in slow motion and I cursed myself for not filming it with my phone so I could watch it over and over again. My eyes surveyed the rugged terrain.

He was divine.

No, heavenly.

Godlike.

"Do you like what you see?" A sexy, seductive smile teased me and I nodded. No words could describe the breathtaking sight.

He placed my hands on his chest. My fingers trembled over the hardness but I didn't let that stop me from exploring every hill and valley. Immediately, my eyes took notice of the large tattoo that covered his right shoulder. Intricately woven branches covered the top of his arm and I followed them with the edge of my finger until it landed on a large black bird.

"A raven?" I studied the design that looked like it had been shattered into a thousand tiny birds.

He shrugged. "Yeah, you like it?"

"I do." It was a work of art and I wanted to snap a picture of it. Resisting the urge to grab my phone, I committed every detail of it, along with his body, to memory. I could never tire of looking at him.

"Do you have any tattoos?"

"All over my body," I deadpanned. "Big and small."

"I don't believe you." His eyes surveyed me from head to toe, causing a tornado to rip through me. I wasn't sure how much more I could handle of this storm he brewed inside of me. "Show me."

My fingers stop mid exploration and I froze. "What?"

"You heard me." With two fingers, he motioned for me to remove my sweater. "It's your turn. Take it off."

"Um, I don't have any tattoos. I was just messing with you." I tried to move from underneath him, but his legs straddled over mine, leaving little wiggle room.

He ogled me. "I know you don't, but I still want you to take off your shirt."

I suddenly felt a little breathless. "Oh... okay." Everything began to spin and I paced my breaths, telling myself it was okay to get undressed for him. I hated that I was so damn nervous. What if he didn't like what he saw? What if he thought my boobs were too small or if my body didn't do it for him? I knew if we were going to have sex, I had to get somewhat naked. Then, I remembered he saw me last night in my bra and panties. That he said I was beautiful.

"Um, alright." I gripped the edge of my sweater and pulled it over my head. He helped me slide it down my arms and then tossed it to the floor. He flashed me a quick smile before a look of disappointment settled onto his face.

"This too." His palm swept over my stomach, pinching the tight tank top and then releasing it. His hands splayed over my waist and he slowly inched up my cami, making my stomach clench with anticipation.

I winked at him. "Who's the impatient one now?"

"A guy can only wait so long." His stare turned hungry and I prayed my body would satisfy his cravings.

"And I've made you wait too long?" I teased, gathering the material around my breasts. I squeezed my arms together, giving him a full view of my cleavage.

If only my boobs looked that good without a push up bra.

"Too long." His eyes sparked with delight and he wet his lips, which told me he was at least somewhat happy with what I had to offer. "But Lexi, you've been worth every minute of it."

My checks flushed with heat and I lifted slightly, removing my tank and letting it fall to the floor. I rested against the couch, keeping one arm tucked behind my head.

"Beautiful." Raven's eyes traveled from my eyes to my chest and then to my stomach, widening along the way. "Your body is so beautiful." His eyes returned to mine.

I shook my head. "It's nothing like yours." I slapped my stomach, showing him my little jiggle. "I'm all flabby and you're like rock hard."

He traced swirls along my mid-section with the tip of his index finger and my stomach quivered. "That's how women are supposed to be. Soft and silky." His hand glided up my stomach and over my left breast, where he gave a slight squeeze. "And believe me, I like it."

He lowered his head and pressed a kiss to the hollow of my neck before continuing to pepper soft pecks all over my chest. I drove my fingers through his short hair, pulling him closer to me as he worked his way toward my breasts. His hand slipped behind me and in one quick pinch, he unfastened my bra. Placing both of his hands on my shoulders, he eased the straps down and slipped it off. Internally, I cringed, only relaxing when he said, "You've been hiding those from me this whole time?"

I titled my head to the side, not knowing how to respond. Dare I tell him my mom had brainwashed me to never let guys see them? He'd laugh at me. "Sorry." I wrapped my arms around my stomach, covering my breasts slightly. A guy had never seen me without a bra. This was so nerve wracking and scary.

His fingers laced around my arms and he lowered them, exposing me fully. "Don't ever be afraid to show me what God has given you." He placed my hands around his neck and lowered against me. Flesh to flesh, his skin seared mine, and my eyes fluttered to a close. We kissed until our lips were raw and our mouths were dry. I couldn't get enough of him.

His taste.

His touch.

His body.

It was what I had been missing all these years. Raven filled every void, every hole, and every missing piece. I just hoped I did the same for him.

When his hand dropped to the button on my jeans, I froze. Was I really ready to do this?

Hell yeah!

He stalled and then looked at me. "Don't be nervous, baby." His lips brushed against mine and I inhaled his tantalizing scent. "If I do anything that doesn't feel good or hurts you, just tell me and I'll stop."

I nodded, unable to swallow the huge lump in my throat.

I can't believe this is finally happening!

"Okay. But I have no idea what to do." I wanted to strip his jeans from his body and explore him further, but I reminded myself to keep calm and not get ahead of myself. I didn't want Raven to think I was another one of his sex-crazed hoes, even though I silently wanted to be.

"Don't worry. I'll show you what to do." His tongue slid into my mouth and I received it willingly. Our tongues fused together in a free spirit that no force could break apart. He was shaping and fastening me quickly, and even though I knew I needed to follow his steps, I couldn't stop myself from coming on to him. Errantly, my body refused to obey my mind and I knew he had me in his trap for good. One thing was certain; I wasn't playing in the peewee leagues anymore. I had made it to the pros.

"Are you ready for me show you what it feels like to feel like you're on top of the world?"

"I already am." I pawed at his chest, feeling the tiger in me come alive.

Raven chuckled low in his throat. "Baby, this is nothing."

Holy shit!

Was Raven referring to what he had told me last night? Even though I had been drunk, I knew what I wanted. I wanted to wrap myself completely around his body. I was ready for him to take me. And this time, I wasn't drunk.

I bit down on my lip, leaned forward, and whispered in his ear. "If you're asking me what I think you are, then the answer is yes. I'm ready to go all the way."

"Are you sure?" He stilled, his body hovering inches above mine. "Because I can wait."

I shook my head. "I don't think I can wait any longer."

"Good, because neither can I."

Σ

Chapter 12

I felt so beautiful next to Raven. Chills poured over me as he traced his finger on my bare back, altering my body to a new and undiscovered sense I had never experienced before. Having sex with Raven was beyond incredible. Magical in every way possible. I never imagined that losing my virginity would feel that good. He definitely knew how to satisfy every need, every desire, in every way possible, and I knew I'd never be the same again.

I liked it.

I wanted more of it.

But the clock flashed ten minutes after midnight and I had to get home. In the faint distance, I heard my phone vibrating and I knew it was my mom.

"Raven?" I raked my nails through his hair, rubbing his head in short strokes.

"Yeah?" He kept his fingers pressed to my skin, continuing to skim unknown patterns on me.

"What are you drawing on my back?"

"Plays," he replied with an impish grin on his face.

"What kind of plays?"

"Winning ones." His head lifted slightly. "And they have you in them."

Excitement bubbled in me. "I'm glad I can be a part of them."

"Me, too."

Silence filled the air as he continued imprinting his mark on me. No doubt, I was totally in The Raven's trap. But I couldn't help but wonder what that looked like. Raven and me together.

I cleared my throat a few times, trying not to spoil the mood. "It's after midnight and I know my mom is probably freaking out. I really need to go."

The moonlight filtered in through the window, casting a glow across his bare body. Raven was so damn sexy. I had to blink a few times because I really couldn't believe I was next to him. I didn't want to leave. I wanted to stay naked with him in bed forever. His fingers slowed as his eyes met mine. Sadness filled them and a level of pain struck the center of my chest. "Do you really have to go?"

Did he want me to stay the night with him? "Well, I—"

"I can't believe I'm about to say this." He latched onto a lock of my hair and wrapped it around his finger in slow turns. "I was hoping you might want to stay with me tonight." He inclined his head and anticipation filled his eyes. "That is, if you want to."

Raven wanted me spend the night with him.

In his bed.

A rush filtered through me and my jaw trembled as I opened my mouth. Was he serious? I tried to answer him but the words caught low in my throat.

"Yes. I do." I about screamed for joy.

Aside from his thrilling question, I couldn't help but focus on his first statement. It twisted in my head and I told myself not to go there, not ruin the moment, but it refused to leave my curious mind alone. Was I just another play in Raven's playbook? "As long as you're sure you really want me to."

He continued twirling my hair around his finger. "I wouldn't have asked if I didn't mean it."

"Do girls typically stay with you?" I blurted and then buried my head in the pillow, wishing I could take it back.

Idiot!

My hair slipped from his fingers and I turned to see his reaction. He rose to his forearms and his head hung low, nearly touching the bed. "Look, Lexi, I'm not really proud of my past, but I'm trying hard not to be that person anymore."

For a brief moment, I wanted to slap myself. "I'm sorry. I didn't mean to shame you." I placed my hand on his back and tried to pull him close to me. He didn't move at first, keeping his body firmly in place. But when I wrapped my leg around him, he shifted his body until he faced me.

"It's okay." Sincerity laced his voice and I knew he meant what he said, but it didn't change the fact that I hated myself for making him feel bad about his past.

"I'm just a little scared." I trailed a finger between his pecks, following the thin line of hair that disappeared beneath the sheets. I stopped near his navel before I lost my train of thought. "I'm afraid that one day you're going to tell me that you don't want to be with me anymore."

"Lexi, the last thing I want to do is hurt you." He laid his hand on top of mine, pressing it firmly against his heart. "There's something in here that's drawing me directly to you and I'm not going to ruin whatever it is." The thumping of his heart pulsated against my palm and drew closer to him.

Tears lingered on the rims of my eyes but I managed to keep them at bay. "That's all I'm asking for, and I want us to trust each other."

He lifted my hand and pressed his lips to my palm. "I'll prove to you that I'm worthy of your trust." His eyes closed for a brief moment and then rested on mine. "Look, I'm in unchartered territory, just like you. But there's no one else I'd rather be with."

Was Raven admitting to me that he was scared? Admitting that he didn't need all those hoes? That he only needed me? This guy was more than I could handle. His trap was totally making me fall for him deeper than I had ever thought I would. Apparently, he was just as nervous as I was.

"Then we'll take it one step at time." I placed my hand on his cheek and pressed my lips to his in a gentle kiss. "There's no rush."

His lips spread into a grin and my heart soared. Was I actually what Raven wanted and more? I tried not to get overly excited, but it was hard keeping my emotions under control.

"That might be a little difficult."

The air left my lungs. *So much for wishful thinking.*

"I'm a big guy and I'm known to take big steps." He traced my lips with the tip of his finger. "Do you think you can keep up with me?"

"As long as you allow me to, I'll try my best." I slipped my tongue across his finger and it awoke every taste bud in my mouth. A low moan escaped him and I knew he was hooked on me, too. There was no turning back now. I had to keep up with him. Even if I died trying.

"Good." He rolled on top of me, encapsulating me with his strong arms. "Because I'm not done with making you feel beautiful." My body fell limp and there was no point in resisting him. But I didn't want to. In deliberate, slow movements, he kissed my forehead, the tip of my nose, and then my lips. He suckled my lower lip and my back arched, pressing me into him further. His lips molded to mine and I took all of him in, one piece at a time. My body was on fire for him. Heat, want, need, and desire had me ready to combust. There was only one thing that would put out the fire.

Raven.

I wanted him to pour himself all over me. Soak up every piece of him until he was part of me. Forever.

Out of the corner of my eye, I saw Raven set my phone next to me on the bed. Muscles flexed with each movement and he looked so damn hot in his boxer briefs. His thighs were molded to perfection and I had to pinch myself just to make sure I hadn't dreamed the whole thing. Raven was one sexy babe and we had just spent half the night making love to each other.

"Good morning, baby." He pressed a kiss to my cheek. "Did you sleep well?"

I nodded. Raven had rendered me speechless by the work of his hands, the tenderness of his touch, and sweet words of his affection. My body hummed with a level of happiness and satisfaction that went beyond words. Chords of joy played over and over in my head and my body was singing an entirely new tune. Last night had changed it all. Nothing would ever be the same again. Raven was a part of me now; a piece I knew I couldn't live without.

"Are you hungry?" He sat on the bed and placed an arm over me. His body hovered close to mine, causing a rush of emotions to filter through me. I had to remind myself to take it slow. Being with him made my hormones soar. I was ready for him to take me again, and again, and again.

"Yes." I swallowed hard, trying to moisten my parched throat. "What time is it?" I held the sheet to my chest as I tried to turn to see the time.

"It's almost noon," Raven replied, not allowing me much room to move. But I didn't mind. "And your phone's been going crazy."

"Oh, wow. I didn't realize it was so late."

"I don't have much in the fridge, but let me see what I can put together." He gave me a quick peck on the lips and then crawled out of bed.

"Thanks." I sighed, glancing at the reminder that my time with Raven would soon be ending. At least temporarily. I always looked forward to Christmas break, but I wished we could skip it and dive right into spring semester just so I could be with Raven. Going home would make it difficult to see each other and I honestly didn't know how long I could go without being with him. I was a lost cause.

Raven opened his dresser drawer and pulled out a pair of Star Wars fleece pants. I lifted up on my forearms to catch a full view of his perfect bubble butt that tensed as he bent to slip them on. I could watch him get dressed and undressed all day. The scene was deific.

He turned and faced me, quickly tying the strings into a perfect bow. The pants sat low on his waist, just below the indentions of his pelvic bone. Knowing what laid under those Death Stars made me want to take the ends of the drawstring in my mouth and pull them off. I was quickly transforming in to a sex-crazed girl and the more I tried not to think about him, the more I did. "I'll call you when it's ready." He left the room and my head hit the pillow.

I had to be dreaming. Being with Raven was unfreakin' believable.

My phone buzzed and I glanced to see a text from Delaney.

Delaney: WTF? Luke said you stayed with Raven. Way to go!

Me: I know! I can't believe it.

Delaney: Do tell.

Me: Nope. Respectful girls don't kiss and tell.

Delaney: Oh, whatever. You threw out that level of conservativeness when you decided to hook up with Raven.

Me: Yeah, I guess you're right.

Delaney: So, did you finally turn in your V card? Tell me. I'm dying to know!

Me: Lol! Yes and it was beyond incredible.

Delaney: Oh hell. Sounds like you're totally sucked in.

Me: Yep. I'm definitely wrapped in The Raven's trap.

Delaney: Have fun! Do everything I would do and more!

Me: Don't worry, I am ⊠

My hand rested against the bed, still holding on to my phone. I giggled internally, reminiscing on what had happened last night. The way Raven touched me. The way he made feel, but most of all, how he showed me what to do and didn't make me feel embarrassed. It was surreal and I wasn't ashamed about giving my virginity to him.

My phone rang, snapping me out of my rumination. I cringed when I saw my mom's picture appear. I considered not answering the phone but knew I'd pay for it later. Hesitantly, my finger hit the answer button.

"Hello?"

"Lexi? Where the heck are you?" I held the phone away from my ear as her voice bellowed loud and clear through the speaker.

"Hey, Mom. I'll be home shortly. I just need to shower and get dressed." I cringed with each word I spoke.

"Where are you?" She pounded question after question, not stopping for a breath of air. "You need to get home immediately. A bad storm is expected to hit in a few hours and I don't want you caught in it."

"Okay. Okay." I sat up and looked around the room for my clothes. I was completely nude and knew if I went to the kitchen in my birthday suite, Raven and I would be back in bed celebrating early. Not that I minded, but I had to be realistic and get home before my parents sent out a search team.

"Who are you staying with?"

"With a friend, near the campus."

"That's not answering my question. Who are you with?" Fury laced my mom's voice and I knew she wasn't happy. She wanted specifics and I wasn't telling her what she wanted to know.

"Look, Mom, I'm fine. I'll be home in a few hours." Picking up the covers, I searched underneath them. There was no sign of my underclothes.

Crap!

"Lexi, why won't you tell me who you are staying with?" Her voice deepened as the tension built between us. Her accusatory tone seeped through the phone, making me nervous. I jumped out of the bed as if she were on the way to pick me up. I had to find my clothes and get dressed.

"Does it matter?" I hobbled around the room, trying to cover my exposed body parts. "I'll be home in a few hours."

"Lexi, are you with a guy?"

Shit!

"I'll be home a little bit. Bye, Mom." I hung up the phone, refusing to answer her question. There was no way to tell her the truth. My only option was to lie and I didn't want to. She'd never understand and she'd tell my dad. Both of them would wear me down, telling me how I was making a huge mistake.

Pressing the phone to my mouth, I tried to recall where I'd left my clothes. That's when I remembered that Raven had removed them in the living room. My bags were in there, too. I'd have to pass the kitchen to get them. I circled the room, vying for the best option when I saw one of Raven's long-sleeved dress shirts hanging on the edge of a chair. My options were few: run out naked and retrieve my clothes, go through his drawers and find something to wear, or put on his shirt. I opted for the most obvious.

And boy was I glad I did.

His scent lingered on the material and I inhaled deeply. My eyes shut as I sucked in every fiber of his smell. It sent tiny shocks through me while relaxing me at the same time. I wrapped the shirt around me, reveling in a paradise that I never wanted to part from. Ever.

"Like the way my clothes smell?" Raven stood in the doorway, holding onto the doorframe with both hands. A flirtatious smile played on the edge of his lips and he looked sexy. Contrary to how I probably appeared. Like an idiot!

Kill me now, please.

"Um..." I relaxed my arms, but made sure the material covered my bare body. "I, um, left my clothes in the living room."

"Correction." His hands dropped and he neared me. "I took your clothes off in the living room."

"Oh, well, yeah, I guess you're right. I mean, you did strip them off of me." I shifted my weight from my left hip to the right.

"I sure did." He cocked a brow. "And I can't wait to do it again."

A low whimper escaped from the back of my throat. My hands relaxed and I allowed his shirt to fall open. His eyes dropped to my chest and he extended his hands. I shuddered as my skin prepared to receive his touch. My knees shook and muscles went limp.

"But you need to eat first." His fingers grasped the top button of my shirt and my stomach let out a rumble, thanking him while my body screamed, *no!*

"Food would be good," I managed to reply, unable to form complete sentences or articulate thoughts. I was in desperate need of food. After last night and this morning, I was totally spent.

Raven's eyes traveled over me, making my cheeks flush with heat. "Damn, you look sexy as hell in my shirt."

"It's amazing how your clothes do that to me." I ran a hand through my matted hair and prayed I looked somewhat decent.

"I think it's the other way around." One by one, his fingers pushed each button through the holes. "You make my clothes look damn good." After he finished buttoning the shirt, he pressed a kiss to my forehead. "Let's eat."

He took me by the hand and led me to the kitchen. On the dining room table was breakfast for two. My heart melted as I took note of the perfectly folded napkin and spoon with two bowls of cereal and orange juice.

"I know it's not much, but it's all that I have." He flashed a lopsided smile. "I wasn't expecting to stay here."

"It's perfect, Raven." I pulled out a chair. "Thank you."

We sat and ate our breakfast, chatting like we normally did. Everything felt so natural and comfortable with him. I still couldn't believe we were together. That I had given myself to him. That I had shared that special bond with him. It was surreal and fabulous. I heard my phone going off in his room and quickly reminded myself that this day would soon end.

I finished the last drop of my juice and set the glass on the table. "I guess I should take a shower and get dressed so you can take me home."

Raven's eyes drifted to his bowl and he pressed the spoon in the small puddle of milk. His chest rose and fell in long, slow paces as his shoulders slumped forward over the table. I waited for him to say something, but he didn't speak.

After several long minutes, I finally said, "My mom said there was a bad winter storm due to arrive in a few hours. She didn't want me to get caught in it." I stood up and took my bowl and glass to the sink.

"I'll get it." Raven followed me to the kitchen, carrying his empty dishes.

"I can help you wash them." I turned on the water and began to rinse my glass.

Raven reached his hand over mine and turned off the water. "Stay with me."

I looked at him, completely caught off guard. "What?"

"You heard me." He turned me to face him. "Don't go."

My heart took flight as excitement raced through me. Raven wanted me to stay with him? Was I dreaming?

"Seriously?" I placed my hands on his chest, fighting to keep my fingers under my control. The tips of my fingernails dragged across his smooth skin, erupting tiny flesh bumps. "You really want me to stay with you?"

"Only if you want to." He wrapped his arms around my waist, splaying his hands along the curve of my back. I leaned back, allowing our eyes to connect. His hands slid down until the edge of his fingers brazed the bottom of my butt cheeks. It sent tiny sparks along my flesh and all of the air in my lungs vanished.

"So, you want to wake up with me every morning?"

Raven's head tilted to the side and my lips followed his. "Is that too much to ask for?" Everything seemed to slip away as I imagined spending the next few days with him. The entire world could've been crumbling around me, but I didn't hear one sound, except for his hypnotic voice that wrapped around me, lulling me deeper into his trap. I wanted his voice to be the last sound I heard every night.

"No, not at all."

"Good." His lips puckered against my mouth in a slow, deliberate motion. "Because I want to see you tomorrow and every day after that, just to start." He smoothed my hair around my face and I fell for him all over again. There was no turning back.

Σ

Chapter 13

Raven stepped out of the bathroom wearing only a towel. I tried not to watch him as I looked through the mirror, applying my mascara, but the scene was more than tempting. He stood with his back to me as he searched through his chest of drawers for some clothes. Droplets of water trickled down the curve of his spine and I wanted lick them off before taking his towel to dry him. Pat him in all the right places and then rub lotion all over his body. My mind focused on one thing only.

Raven.

He released his towel and I dropped my mascara wand. His ass was so plump and round, exactly how a football players rump looks underneath their tight pants. I quickly retrieved the wand and tried to focus on my face, but my eyes continued to wander to the reflection of Raven getting dressed behind me.

He put on his jeans and I let out an audible sigh. "What's that noise?" Inclining his ear in the direction of the window, he paused as he listened for a moment.

"What?" I had been so consumed by his presence that I hadn't noticed the sound of pellets beating on the window.

"Is that ice?" He pulled on a sweater and went to the window. "Damn, it's sleeting," he said, peering outside.

I zipped up my makeup bag and walked toward him. Glancing over his shoulder, I saw the ground was covered in tiny white BBs, making it look like a blanket of snow. It was coming down hard and fast, slashing against the window. "If it freezes tonight, it's going to be an ice rink outside."

"I know." He let go of the blinds and faced me. "We better hurry up and get to the store. Otherwise, we won't have anything to eat."

"Okay, let me get my shoes and we can go." I darted to the living room and put on my boots and coat. Raven pulled on his jacket and grabbed his keys.

"Ready?" he asked as he fit the cap over my head. "You're so beautiful." Leaning forward, he kissed the top of my head.

I smiled uncontrollably. "And you're one sexy babe." He knew how to strike all the right chords, making my body hum in delight. I slipped on my gloves and picked up my purse.

"Then that means we make one awesome looking couple." Raven winked and then opened the door. A gust of frigid air swept over us and we both gasped. It prickled my skin and my teeth began to chatter uncontrollably. "Damn, that's cold." He shoved the key in the slot and locked the door behind us.

We walked to the parking lot, our feet sliding on the ice that had already started sticking to the pavement. "This is going to be bad," I said, moving to the wet grass. The last thing I needed was to fall and break my leg.

"It sure is. Perfect weather for sleeping in, watching movies..." Raven wrapped his arms around me and placed a kiss on the nape of my neck, "and having sex."

"Raven..." A giggle escaped my mouth and a shiver danced down my spine as his warm breath radiated along the back of my neck. "Don't tempt me."

"Oh, baby, I'll do more than tempt you." He hugged me tighter, continuing to nibble on my ear and neck.

I wiggled in his arms until I was able to turn and face him. "Are you sure you want to go to the store?" I latched on to his bottom lip and sucked on it, kneading it between my teeth as I glided my tongue into his mouth.

"Shit." He moaned low in his throat and I let go. "I guess I shouldn't tease you unless we are both ready for some action."

I placed my glove-covered hand on his cheek. "But don't you like knowing what's to come?" I raised my brows, trying to entice him.

His eyes widened and he smiled. "Hell yeah."

"Then don't stop."

"I won't." He planted several kisses all over my face in a hurry as if he couldn't get enough of me. I laughed at the feeling of his stubble brushing against my skin. It tickled my skin and I couldn't wait for him to do that to my entire body. Not releasing me, he began to walk and I treaded backwards, trusting him to guide me. "But if I don't keep my focus, we'll never make it to the store."

"Is that a bad thing?"

"It might be if we're iced in." He lifted me in the air, but my feet automatically searched for the ground. "Curb ahead."

I yelped when I lost my footing and nearly tripped when my feet touched the asphalt. We stumbled to the car, laughing uncontrollably. My butt tensed when Raven pressed me against his car. Coldness seeped through my leggings and my body shivered.

Raven quickly pressed the button on his remote and opened the door for me. I got in and rubbed my hands together, trying to warm them through the knitted fabric. The coldness seeped through the holes, numbing my fingers. He started the car and cranked up the heat. I wiggled my toes, trying to restore the blood flow. In the short amount of time it took to get to the car, my body had turned into a popsicle.

Raven pulled out of the parking lot and drove to the main road. The ice crunched beneath the pressure of the tires and I could feel the back of the car fishtailing along the way. "Shit, it's slick."

"Can you make it to the store?"

He gripped the steering wheel tighter and his skin cracked. "Yeah, I can make it. I just need to drive slowly." He rolled his shoulders and I could tell he was trying his best to stay calm. "I just don't want to wreck this car."

"I understand. If I had a car like this, I'd make sure to take care of it, too." I internally questioned how he could afford to drive a nice car. To my knowledge, he didn't have a job and after learning more about his mom, I was certain that she didn't have the money to buy him a vehicle. I hoped he wasn't involved in anything illegal. Recalling the wad of money I'd seen him pull from his pockets, it made me wonder.

"Since this car is a lease, I have to take care of it," Raven openly admitted and it chiseled away some of my concerns.

"Oh, so you're leasing it?"

"Not exactly. It was given to me to use and it's paid for monthly," he turned to look at me, "but you're not supposed to know that."

"Who pays for it?" I questioned, eager to know more.

He tapped his finger repeatedly along the steering wheel as he kept his gaze straight ahead. I could sense his reluctance to tell me the secret he hadn't shared with anyone.

"I'm sorry, I don't mean to pry." I shifted in my seat and readjusted the seat belt. A part of me wished I hadn't asked, but another part couldn't help but wonder what the story behind the vehicle was. I averted my attention to the cars that surrounded us, not wanting to press the subject further. Several cars were headed in the same direction we were, crawling along the way. The sky was grey and to the northwest, a row of thick, ominous clouds proved that the storm was far from over. The wind whistled and howled, rocking the car like it was a toy.

"I can trust you, right?" He broke the silence and I quickly turned toward him. He looked at me for a quick second before returning his focus to the road.

"Of course. I'm not going to tell anyone."

"I won the use of this car in a bet. A bet that was illegal and could get me kicked out of school and off the team for good."

"Raven," I gasped, surprised that he would do that. What else was he involved in? Was I placing my life at risk by associating with him? Things had definitely changed since last night and I prayed I hadn't made a huge mistake.

"I know. I think about it every time I get behind the wheel." He drove cautiously around the traffic circle, making sure to keep a safe distance from the other cars around us. I was glad that he wasn't trying to show off. It proved that he truly cared about our safety and the protection of the car he didn't own.

"So, give it back." I extended my hand and rested it on his shoulder. I ran my hand up and down his arm in long, slow strides. "It's okay to tell someone 'no, thank you'." Something inside me propelled me to give him that bit of advice. To reaffirm that even through peer pressure, we have to stand firm in our beliefs. It made me think twice about what I had done and why I was with him at that very moment. Why was I questioning losing my virginity to him? It was what I wanted to do and I didn't regret it. Or, so I told myself.

"Yeah, but some things aren't so easily done." He parked and turned off the car.

"I know." I let out a silent sigh. "I get it. I really do."

He gave me a meek smile and then opened his car door. I got out, unsure of what was going through his mind. Not saying a word, he took me by the hand and we trudged toward the entrance of the store. The wind whipped against us and the ice scraped our faces, showing us no mercy. The store buzzed with people shopping frantically as if the zombie apocalypse was among us. The bread aisle was ransacked and we settled for a nine-grain loaf that looked like it had birdseeds sprinkled all over it.

"So, what do you like to eat?" I pushed the cart as Raven strolled next to me. Despite the chaos around us, we took our time, going from aisle to aisle. I could tell he was still processing what I had said so I gave him some space, allowing him to sort through it.

"I'm not picky," he said, grabbing a few boxes of macaroni. "What about you?"

"I'm easy."

Raven laughed and pressed a hand to his stomach. "No, you're really not, Lexi."

I frowned, realizing I had used the wrong words — again. "Okay, I get it." I slugged him on the arm and he stumbled to the side, feigning hurt.

"Please don't beat me up." He clutched his arm like a broken wing, twisting his face in fake agony.

I pressed my lips together before saying, "And please don't disappoint me." My voice was full and thick with undisclosed meaning that I hoped he understood without me telling him.

His playful look turned serious and I immediately pushed the cart forward, leaving him behind in the process. I wasn't good at confrontations and I wasn't sure why I brought up the subject in the grocery store of all places, especially after what I had just told him. Doubt clouded my mind and an onslaught of tears hit me. I swallowed the huge lump forming at the back of my throat and shoved my nose into the beef section of the meat cooler.

"Hey, what's wrong?" Raven placed his hands on my shoulders and leaned forward, trying to get my attention.

I kept my focus on the packages, shuffling through the various selections. "I like spaghetti." The tears escaped and I quickly wiped them away. "I can make spaghetti for dinner."

Raven took the meat from my hand and turned me to face him. "Lexi, tell me what's wrong? Why did you say that?"

Not wanting to answer him, I quickly shuffled to the other end of the cooler where the chicken was located. I scanned through the wrapped offerings and picked up a package. "We can make grilled chicken one night." I tossed the chicken breasts in the basket.

"Lexi." Raven's voice deepened and it stopped me in my tracks. I had never heard him speak in this tone. I sighed, knowing I owed him an explanation before things got ugly.

I turned and faced him, wrapping my arms around my middle for support. A few people stared at me as the tears dribbled from my lower lashes, but I didn't care. "I'm sorry."

"It's okay." Raven cast a few of the nosey people a dirty look and then took my hand and led me away from the open area to an aisle. "But that doesn't answer my question." He pulled me into his arms and his caress eased the fear and worry that had been building up inside of me.

"I guess I just started questioning whether I really know you. It scares me, that's all." With the pads of his thumb, he wiped my tears. His eyes softened and I could see his desire to make everything safe for me.

"Lexi, when I told you that I'd never hurt you, I meant it. I'll tell you whatever you want to know, but you might not like what you hear." His voice lowered and he leaned in closer. "I have done some bad things that I'm anxious to leave behind. Like I told you, being with you makes me want to do everything right. Makes me want to prove that I'm worthy of a girl like you."

"Oh, Raven. I'm not that special." My heart sunk and I hated that I had doubted him.

"Yes, you are. And I think you might be able to help me. That is, if you want to."

He was beyond incredible. I just had to remember what he had already told me about his past and how he grew up. Raven deserved to make things right in his life and I wanted to help him do that, no matter what it took.

"Of course I want to. I'll go anywhere for you, *do* anything for you. As long as I can be with you."

"Good, because that's all I want." His lips turned upward in a full smile. He wiped my remaining tears and kissed both cheeks.

I took in a deep breath and sighed. I couldn't imagine my life without him. He was a piece of me now, a piece that I knew I had to help fix. "We're going to rewrite your story. It might be painful and hard, but if you allow me to help you, I know we can do it."

"You're the only one I want to help me." Raven reached behind me and pulled something off the shelf. "And, we're going to need a lot of these if we're going to be staying with each other for the next few days."

I looked at the boxes of condoms he threw in the basket and laughed.

"Yeah, I think that's a must have."

It took us longer to get home because the ice was accumulating quickly. The roads were congested. It seemed that everyone had the same idea we had. Get to the store, stock up, and get home before nightfall. Raven bought enough food to last a week or maybe longer and refused my offer to help pay for it. Even though I didn't have much money left in my savings, I wanted to contribute. Though, he did allow me to pay for the movies we rented at my insistence.

I didn't regret my decision to stay with him. Even if it meant taking the risk that my parents would lock me up forever once I got home. I had sent my mom a text that the storm had already hit Fort Worth and I'd be home as soon as the roads were safe. She didn't like the fact that I had hung up on her and refused to answer my phone. She continued to question whether I was with a guy and I continued to ignore her pestering question.

After we got home, we watched a movie and managed to finish it with our clothes still intact. Being next to Raven was so tempting, but I knew I had to control my urges. My body was silently screaming for him while also begging me to take it easy since I had just engaged in sex for the first time the night before. Raven had something that my body wanted, over and over again.

As I took the carton of milk from the refrigerator, I got a whiff of the food cooking. "Wow. That smells wonderful." Raven stood over the stove, stirring a big pan of Jambalaya. The smell of creole seasoning and shrimp swirled around me, making my mouth water.

"Thanks. It's my grandma's recipe. It's been a family favorite for years." He took a small spoon from the kitchen drawer and lowered it into the pot. Retrieving a spoon full of food, he blew on it and tasted it. Then he brought it to my mouth. "Taste it and tell me what you think."

I smiled internally. It felt good to know that he didn't mind sharing his food with me. Cautiously, I tasted the Cajun paella, making sure not to burn my tongue. The seasonings exploded in my mouth, dousing my tongue with fire and a bit of sweetness. "Oh my gosh. That's delicious, Raven."

His lips spread into a huge grin and by the sparkle in his eyes, I knew he was proud of his accomplishment. "Thank you. It's been a while since I've made this. I wasn't sure if I'd remember how."

"It tastes fabulous." I added the milk to the cornbread batter and mixed it. "Did your mom teach you or your grandma?"

"Both." Raven placed a lid on the pot and wiped his hands on dishtowel. "I really enjoy cooking so I slip into the kitchen every chance I get." He leaned against the counter, keeping a watchful eye on me as I poured the batter in a pan. It made me a little nervous and I hoped I was doing everything right. Since I wasn't a pro in the kitchen, I questioned everything I did several times. I guess a tiny part of me wanted to impress him even though I didn't have much to offer.

"That's great. I wish I would've taken the time to learn some of my grandma's recipes before she passed, but I was only in middle school. To be honest with you, I really don't cook much." I tried not to think about the conversation I had with my mom a few months prior. She promised to give me a crash course in cooking before Collin and I got married. Now that things had changed, would she still be willing to teach me?

"That's okay. I don't mind cooking." Raven opened the oven door and I placed the pan on the rack. He closed the door and I set the timer.

"As long as you're okay with it." He handed me the dishtowel and I wiped the batter from my fingers.

"Yeah, sure." I looked at my side of the counter noting the mess I had made versus Raven's nearly spotless work area. "You can cook and I can clean."

"Deal." Raven took a step closer to me, backing me up against the counter. The small kitchen narrowed around us as he rested one hand behind me and slipped the dishtowel from my grip. My knees weakened and I waited anxiously for his next move. I liked the feeling of being trapped between his arms. It was thrilling and nerve wracking at the same time. "Because you kind of make a mess when you cook." He dotted the tip of my nose and showed me the flour he had removed.

"Sorry." My body stiffened. Did I have more batter on me? The urgent need to flee to the bathroom to check myself took hold of me, but he had me barricaded. His scent engulfed me and my stomach unfurled. Raven smelled so damn good, I wanted to rub against him and carry his scent with me all day long.

"You look kind of cute, actually." He smiled as he rubbed my cheek a few times and then my forehead.

"Do I really have that much batter on me?" I tried to see my reflection on the microwave, but he moved his head along with mine, preventing me from catching a glimpse. "Raven, I'm trying to see." My hands gripped his arms and I tried to push him to the side but he continued to follow my movements.

"What's wrong? You don't like to get dirty?" His voice lowered and his eyes turned dark. Maybe being messy wasn't so bad after all. As long as I could get dirty with him.

"If you put it that way, the answer is yes."

"Good, because you have some right there." He pointed to my neck and I became more self-conscious.

"Where?" I rubbed the spot his finger touched but didn't feel any food.

"Right here." He lowered his lips to my neck and kissed the spot right below my ear, brushing his tongue along the sensitive area that awoke every nerve within my body.

A whimper escaped my lips and my head relaxed against the kitchen cabinet. "Are you sure?" I wrapped my arms around him and pulled him closer. Even through our thick sweaters, I could feel his chest move in the same rhythm as mine, the erratic pounding of our hearts synchronized.

"Yes." His mouth worked downward, pinning me with his incessant need for me. "And right here." He kissed the hollow of my throat and my lips trembled. With the tip of his tongue, he traced the curve of my neck until his lips met mine. Our lips locked and our tongues thrashed against each other. He cupped my jaw and his other hand dove into my hair. My hands rested on his chest and I gathered a fistful of his shirt in each hand, eager to rip it off his body. Everything seemed to fade away as my mind focused in on my target.

Raven.

He kissed me long and hard, like he couldn't get enough of me, and I allowed him to devour me until I was breathless. I slid my hands underneath his T-shirt, allowing them to blindly travel along the rock-hard terrain. I was ready to be wrapped in his net and never allowed to leave until I breathed my last breath.

"Damn, I want you now," he growled. He picked me up and sat me on the counter. The timer for the cornbread sounded but neither one of us paid it any attention. I didn't want to miss one second of his searing touch and my hands refused to break away from their exploration of Raven's body. After a few minutes, the buzzer finally stopped. With his free hand, he fumbled with the knobs on the stove and the oven until several beeps sounded. A sexy grin played on the edge of his lips. "Dinner will have to wait because I want dessert first."

Σ

Chapter 14

The sound of a text message from my phone woke me. With sleepy eyes, I looked at Raven. His hair was a disheveled mess from my fingers raking through it most of the night and he breathed heavily, on the edge of snoring. The covers draped below his bare chest and I seriously considered snapping a picture of him. I had to be the luckiest girl in the world.

I never thought sleeping next to someone you cared for would be so restful. His presence brought a calmness that settled every concern and released every worry. We were connected on a new level and I prayed our time together would never end. It was magical and unbelievable, and I thanked God for bringing us together.

Glancing at my phone, I saw that it was a text from Luke.

Luke: Mom is freaking out and driving me crazy. You had better get your ass home as soon as the roads clear up.

My mom knew how to ruin a good thing.

Me: What's she saying?

I waited patiently for Luke to reply. It took a long minute before I received his message.

Luke: She wants to know who you're staying with and so does Dad.

Me: Please tell me you didn't tell them!

I watched my phone, hoping that my brother hadn't revealed to my parents that I was with Raven. I knew they wouldn't be ready to accept the fact that I had moved on from Collin, and he would no longer part of my life.

Luke: Damn, give me some credit. I told them I didn't know anything.

I released the tight hold of air in my lungs and sighed.

Me: Thank you. I didn't mean to put you in the middle of this, but I guess there's nothing I can do about it now.

Luke: Whatever. It's between you and them. Later.

My natural tendency was to continue questioning Luke and find out exactly what my parents were asking, but I knew that would only aggravate him. Instead of texting him back, I checked the weather app on my phone for the latest report. The high was only twenty-five degrees with continual snow showers scattered throughout the day.

I eased out of the bed, careful not to wake Raven, and walked to the window. I opened the blinds and the bright light filtered in, casting a peaceful glow in the room. Outside had been transformed into a winter wonderland. Snow covered the ground, cars, and rooftops of the apartments, making it look like a tiny village in a snow globe. It was so beautiful and peaceful. I couldn't remember the last time north Texas had seen a winter storm like this.

Raven let out a yawn and I closed the blinds. "Sorry, didn't mean to wake you." I sat on the edge of the bed next to him.

"It's okay." He blinked a few times and stretched. It was a sight I would never get tired of. Ever. "As long as you're the one waking me up, I don't mind." Picking up my hand, he placed a gentle kiss on the top of it.

"Did you sleep well?"

"I've never slept better." He rested his arms behind his head. "What about you?"

With every breath he took, the ripples on his stomach moved like the waves in the ocean and it pulled me in, one movement at a time. Damn, he was so freakin' hot.

"I don't think I'll ever be able to sleep alone again." I laid against his chest and allowed the subtle movements to relax me. The warmth of his body eased the chill over my skin and I snuggled closer to him.

"Me either." He lowered a hand to my back and stroked my hair in long, slow strides. The brown in his eyes softened and the green sparkled as our gazes connected. "In fact, I could really get use to this."

My heart skipped a beat as I clung to each and every word he spoke. Raven knew how to say all the right things leaving me, the English professional, wordless, once again. I knew the weather would eventually clear up and I'd have to go home, but I ignored the obvious fact that would come to pass and cherished the moment.

"Me, too." I allowed my finger to trail up the curve of his tattoo until I reached his shoulder. With the tip of my fingernail, I traced a few of the black birds that scattered along his skin. His body shuddered at my touch and a small moan escaped his lips. "I love being here with you, but eventually I'll have to go home."

"No you don't." He blinked his sleepy eyes at me. "You can stay here with me as long as you want."

"Yeah, right." My finger stopped as I thought about what he said.

"I'm serious." He pulled me closer, holding me tightly in his clutches. "Now that I finally have you here, in my space, I'm not letting you leave."

A laugh escaped because he sounded so serious yet desperate at the same time. "So, you're going to keep me here?" I stared deep into the center of his beautiful eyes. I had to know his true motive. "Like some kind of sex slave?"

"What?" Raven's chest collapsed as he sighed heavily. Disappointment filled his eyes and I knew I had said the wrong thing. "Lexi, that's not why I want you here."

Damn!

My alter ego really hoped that was what he wanted, while the practical side hoped there was more to it.

"Sorry." I shifted within his embrace, but he didn't release me.

He kept his gaze steady on me. "Don't get me wrong, the sex has been great, but I really like spending *all* of my time with you." He rubbed my arms in slow, caressing strokes. Chills dotted my skin and I was totally shackled in his embrace. "I feel so close to you and I like it." His mouth parted and he rolled his tongue against his lips, wetting them. I was such a victim for his affection. "I don't know what you've done to me, Lexi Thompson, but you totally latched me for good."

My heart lifted and then exploded into thousands of tiny hearts with wings. They took flight, making my entire body feel as light as a feather. "And you've totally locked me in The Raven's trap." My hands dropped to his cheeks and I cupped his face. "And there's nowhere I'd rather be."

"Good." He smiled. "So, you're going to stay here with me?"

I gave him a quick kiss on the lips and then released my hands from his face. "Maybe," I teased, even though it was what I wanted more than anything. If I eagerly agreed, I knew I'd be just another one of his hoes.

He twisted his lips and a frown formed across his face. "Damn. What do I have to do to convince you to stay?"

I shrugged. "I'm not sure."

"What's today?"

"Tuesday, I think. Why?"

Raven counted on his fingers, throwing out days and dates. "I think we have eight days until Christmas, if I have my dates correct. Stay here with me until Christmas Eve. I'll take you home so you can be with your family and then I'll pick you up Christmas day. We'll spend the week together and then we can bring the New Year in the right way."

A flutter danced through my stomach and swelled inside of me. Was Raven unofficially asking me to move in with him? I averted the question I really wanted to know and instead, focused in the next enticing suggestion. "And what's the right way?"

"You'll have to wait and see." Raven's eyes deepened with intent and his voice was full and resonant. He was definitely serious and I couldn't wait to see what that night would hold.

"Sounds exciting." I raised a brow. "Then I can go back to the dorms once they reopen," I casually commented, wondering what he would say.

"If you want, or you can just sleep with me every night." He waggled his brows at me and my heart stuttered.

Holy shit!

"Raven." A throaty laugh escaped from me. "And what will Josh say?"

He shrugged. "Hell, I don't care. Shelby practically lives here."

"He won't mind?"

"I doubt it."

I was really considering his offer, so much so, that I said, "Okay."

"Then, it's settled. I'll take you home in a couple of days, unless you'd rather wake up in my arms every day."

"Don't tempt me." I ran my hands along his chest in a slow, sensual manner, squeezing his pecs simultaneously. "Because I don't mind skipping Christmas this year, if it means I can be with you."

"That's what I thought," he laughed. "What did the weather do last night?"

"It's beautiful outside. Snow everywhere."

"Really?"

"Yeah. Go look out the window." I lifted off him, even though I didn't want to.

Raven threw the covers off and got out of bed. His boxer briefs clung to his skin and his butt cheeks squeezed with every stride he took. He peered out the window and said, "When's the last time you played in the snow?"

"I don't know." I approached him and peeked over his shoulder. "I've never seen snow like this in Texas."

"Me either." He wrapped his arms around me. "Let's go play in the snow, baby."

"Sounds fun."

Raven and I ate a bowl of oatmeal and then got dressed, layering our clothes to protect us from the elements. We trekked down the icy stairs and walked to the front of the apartment complex. Several inches of white, fluffy powder covered the ground, trees, and shrubs. Everything else was capped with a white covering, making the world outside monochromatic. An eerie silence filled the air and it seemed like the entire city had vanished due to the storm. The roads were desolate, making it difficult to tell where the curb ended and the street started.

"It's so beautiful." The snow crunched beneath my boots, but I knew underneath the beautiful covering was the treacherous ice.

"I feel like we're in Colorado, even though I've never been there." Puffs of white smoke filtered from Raven's mouth as he spoke. The air was cold but since there was no breeze, the dry coldness made it more tolerable.

"I've been a few times, since that's where my parents prefer to vacation. It's somewhat like this, except there's a lot more snow and people. Everyone is headed to the slopes to take advantage of what the latest storm has left behind. Not hiding inside, like everyone is here."

"Hey, there are some people over there." Raven pointed to the small park at the end of the street.

"Wanna walk over there?"

"Yeah, let's go check it out."

We walked down the street, treading carefully along the pavement. A couple of guys were having a snowball fight with some girls and from what I could tell, the girls were winning. A family was on the other side, making a snowman, but having trouble with the head.

I passed a few trees to an open area. Small dunes of snow piled along the outer wall that encompassed the park. "Wow, there's more snow over here. That's weird."

"Maybe because there aren't any buildings?" Raven queried.

"Possibly." I surveyed the area, noting the huge icicles that hung from the trees. They looked like daggers and I made a mental note not to walk underneath them.

I lunged forward when something hit me in the back. Snow splattered to the sides of me and I heard Raven laugh. I turned around, somewhat shocked. "Did you just peg me with a snowball?"

He whistled like a bird as he stared off into the trees. I quickly scooped a handful of snow and made a tight ball. I pounded it against my palms as my fingers pressed it into a perfect weapon.

"You wouldn't." He stood with his feet spread and his hands on his hips, with no visible fear

I cocked my head to the side and huffed. He may have been used to taking hits from his fellow teammates or opponents, but I was neither. The cockiness was a little much and I decided to remind him that he wasn't invincible. Recalling how he showed me the proper way to throw a ball, I retracted my arm and flung the snowball, hitting him square in the chest.

"That's it." His eyes widened and his nostrils flared. "You've done it now!"

I screamed when Raven came barreling toward me. I tried to run from him, but it was nearly impossible with my boots sinking into the snow. His arms wrapped tightly around my waist as he tackled me to the ground. We hit the soft snow, but he managed to keep me on top of him, protecting me from his weight and the ground. I felt like his special football that he shielded with all of his ability.

I was totally enamored with his love.

"Are you okay?" He gathered the strands of hair that stuck to my face and tucked them behind my ear.

"Yes." I took a deep breath, trying to steady my erratic heart. "I just didn't expect you to tackle me."

"Let's do it again. That was fun." Raven tried to get up but I shoved him to the ground.

"What?" I grabbed the edge of his knitted cap and pulled it over his eyes. "Fun for you, maybe."

He laughed hard and I got off him. I crossed my arms and pouted. I really wasn't that upset, but I wanted to give him a hard time. Readjusting his hat, he said, "Oh, baby, don't be mad. I just want to have a little fun with you."

I lowered my arms, unable to hold the fake expression any longer. Raven was just too irresistible. "Then let's do a something more my style."

"What's that?" he said, standing and shaking the snow from his body.

Grabbing his hand, I pulled him to the ground. "Make snow angels."

He rolled his eyes. "Oh, lord."

Raven and I goofed off for about thirty minutes making snow angels, snow monsters, and various non-existing creatures. We threw a couple of snowballs at each other and attempted to make a dragon, even though it looked more like a fat cat lying in the snow.

I held my hands up to my mouth and breathed hot air on them. The coldness had made them go numb.

"Are you ready to go?"

Nodding my head, I said, "Yes."

"Then let's go." He extended his hand and helped me stand. "Hey, look, the donut shop is open. Want something hot to drink?"

"Sure, that sounds good." We crossed the street to the shopping strip. Raven's eyes lit up when he saw the door to the comic book store open and a guy walk out. "Do you want to go?"

"Yeah, I need to get my latest issues."

"I can't believe you read comic books."

Raven opened the door to the donut shop and I walked in. "That's why I never read my assigned books."

"Aww, so the truth finally comes out." I snickered.

"What can I say?" He shrugged. "Comic books are more fun to read than Booker T. Washington."

"I guess it depends on what you like to read, but I won't argue with you on that one."

After buying two cups of hot chocolate, we headed next door. To my surprise, a few people were shopping, even though there were no cars parked outside. I figured they had walked there like we had. A table top Christmas tree decorated in Star Wars figures immediately caught our attention.

"Wow, this is cool." Raven tapped a mini figure of Chewbacca.

"It sure is," I said, showing him a Princess Leia figure.

"I think we should buy it."

"Really?"

"Yeah, we need one for the apartment." He did a quick sweep, checking all the figures. "It's not Christmas, unless you have a tree."

The guy behind the counter greeted us and by the handshake he and Raven exchanged, I knew Raven frequented the place.

"I didn't think the store would be open today." Raven leaned over the counter, strumming his fingers against the glass.

The guy pulled out a stack of comics and handed them to Raven. "Since I live in the apartment's right behind here, I was able to walk to work."

"Really?" Raven flipped through the stacks of books. "What building are you in?"

"Building four." The guy took a sip from an oversized coffee mug that was the head of Spock from Star Trek.

"I'm in building two."

"Kick ass."

Raven motioned with his head. "How much for the tree?"

"Seventy-five bucks."

"Does that include the ornaments?"

"Yep."

"I'll take it."

"Alright." The guy walked to the small tree and took it to the counter. He continued talking to Raven while he removed the ornaments and wrapped them for us.

I looked around at all the cool stuff I knew my dad would love. They had a variety of action figures and my eyes zeroed in on the Walking Dead figures that my dad had recently started collecting. I quickly spotted a figure of Daryl on his motorcycle and knew that my dad had been searching for it on Amazon. The price seemed reasonable so I decided to buy it for him for Christmas. Then, my mind drifted to what I should buy Raven. I hadn't even thought about buying presents since I'd been so caught up in spending time with him. With Christmas eight days away, I needed to think of something.

I casually neared Raven to see if I could hear him saying anything about something he wanted when two guys walked in.

"Woot! Woot! The Raven is in the house," a large guy with dreadlocks ranted and I quickly recognized his face. He was one of the guys that had entered the taco restaurant when Macy had decided to interrupt our conversation.

"What's up?" Raven fist bumped both guys and I knew they played football for PHU. I kept a discrete distance behind one of the aisles, listening to their conversation.

"Damn remote broke to my Xbox. Thought I'd stop by and see if they had one." The guy ran his hand over his short buzz cut and I noticed the diamond rings on his fingers.

The guy behind the counter smiled. "You're in luck, Jared. We got a few last week."

Jared made a fist and pumped his arm in a backward motion. "Yes."

"Good. Now we don't have to take turns like little kids," the larger guy added. "Rimmy, when does Halo: Spartan Assault come out?"

"December twenty-fourth," the clerk answered.

"Fuck. Seven more days?" The large football player stomped his foot on the ground, reminding me of a big baby Huey. He pouted and sighed like he couldn't wait that long.

"Sorry, man. We don't open until nine, but I'm sure you can camp out at Game Stop if you want it that bad."

"Nah, that's okay. They don't give student discounts."

"Let me check on something." Rimmy went to the computer and typed in some information. "Hey, Cage, I can preorder it if you want."

Cage. Calvin 'Cage' Rutherford.

The name was familiar and based on his build and size, I knew he was probably a defensive tackle.

"Alright, let's do it." Cage's voice instantly transformed into a deep, husky tone that matched his large, stoutly built. With each step he took, the floor shook and I couldn't imagine being tackled by something that size. Raven was about two sizes smaller than him and for me, he was still a big guy.

"Hey, man, why don't you stop by tonight? We're gonna' play some Madden and have a few bitches over," Jared told

Raven and my ears shot up like a hunting dog on high alert. I quickly stepped from behind the aisle, making myself present.

"Yeah, uh, well..." Raven stumbled to answer Jared. Raven shot me a quick glance and then turned to his friend. "I, um..." His friend ignored him and instead, locked his eyes on me. He scanned me from head to toe in a slow and deliberate manner. A chill shot up my back and my stomach clenched. A devious, dark smile covered his face and I inwardly cringed.

"Who's this?" Jared kept his gaze on me, but I didn't flinch. I wasn't sure what went on between Raven and Jared, but I wasn't one of the hoes made for sharing and I wanted to make sure he knew that.

"Hi." I kept a straight face and stuck out my hand. "I'm Lexi Thompson."

Jared's brows arched. "Oh, you're Lexi." He shook my hand in a polite manner. "Nice to meet you."

"Likewise," I said, keeping a watch on him. I didn't trust him and something in the pit of my stomach told me he was bad news. I recalled some of the articles I had read in the newspaper and swore I saw his name listed. I made a mental note to check when Raven wasn't around.

"Yeah, so I don't know, man. Lexi is staying with me and—"

"Oh, you are?" Jared continued shaking my hand and I finally had to tug to get him to let go of it. I wanted to wipe the sweat from his hands on my pant legs but refrained.

"Yes. I am," I said, matter of fact.

"Then you should come." A sly smile played on the edge of his lips and I shuddered. "We're gonna hang out, play video games, and drink."

Raven placed his arm around me and pulled me close, as if showing Jared that I was with him. It eased the tension going through me and reassured me that he would protect me at all cost. "Okay. We'll stop by." He picked up his sack from the counter and the tree that Rimmy had wrapped up. "Ready?"

"Yeah, I just need to pay for this and we can go." I walked to the counter and paid for the figure. The entire time I stood at the register, I sensed Jared was watching my every move. When I turned around, my intuition proved right as Raven's friend kept an unsettling gaze on me.

"Excuse me," I said as I shouldered past him.

"Sure." He barely moved and his hand brushed against mine. A sickening shiver rushed down my back and I quickly jerked my hand away. Everything about this guy screamed trouble. Jared smiled at me. "I guess I'll see you tonight."

Uh, no.

Even though the comment was directed at me, Raven responded, "Yeah, man, see you later on."

"Let's go." I grabbed Raven by the hand and quickly bolted out of there as fast as I could.

Σ

Chapter 15

After we put up the miniature Christmas tree, Raven and I had a slight argument about going to his friends' apartment. I truly felt that it was a bad idea. At first, I told him that we shouldn't drive because the roads were still iced over and he could wreck his car. But he retorted with the fact that his friends' apartment was just on the other side of the park and he'd drive slow. When that didn't work, I told him that Jared made me feel really uncomfortable. Again, Raven discounted my comment by telling me that Jared flirted with every female he came across. Since I didn't want to be the girlfriend that told her guy that he couldn't hang out with his friends, I agreed to go. I just hoped that my decision wouldn't be one that I'd later regret.

We pulled up to a fairly new apartment complex and I remembered my brother checking in to them at the beginning of the semester. My parents refused to pay the monthly rent because it was about five-hundred dollars more than most apartments. Cautiously, Raven entered the parking garage and drove to the top floor.

We got out of the car and walked to the entrance of the apartments. The sound of hip-hop music echoed through the top floor as we approached Jared's apartment, reminding me of some of the frat parties I'd been to. We passed a really nice workout facility and a rooftop lounge that was obviously closed because of the weather. There were a few apartments along the way and I noticed that each door was somewhat distant from each other, telling me that these apartments must be fairly large.

"Did I tell you that you look really beautiful tonight?" Raven commented as we reached the door.

I unzipped my jacket and gave myself a quick look over. I wasn't wearing anything special, just an oversized sweater and leggings. My typical attire during the winter. "Thanks."

"If things get too crazy, we'll leave, okay?" Raven raised his hand and I tried to stop him, wanting to know what he meant by *too crazy*, but it was too late.

The door to the apartment opened and Cage stood in the doorway with a huge glass stein filled with beer in his hand. "What's up?" He smiled and his cheeks puffed. He had on a football jersey, sporting the number forty-five on the front.

"Hey, man." Raven exchanged a fist bump with him and then led us into the huge loft apartment. It looked like a mini-penthouse decked out in shaggy rugs, modern furnishings, and bright colors. Canvas painted art of naked girls lined the walls along with neon lights, trophies, and football paraphilia enclosed in glass. A football player's dream with a playboy accent.

Great.

And I had willingly walked into it.

To my surprise, the place didn't reek of cigars, liquor, or any other funky smell, but something turned my stomach and I instantly got another bad vibe. Several girls were playing a dance video game in the living room, screaming and yelling as they shimmed against each other. Two guys, who looked like football players, were sitting on the couch with a couple of trampy-looking girls surrounding them. They nodded their head at Raven, exchanging a typical guy hello. The girls wore short skirts and tiny shirts that barely covered their stomachs. I looked homely compared to how much skin they were showing. How the heck could Raven think I looked beautiful?

Past the living room was the kitchen where Jared sat at a glass dining table with a girl on each side. A silver pipe hung out the side of his mouth and he took long draws, puffing on it as a small billow of smoke swirled above his head. I couldn't help but question what was in the pipe. His eyes were red and he had a sly smirk on his face. In a slow, deliberate fashion, his eyes surveyed me from head to toe and my skin crawled, remembering what it felt like when he touched me.

"Glad you guys could make it." Jared pulled the pipe from his mouth and smiled at me. His large, gold tooth sparkled and it looked like a diamond was in the center of it. Was Raven was involved in any illegal activities with him? Based on his pad and the red Corvette I saw parked outside the comic book store, I was confident this guy was more than a student and football player.

"Don't even think about it, Jared," Raven quickly replied, pulling me closer to him. "She's not for sharing."

"Ah, hell." Jared slapped the glass and the table shook beneath his large hand. "I thought I'd get to try a piece of her tight ass." He snickered and my blood boiled. Who the hell did he think I was? One of Raven's ex-hoes? Clenching my jaw tightly together, I held my tongue, knowing that he was trying to get a reaction out of me. I'd be damned if I gave him that pleasure. For all I cared, he could go eff himself.

"Trust me, Jared, I've already tried." The girl on his left side ran her slender hand down his arm and across his chest. Her gold bangles clanged against each other and her long, pointed fingers trailed a path to Jared's mouth. Her nails razed his thick lips and his tongue swept across her finger, as if he were licking a lollipop. She released a low moan while keeping her eyes directly on Raven. "For whatever reason, Raven's really hung up on this one."

"Shut the fuck up, Macy," Raven barked as he rolled his eyes at her.

I did a double take, realizing that it was Macy from the restaurant. Her hair was jet black and pulled into a high ponytail with braids on each side that trailed down her back. A huge contrast from the blonde hair she had a few months ago. She had on a black, silky tank top with no bra, paired with a cheetah print micro-mini skirt. She was an animal ready to rip apart her prey. I held on to Raven's arm tightly, because there was no way in hell I was letting that puma pounce on my man.

"Do you want something to drink?" The girl hanging on the other side of Jared's arm stood. She had a big afro that was highlighted with a gold color on the tips that made her almost as tall as Raven. Her smooth mocha skin radiated under her bright, peachy blush and glossy lips. Her eyes were light green, almost like Raven's, and I noticed how she caught his attention.

"Yeah, sure." I tucked my hair behind my ear, wishing I had fixed myself up more. There was too much skin and too many head-turning girls, making me feel totally out of place. Danger lurked in the air and I knew then that we shouldn't have come.

"I'm Reece," she smiled and it was mesmerizing. The girl was absolutely gorgeous. I feared that Raven had hooked up with her and by the way she studied him, I knew the answer.

"I'm Lexi Thompson, nice to meet you," I said, remembering to keep my enemies close. Raven and I followed her to the kitchen. She towered over me in her four inch stilettos and I promised myself to buy a pair of stacked heels the next time I went to the mall. I seriously needed a wardrobe makeover. Where the hell was Delaney when I needed her?

"What do you want to drink?" Reece showed me a few bottles of liquor and I immediately zoomed in on the one that I was most familiar with — Malibu Rum.

"How about Rum and Coke?" I pointed to the white bottle among a few other liquor bottles.

"Sure." She turned around and said, "What about you, Raven?"

My stomach dropped when she said his name in a familiar tone. It confirmed my theory. She was probably one of his tramps.

"I'll just get a beer." Raven opened the fridge and took out a bottle.

I watched her make my drink, but hesitated to take it from her, knowing that I shouldn't. However, I really needed something to take the edge off.

"Thanks," I said, taking it from her.

Raven sat at the table with Jared and I reluctantly stood behind him. Macy was still clinging to Jared's side, petting him while maintaining one eye on Raven. It made me sick.

"Let's play some poker." Jared picked up a stack of playing cards and shuffled them several times in his hand. I tried not to watch his skillful hands, but it was hard not to. The cards fluttered through his fingers with precision and speed, like a professional dealer at a casino. I wondered how many times he'd been to Vegas and if that's how he earned his money or if my intuition about drugs being involved was true. "Come on, Lexi, don't be shy." Jared winked at me and I cringed. "Sit down and play with us."

"I'll play." Macy's voice was seductive and her body language expressed what she truly meant by her words. Pulling the empty chair next to Raven, she eased down on it while purposefully sticking out her behind for everyone to see. She whipped her long ponytail to the side and then leaned forward, giving everyone a clear shot of her cleavage. Her fingers wrapped around a dark purple glass and she took a sip.

Why the hell did I agree to come here?

"Now that's what I'm talkin' about." Jared placed the cards in the center of the table. "Well, what's it going to be, Lexi?" He took another puff from his pipe and motioned at the cards. "Are you going to cut them?"

"Jared, leave her alone." Raven shook his head. "You don't have to play if you don't want to." He eased his hand around my waist and pulled me close to him.

"Um, I guess..." I cast a doubtful look at Raven but before I could sit down, Reece grabbed my hand.

"Let's have a dance off."

"What?" I looked at her and then at Raven. Was it safe to leave him with Macy? I didn't trust her and even though I wanted to trust Raven, I wasn't sure if I should. I reasoned with myself that I would be in the next room with a clear view of what was going on in the kitchen. If things got out of control, I could end it quickly. With that, I hesitantly followed her.

"Come on, it'll be fun." Reece pulled me toward the living room where two girls were dancing with each other as Cage humped one of them from behind. The only time I had danced in that way was at the frat party with Brian and I was somewhat drunk.

"I guess." I downed half my drink and decided to make the best of it while I was there.

"Cage! Get your ass over here," Jared yelled.

"Shit." Cage's smile quickly turned into a frown and he sighed. "I guess."

Cage dragged his feet past us toward the kitchen and I breathed a sigh of relief. Maybe he'd take Macy up on her offer and she'd forget about Raven. I sat on a white leather chase and looked around for the other two football players that were sitting on the couch with the girls that were hanging on them. My eyes navigated down the hallways and I listened for any signs that would tell me if they were in a room with them or if they had left.

I watched Reece get down with the two girls. I laughed as they fought to keep up with the video game while continuing to sip the remainder of my drink. The door to the loft opened and another football player walked in, carrying a bag. The girls stopped dancing for a moment, eager to see who had entered. One of them exchanged a silent look with him and he cast a crooked smile, giving her a quick wink.

"Shawn, my man," Jared greeted him from the kitchen.

"What's up?" Shawn slammed the door behind him. He walked to the kitchen and opened the refrigerator door, placing his brown paper sack inside. When he shut the fridge, he had a beer in his hand.

"Have a seat," Raven placed his cards face down on the table, "we're just getting started."

"That's okay." Shawn patted Raven on the back. "I'm gonna chill and drink my beer."

"Alright." Raven tipped his beer to Shawn's. "I get ya."

Shawn took off his letterman jacket and tossed it on a chair near the patio doors. He had on a short sleeve polo-style shirt and jeans. His bicep muscles cut into the sleeves of his shirt making his tattoos stick out more. He sat on the couch and propped his feet on the leather ottoman in front of us. I tried not to stare but I wanted to know what the annotation on his arm spelled. When he caught my gaze, he leaned forward.

"Hi, I'm Shawn." He held out his hand. I shook it, not wanting to be rude. His thick, warm hands swallowed mine and the callous from his palm scraped my skin.

"Nice to meet you, I'm Lexi."

"I've never seen you around before." He cast me a dubious stare as though trying to place me. He ran his hand over his short hair and reclined against the couch.

"That's because you haven't," Raven yelled from the kitchen.

Shawn looked over his shoulder. "Oh, okay." His brows lifted as though he knew what Raven meant. I was his girl and hands off. It made me feel good but also cheap when he rubbed the stubbles on his chin a few times as if contemplating what Raven was doing with me.

"And she's a really good girl," Jared sneered.

I rolled my eyes and sighed. Eventually I'd break and tell Jared how I really felt about his comments, but I knew right then wasn't the time.

"How do you know Raven?" Shawn held the beer bottle up to his mouth.

"I used to tutor him," I admitted, hoping that set the record straight for every football player in the room.

Shawn cut his drink short. "No shit." He turned around toward Raven. "This is the girl you were talking about?"

Raven shot a quick glance in our direction. "Yeah."

A flutter swirled through my body. Raven had told Shawn about me? How many of his friends knew about me?

Shawn leaned forward and whispered. "Keep him in line, okay?"

I smiled and was glad to see that Shawn wasn't like the other football players in the room. "Don't worry, I will."

"I heard that," Raven commented and I held up my hand, trying to cover my giggle.

Shawn pointed to himself and then to me, while mouthing, "It'll be between you and me."

I nodded and shot him a quick wink. Returning my focus to Reece and the girls, I observed the huge TV on the wall. I had never seen a screen so large with a picture so crisp and clear. My dad would've loved it. I continued watching the girls dance and made a conscious effort to check on Raven every chance I got. Thankfully, Macy had taken a keen interest in pleasing Jared and left Raven alone.

Two drinks later, I finally began to feel the effects of the alcohol and relaxed enough to start dancing. The girl who was eyeing Shawn when he walked in sat next to him on the couch when I asked Reece if I could join the fun. For the next hour, Reece and I danced with the other girl, laughing, and having way too much fun. The good thing about playing the game was it taught me some good dance moves. I couldn't wait to show Raven.

"Lexi." Shawn got my attention and I stopped dancing. He motioned with his head down the hallway.

My stomach flip-flopped and a sickening feeling overcame me. Raven wasn't in his chair and neither was Macy. I tossed the remote to the video game on the couch and rushed down the dimly lit hallway. Standing at the end of the narrow passage was Macy. She was knocking on the bathroom door.

She rolled her eyes when she saw me coming. "Not you again."

I was ready to pull her by the hair when the door opened. Raven looked at Macy and then at me. "What do you want, Macy?" Raven shouldered past her.

She bit her lower lip and gave him a more than thorough look over. "You know what I want."

"You bi—"

"She's not worth it. Trust me, baby." Raven wrapped his arms around me and forced me away from her. I had never fought a girl, or guy for that matter, in my entire life, but I was ready to show Macy that Raven wasn't available and she needed to stop. When Raven's lips covered mine, I quickly forgot about the tramp behind us.

His kiss was deep and tasty. It sparked a calling that made me want to pull him into one of the bedrooms. Not wanting to fall in the same category as Macy, I decided to let that lustful desire go. I could wait until we got home.

"Damn, you taste good, baby." Raven spoke across my lips and my body shivered in excitement.

"I was thinking the same thing." I eyed him hungrily, ready to leave.

"Raven, c'mon man. This shit is good." Jared coughed and sniffed a few times.

Raven quickly released me and that's when I noticed in the bright light how his eyes glassed over. "We'll leave in a little while." He planted a quick kiss on my cheek and I heard the slur in his speech. Was he drunk?

I reached for his hand but his fingers slipped from my grip as he walked toward the kitchen. I was a little disappointed that Raven preferred to return to his Poker game and not to me. I picked up the remote and decided to return to my dance game with Reece.

"Raven, I think you need to leave," Shawn commented and I turned around.

"Nah, I'm good." Raven eyed his friend and I watched for a moment, trying to gauge his next move. His behavior was vagarious, but I had never been around Raven when he was drunk, so I had no idea what to expect. My heart rate picked up and I took a few deep breaths. I could handle this.

"Don't do it, man. Just walk away," Shawn insisted and that's when I noticed the white lines that reflected off the square mirror on the table. Raven's eyes widened in delight and I knew being in that apartment was a bad idea.

We needed to leave. Now.

"Leave me alone, Shawn." Raven bumped his chest against his friends, trying to push him out of the way.

"Fine. It's your life. If you want to fuck it up again, be my guest." Shawn stepped to the side and then stormed out of the kitchen. "You're a dick, Jared," Shawn yelled and grabbed his jacket. He passed by me and then stopped and turned around. "You better do something and save your boy."

"Shawn, don't go." The girl chased after him and I couldn't help but wish he had stayed to help me.

I didn't know what to do. If I grabbed Raven by the hand and yanked him out of there, I'd probably piss him off and since he had been drinking, I wasn't sure how he'd react. I also knew that doing that would make him look whipped in front of his friends and that was probably a bad idea. So, I decided to use the next best thing. The one thing that would persuade him to leave with me and not touch the stuff that would destroy him.

I whipped out my cell phone and text him.

Me: Hey, sexy, you look damn hot in those jeans. Care to show me what's underneath them?

His phone chimed and he retrieved it from his pocket. He studied the screen for a moment as though trying to focus on the words. His eyes widened and he grinned. Pressing his lips together, his fingers worked furiously, typing a message.

Raven: Baby, I'll show you anytime. Just say the word.

He tucked his phone in his back pocket and shot me a wink.

"Are you going to snort or what?" Jared chopped the powder repeatedly with a straight razor blade, forming a few perfect, thin lines.

Raven sat down in the chair and my stomach dropped. "Yeah, cut me two."

No!

My fingers worked diligently as my brain communicated the right words that would lure Raven away from the past, begging him to come back. I had no idea how to deal with people who had drug addictions, but I had to do whatever I could to stop him from making the biggest mistake of his life. The music from the video game blared loudly and the words being sung gave me the perfect idea.

Me: Talk dirty to me.

I waited eagerly for the text to arrive on his phone. With each passing second, I held my breath as I watched Jared slice and dice the white powder with precision. Raven's phone sounded and he titled to the side, pulling the phone from his back pocket. He eased back in his chair as he read my text. His brows rose and his eyes lifted, pinning me with a hungry desire that undressed me with one sweep. He took a drink of his beer and set the bottle on the table. His fingers dragged across his phone and I gripped my phone tighter when Jared moved the mirror in front of him. I prayed for the next words that would keep him preoccupied.

"What the fuck, man? Are you going to text all night or what?" Jared twisted his mouth in frustration.

"Go ahead, man. I'll do the next one." Raven waved him off and I sighed silently in relief.

A few second later, my phone chimed.

Raven: So, you want me tell you nasty, dirty things I'd love to do to you? A sly grin played at the edge of his lips and I knew I was on the right track.

Me: Yes. Tell me, baby. Tell me how much you want to kiss and lick me.

Raven let out a low laugh and then licked his lips. He rolled his shoulders and kept his gaze steady on his phone.

Raven: You like what I do to you with my tongue?

Me: Hell yeah. It's freakin' awesome. But tell me how you like it. Tell me what you want me to do to you. How you want me to touch you...

Raven shifted in his chair and adjusted his jeans.

Yes! He wants me!

Raven: Shit, baby. Why don't I just show you?

The chair skidded across the tile and Raven stood. "I gotta go, man."

"What?" Jared sniffed and snorted, rubbing his nose with his hand as white powered drifted in the air. "This party's just gettin' started."

Raven barreled across the dining area and into the living room, heading directly toward me. The tension in my stomach unwound like a tight string being released and I let out a deep breath. I had done it. I tucked my phone in my pocket and smiled at him.

"That's okay. I've got my own party that's waiting for me." Raven picked me up and hauled me over his shoulder.

"Raven!" I yelped, totally surprised by his actions as he rushed out the door with me in tow. He raced through the hallway and I wrapped my legs firmly around his waist. We passed the lounge and weight room at lightning speed with my body clung to his. Did he want me that bad? I laughed as a rush of adrenaline flowed through me for a different reason.

The beep of his remote echoed through the quiet parking garage and Raven had the door opened before my feet touched the ground. He dropped me in the passenger seat and I barely had time to pull my legs up before the door shut.

Damn, I had created a monster!

Raven got in the car and shut the door. "Damn, Lexi, you sure know how to distract me."

"I guess that's a good thing."

He started the car and his eyes blinked slowly. I silently questioned if he was drunk or if he had taken something when I wasn't looking. "I'm sorry... it's just that—"

"Let's not talk about it right now."

"You promise not to say anything." He pressed a finger to my lips.

I nodded and then dotted his finger with small pecks, working my way to the tip of his finger. When I reached the end, my lips parted and I took his finger completely in my mouth, sucking on it.

"Oh shit." Raven moaned low in his throat. "I don't think I can wait to get home."

"Mm, me either," I muttered as I rolled my tongue up and down his finger.

His hands flew to my face and he pulled me toward him. I threw my arms around him and our lips crashed in to one another. Need, desire, and want worked through my lips as I kissed him. He responded favorably, kneading my lips between his. When his tongue thrust in to my mouth, I received it willingly. It was warm and had a peculiar taste, but I didn't care. I couldn't get enough of him.

Inch by inch, his hands threaded through my hair and he massaged my head with long, deep strokes. My hands slid down to his chest and I was ready to rip off his shirt.

His fingers trailed down my shoulders and to the edge of my sweater. With haste, he pulled my sweater off and tossed it behind him. With a quick tug, I grabbed his shirt and yanked it off. My hands splayed across his chest and my fingers grazed his taunt skin. Big, strong hands gripped my waist and he lifted me out of my seat, straddling me across him. My back pressed against the steering wheel and the radio turned up. The music echoed across the speakers and I knew all the empires of the world would be uniting tonight in his car.

Σ

Chapter 16

We spent the next three days wrapped in each other's arms. We got up to eat, workout in the apartment complex gym, shower, watch a little TV, and then we were back in bed, making love to each other all day and night long. I never thought being loved could be so good. That being touched so pleasing. But I guess when a guy's not afraid to show you, the experience is beyond incredible.

I stared at my weather app, cursing the sun in the forecast for the next few days. The temperature had risen and partly cloudy skies had allowed some of the snow and ice to melt. With the sun out, the roads would definitely clear up and even though Raven had asked me to stay until Christmas Eve, I knew my parents would be calling for me to come home immediately.

"What's wrong? You're quiet this morning."

I shrugged and forced a smile. "Nothing."

"If it's about the other night, I'm sorry." Raven stroked my arm, dragging his finger up and down in slow movements. We had avoided the whole incident, mainly because he hadn't brought it up and I didn't know what to say. I was treading through treacherous waters and I knew one wrong comment might set him off. That was the last thing I wanted to do.

I set my phone next to me and looked him straight in the eyes. "Promise me you won't let your friends influence you."

His gaze drifted downward and he sighed. He took a deep breath and said, "I don't know why I let Jared try and talk me into..."

"You're so much better than that and you know it." I lifted his chin with the tip of my finger but he refused to look at me. "Raven." I demanded his attention and remained silent until he met my gaze. "I don't want to see you throw your life away." I cupped his face with my hands. "I want to see your dreams come true. You have so much potential."

He let out a smirk. "Yeah, I don't know."

"Listen to me." I gave his face a slight shake and his jaw tightened. I knew I was pressing my limits, but I wanted him to know that I was serious. "You know you have what it takes to land a contract with the NFL, and I'm not going to allow you to think otherwise. And I sure as hell am not going to let you risk losing that opportunity just for a chance to get high."

"Why do you care about me so much, Lexi?" His voice broke and his eyes glassed over with tears.

"Because you're not afraid to show me how you feel about me."

A small tear seeped from his right eye and I brushed it away. A pain struck the center of my chest and it rippled through me, creating an unfamiliar agony. I had no idea what Raven had experienced in his life and I knew it couldn't have been easy, but doing drugs wasn't the answer.

"And that's enough to want to be with me? Despite all my faults?"

"More than you know." I pressed my lips to his. "As long as I got you, babe, I'm happy."

"So when your parents ask you what you did this past week, what are you going to tell them?"

"I spent it with you."

He let out a low laugh and he shook his head. "Am I really worth it?"

"I'm willing to risk everything just to be with you, Raven. Does that answer your question?"

"Completely."

But the question was: did Raven feel the same about me?

I had to know.

"And what about you?"

His brow raised and he inclined his head. "Lexi, you are all I've ever wanted and more."

I smiled for a second and then my mind quickly reminded my heart that I wasn't one hundred percent convinced.

"What? You don't believe me?"

"I want to. It's just that... I hate that girls won't leave you alone." I grabbed my phone and started scrolling through my Facebook page. Pictures of us that Raven had tagged me in dominated my page. It at least told me that he wasn't afraid to show everyone he was with me. "Can't they see that I'm with you?" I showed him a picture of us.

"Maybe I need to make it clear that I'm with you." He picked up his phone from the nightstand and went to his Facebook page. His fingers danced across the keyboard at a quick speed.

A notice appeared on my Facebook feed and I gasped. Raven had changed his status to *'in a relationship with Lexi Thompson'*. I held my hand up to my mouth, trying to conceal the huge smile.

"You didn't have to do that."

"I wanted to." He winked at me and then tossed his phone to the side. "And now I think I need to show you again." Raven pulled me on top of him and I squealed.

"Hold on, wait a minute." I tried to scroll to the correct screen to edit my information as Raven tried to pull my shirt off. "I need to change my status, too."

He pulled the phone from my hand. "You can do that later. Right now, it's you and I, baby.

After we ate a late breakfast, we showered together and got dressed. I never imagined that I could feel so comfortable being naked in front of Raven, but I did. He made me feel so beautiful, even though I knew he had been with girls that put my body to shame. But what mattered most, was that he showed me how to love my own body and be proud of it.

"Hey, my mom just text me." Raven ran his hands through his short hair as he applied gel to it. He looked so damn hot that I had to turn away. Otherwise, he'd know I was gawking at him. "She wants me to take her Christmas shopping. Do you want to go?"

I placed a rubber band around the end of my braid, happy that I had finally learned how to do it. "Yeah, I'm up for a little shopping. Besides, I need to get you something for Christmas." I placed a quick peck on his forehead and sat down on the edge of the bed to put on my socks and shoes.

"Oh, hell. Are you mad?"

"What?" I grunted as I pulled on my suede boots.

"I haven't asked what you want for Christmas." He handed me my other boot. "I know girls are all about the presents."

I took the shoe from his hand. "Well, I'm not the typical girl, so you haven't messed up."

"Whew." He pretended to wipe the sweat from his forehead. "But seriously, what do you want?"

I shrugged. "I don't know. Surprise me."

"Um, can you give me some hints?" He followed me out of the bedroom. "Nope."

"Then how will I know if I'm buying you something you like?"

"As long as it's from you, I know I'll love it." I grabbed my jacket and he helped me slip it on. "Come on, let's go pick up your mom." I opened the door and we headed downstairs to the car.

The sun was shining brightly and I had to shield my eyes from the glare. The sound of water dripping echoed all around us as the ice from the buildings, trees, plants, and cars melted away. The winter wonderland would soon be a memory as north Texas' bipolar weather returned.

My phone chimed and I hesitated to look at, knowing my time was up.

Raven opened the car door for me. "Who's that?"

I retrieved my phone from purse as I got in the car. "It's my mom."

Raven leaned against the car. "What did she say?"

I showed him the message.

Mom: Get home now.

"Do I need to take you?" He shifted his weight from one foot to the other as he leaned further into the car. "I don't need your parents mad at me."

"I think it's a little late for that," I admitted. "But don't worry, I'll take the blame. After all, I'm the one that refused to go home, remember?"

Raven twisted his lips to the side and his eyes narrowed. "I thought I was the one that didn't want you to go home."

I shrugged. "She doesn't have to know that."

We both smiled and then he shut the door. He drove to his mom's house and we picked her up, along with his brothers. I guess everyone was sick and tired of being trapped indoors because of the weather. Most of the snow on the roads had melted away, but the bridges still had patches of ice on them, making them somewhat tricky to travel across. Since it was only noon and the sun was in full effect, the roads would continue to clear through the day and there wouldn't be an excuse for me not to return home.

The mall was packed and it appeared that everyone had the same mission as we did — Christmas shopping. Raven dropped us off at the front of the mall while he parked the car. His mother, Trish, and I walked in and window-shopped while we waited for Raven and his brothers.

"I'm so glad you're with my son," she commented as she looked at a pair of shoes.

I smiled, because it felt good to be approved of, even though I didn't need anyone's approval to be with Raven. Nonetheless, hearing his mom say that made me feel good. "He's really a special guy."

She laughed and gave me a strange stare. "No doubt he is, but he's also a handful."

"Yes, he is." I nodded. "But I think I can handle him."

"If you ever need any advice or help, just give me a call." She reached into her purse, scribbled her number on a piece of paper, and handed it to me.

I took the paper from her and stared at the number for a second. Did she know what had happened a few days ago or was she preparing me for what was to come? A shiver of fear sprouted it's ugly head, but I warded it off, telling myself that Raven was changing for the better. At least, I hoped he was.

"Where to first?" Raven appeared from behind me and I shoved his mother's number in my purse.

"Let's head down to Macy's. They are having a big sale and I want to get you and your brothers some nice shirts," Trish said.

"Okay," Raven replied. We followed her to the opposite side of the mall and as we passed by Victoria's Secret, Raven stopped. "We'll catch up to you later."

She winked at me and then said, "Make sure your phone is on so I can find you later."

"It's on," Raven said before leading me into the store.

The store was filled with people, both male and female, shopping for the right present for their loved one. Several of the store clerks wore pink Christmas stockings on their heads and raced around the store, helping shoppers. Holiday music blared over the speakers, putting me completely in the holiday mood. There was a white and pink Christmas tree decorated with bras and underwear and it caught our attention.

"Now that's a Christmas tree." Raven eyed it for a moment, skimming it from top to bottom.

I laughed. "I think I like ours better."

"Yeah, but this one, we could use."

"Maybe." I grabbed his hand and dragged him to a rack of lingerie. "I like this." I picked up a sheer black nightgown that had in a built in push up bra with lace.

Raven's eyes lit up. "I like that, too." He leaned forward and whispered in my ear. "And I'd love to see you in it."

His lips skimmed the nape of my neck, causing goose bumps to spread down my arms. "Do you want me to try it on?"

"Yeah, but let's see what else they have." He pulled me to another display and showed me a racy teddy with a thong and garter belt. His brows lifted and he grinned. "Now this is sexy."

"There's barely anything there," I commented, touching the delicate fabric.

"Which is the whole point." He skimmed through the different sizes and handed me a small.

"How do you know what size I wear?"

"I pay attention." He strolled off and I followed him. "Really? You've been looking at my clothes."

"Maybe." He pointed to a collection of beautiful lace push up bras and matching panties in a variety of colors. "And I like these, too."

No doubt, my underclothes needed an overhaul and I couldn't but wonder what he thought of my flowered cotton panties and plain white bras. He helped me pick several different styles and colors and I tried them all on. From bras to nightgowns and sexy lingerie, I modeled them all for Raven. They made me feel sexy and pretty, and I was anxious to wear them for him. He insisted that I buy everything I had tried and refused to let me pay for them, stating they were part of my Christmas present.

I still hadn't bought him anything, so while he waited in line, I walked to the body shop at the back of the store. The store clerk showed me a couple of different colognes for men and I selected one for Raven. Although I loved the way he smelled, I wanted him to have a new scent. One that he had never worn and women hadn't smelled on him.

"What did you get?" he asked looking at the bag in my hand.

I winked. "You'll see."

"Oh, okay."

We walked out of the store and met up with his mother and brothers. They were in the young men's department of Macy's, purchasing some clothes for Ashton.

"Hey, I'll be back shortly. I'm going to pick out something for my mom." Raven gave me quick kiss on the cheek. Trish glanced out of the corner of her eye and smiled at us. It was nice that Raven didn't hide his affection for me, even in front of his mom. "Jared, Ashton, wanna come with me?"

"Do you want me to hold the bags?" I asked, motioning to the two large Victoria Secret sacks.

"I got it." He winked and then walked off with his brothers.

"I never get to shop with any females unless I'm with my sister and mother." Trish smiled and I could see the excitement in her eyes. "Let's go pick out a couple of different shirts and pants for Raven."

"Sure." I followed her to the men's section.

We talked while we searched for a few outfits for Raven. She shared stories with me about Raven when he was a child and how hard he worked at becoming a great football player. The pride in her eyes told me how much she loved him and cared about him. It was evident that whatever had happened in the past and the bad choices he had made, she had forgiven him and stood by him regardless.

An hour later, Raven and his brothers returned with a few more bags.

"I guess you're done with your Christmas shopping," his mom commented, looking down at her two bags.

"Yes, I am." He sat his bags down and took an interest in the clothes I held in my hands.

"We picked out a few things for you to try on." I showed him a couple of the shirts.

"I like them." His surveyed them quickly and then turned toward his mom. "You did good this time."

"Maybe because I had help from your girlfriend." Trish gathered them from my hands. "Now, go try them on." She urged him toward the dressing rooms and I followed. Raven tried on all the outfits we had selected for him. It was fun watching him model them because every inch of his body was perfect from top to bottom. Raven practically looked good in anything he put on.

"Are you going to check that?" Raven looked at my purse and I knew he was referring to my phone. It had gone off at least three times since he had stepped in the dressing room.

"No." I stood on the tip of my toes and helped him flip down the collar of his shirt.

"Why not?" He adjusted the sleeves one at a time, buttoning them.

"Oh, you look so handsome in white." Trish commented and I couldn't deny how sexy Raven looked.

"Because it's probably my mom," I said in a low voice, trying to keep his mom from hearing me.

"Don't ignore your mom," she scolded, "we worry about our children and not answering your phone or texts makes it worse."

Grudgingly, I reached into my purse and retrieved my phone. She didn't know my mom and I was sure she wasn't unaware of how controlling she was or why I was better off ignoring her.

To my surprise, it was Luke.

Luke: Great job, genius. Mom and Dad know about Raven and they are pissed. You better tell him to bring you home NOW.

"Oh no," I muttered under my breath as I typed the obvious question.

Me: What did you tell them?

"Is everything alright?" Trish asked.

"Um..." I avoided her question and kept my eyes glued to my phone. I could feel Raven's stare radiating through me and I prayed Luke responded quickly.

A few seconds later, Luke's message popped up.

Luke: I didn't tell them shit. Mom saw the pictures on Facebook and the change in your status.

Shit.

Me: Since when is Mom on Facebook?

Luke: I don't know. I'm just telling you what's going on so be prepared. Later.

My phone rang and I silenced the call from my mom. There was no way in hell I was talking to her in front of Raven and his mom. She'd be irrational and I knew the only way to get through to her was to talk to her in person. I had to introduce Raven to my parents and tell them that I was with him now and it was my decision, not theirs.

A short tone sounded, telling me I had a voice mail. I also noticed that I had seven missed calls and voice messages, all from her. I cringed. This wasn't going to be easy.

"What did she say?" Raven leaned forward, trying to read my phone upside down.

I pulled it closer to me, embarrassed about the situation. If only my mom could be understanding like his. My phone chimed and another message from my mom appeared.

Mom: If you don't get home now, I'm calling the cops.

"Fuuuu—" I stopped before cussing in front of Trish. "I'm sorry, it's my mom." I quickly typed a message, telling her that I was at the mall and would be leaving ASAP. "She wants me to come home now. She's freaking out over stupid stuff."

"Oh. Raven better take you home."

"What did she say?" Raven reached for my phone and I quickly dropped it in my purse. If he saw what she typed, he'd freak out.

I turned toward Trish. "I'm sorry. I know you're right in the middle of Christmas shopping and—"

"Don't worry about it." Trish placed her hand on my arm. "I can finish up later. Besides, I think we picked out a few things for Raven, Ashton, and Trey. I just have a few more things that I can buy later."

"Are you sure? I'm so sorry."

She waved a dismissive hand in the air. "Don't worry about it.

Trish purchased the clothes for her sons and we left the mall. The entire way to his mom's house, Raven was abnormally quiet. I knew he was disappointed that he had to take me home. I didn't want to leave either. I had gotten so used to being with him that I wasn't sure how I'd make it without seeing him every day.

We pulled up to his mom's house and dropped everyone off.

"Wait just a minute," Trish said before Raven shut the door. "Delaney stopped by and left something for you."

"Okay." Raven removed his hand from the gearshift.

My heart stopped for a second, but I reasoned with myself that there was nothing to be alarmed about. Delaney had done that class project on him and I knew it was probably something related to that.

Trish returned with a large silver bag and handed it to Raven. "Be careful, Raven. The roads are still icy."

"Don't worry, Mom. I will." Raven tried to ease the fear in her voice.

"Lexi, it'd be nice if you could join us Christmas evening for dinner. My mom and my sister, along with her family, will be coming in town. I'm sure Raven would like to introduce you to them."

"Thanks, I appreciate that." I turned to Raven and waited for his response.

"If it's okay with her parents, I'll pick her up," Raven told his mom and I smiled.

"See you soon." Trish went inside and I waved bye.

Raven looked at the bag in his hands and then at me. "Should I open it?"

"Yes, I want to know what she bought you."

Raven plucked out the purple tissue paper and removed a large black portfolio. I sighed under my breath in relief that it wasn't anything more and wanted to punch myself for thinking it might have been. He untied the ribbon binding the thick stack of cardstock boards. Delaney had laid out Raven's life in a variety of pictures. Each one of them depicted him in a variety of different poses with different headings.

"Wow. These are awesome," he sighed. "She really did a great job."

"Yes, she did." I looked over his shoulder as he flipped through them. I sighed when I saw the picture of us on the lawn playing football together. It was a black and white photo that focused on our faces. The contentment in both of our eyes was evident.

"I'm framing this one," he said with a smile.

There were a few more photos of us together and several with his mom and brothers. In all, Delaney had captured highlights and low points in Raven's life, telling his story through vivid pictures that made me want to laugh and cry. The expression on his face indicated that he was more than pleased and maybe a little dissatisfied with some of the twists and turns his life had taken.

"Will you send her a message and tell her I said thank you?" Raven's voice cracked and I could tell he was holding back his emotions.

"Yes, of course."

He stacked the boards evenly together and placed them in the sack. "She's an amazing photographer and storyteller."

I nodded and took the sack from his hands, placing it on the floorboard next to me. "Yes, she really is."

Raven drove off slowly and headed toward his apartment. We didn't say anything and I think it was because neither of us wanted me to go home. The mood between us had turned somber, a stark contrast from the past week. After the quiet walk up the stairs, we reached his door. It creaked opened and our small Star Wars Christmas tree twinkled in the darkness. I placed his gift under the tree and trudged to his bedroom to pack my stuff.

"Can I help you?" Raven voice was thick and the sadness was audibly present.

I didn't want to leave, but I had to. My face became wet with moisture and I quickly patted it dry with the back of my hand. Keeping my head down, I focused on my task.

"Yes, can you please get my stuff from the bathroom?"

"Sure." Raven walked slowly out of his bedroom. In the silence, I could hear him gathering my bottles of shampoo, mousse, and hairspray. I don't know why, but it felt like I was leaving for good, even though I knew I wasn't. "Here you go."

He placed my toiletry bag on his bed. I checked to make sure everything was there and slowly zipped it up.

"Thanks." I closed my large duffle bag and he helped me pick up the other one. I stuffed my shoes and dirty clothes in it, but before I could close it, he motioned for me to stop.

"Please take the things I bought for you today." He darted out of the room and returned with the two Victoria Secret bags and a small burgundy one.

"I can leave them here. Unless you don't want me to come back." I hesitated to take them.

"Of course I want you to come back." He pulled me into his arms and I draped mine around his neck. "I haven't changed my mind, unless you have."

"No." I shook my head. "Just because I have to go home sooner than we planned, doesn't mean my decision has changed."

A smile stretched across his face from ear to ear. "Good. That's exactly what I wanted to hear."

His lips met mine and my eyes fluttered to a close. He kissed me with so much passion and intensity, my knees weakened. I was completely and utterly swallowed up by his emotions that I ignored my phone ringing in the background. Being with Raven made the world around us disappear. There wasn't anything I wanted more than him. Nothing mattered to me any longer.

Our lips parted and I rested my head against his chest. His hand stroked my hair and I let out a heavy sigh. I held him close to me, listening to the beat of his heart. I'd miss laying my head on his bare chest and listening to his ragged breathing. My eyes watered and this time, I didn't bother to wipe the evidence of my torment away.

My phone chimed and Raven kissed me on the forehead. "Come on, I better get you home before your parents send out a search team."

I let out a nervous laugh, hoping that wasn't the case. "I know." I sniffed and Raven moved his head back, capturing a better glimpse of me.

"Don't cry, baby." He pulled me tightly in his arms and I wrapped myself around him, not wanting to let go. "I'll see you in a few days. Or, if you want, I'll pick you up tomorrow and we can spend the day together."

"Okay." I nodded and wiped my eyes. "As long as you promise."

"I promise, baby. I promise."

Σ

Chapter 17

Raven drove me to Dallas and we spent the entire time laughing and talking. Thankfully, the roads weren't as bad as we had thought and we made it there without encountering any incidents.

Raven pulled up to my house just as the sun was beginning to set. "Promise me you'll go straight home?"

"I will." He gave me confused look. "Don't worry."

"It's hard for me not to," I admitted.

"Well, I don't want you to." He took my hand in his and kissed the top of it.

I closed my eyes, committing the softness of his lips and the strength of his touch to memory. It was something I never wanted to forget. He turned my hand over and placed something in my palm. When I opened my eyes, a flat burgundy box was in the center. My heart rate picked up and joy overfilled me.

"What's this?"

"An early Christmas present." He smiled. "Open it."

"Raven," I said, trying to conceal the happiness bubbling up inside of me. Aside from receiving an engagement ring from Collin, which I had given back, and some jewelry when I was younger from my mom and dad, I'd never been given jewelry as a present. "You already bought me enough from Victoria's Secret."

"I know, but when I saw this today, I just had to get it."

I opened the box and my eyes automatically filled with tears. A silver dove with a small diamond for an eye was attached to a dainty chain. "It's beautiful." I swallowed a few times, trying to free the lump in my throat. I carefully removed it from the box. "Thank you." I pressed a kiss to his cheek.

"I'm glad you like it." Raven motioned for me to lean forward so he could help me put it on. "It's a dove, you know."

"Yes, I noticed that. I guess you have a thing for birds."

He laughed. "Maybe, but do you know why I chose it?" He clasped the chain around my neck and I looked at it, touching the wings with the tips of my fingers.

"No, why?" I pulled down the visor and admired it through the vanity mirror.

"Because doves are pure and innocent. Just like you, Lexi."

"Raven..." I closed the visor and fought the tears once again. "You're going to make me cry."

"Don't cry, baby." He cupped my face with his hands and tilted my head back as he pressed a soft kiss to my lips. Tears seeped from my eyes onto my temples and into my hair. "I'm so grateful to have you in my life." His eyes drifted downward and he smirked. "I just don't know why you want a guy like me. I'm a raven, tarnished and dark. You're the exact opposite of me."

"Look at me, babe." I lifted his chin so our gazes aligned. "You're not tarnished and dark. That's just a name your mom gave you. A pretty cool name, if you ask me. In fact, did you know that ravens mate for life, just like doves, and defend their territory?"

"Really? I didn't know that." He wiped the tears from my face.

"Yes, so see," I sniffed, "a dove and raven go perfectly together."

"It's hard to picture that. All I know is that I can't be without you, Lexi. You've trapped me for good."

I laughed. "It's about time, because I got caught in The Raven's trap a long time ago." I wrapped my arms around his neck. "And there's nowhere I'd rather be."

He kissed me again and just as his hand eased to my breast, a knock startled me. Raven pulled back and we immediately stopped kissing. I turned to see my mom and dad standing outside. My heart thundered in my ears and I turned hot and sweaty.

I unlocked the door and opened it. "Hey, Mom... Dad, um this is Raven and—"

"Get out now." My mom grabbed my arm and yanked me out of the car.

"Mom!" I fell to the ground and heard Raven call my name.

"Take her inside," she demanded. Before I knew it, my dad was pulling me inside.

"Dad, no. Wait!" I tried to stop him, but didn't want to physically start a fight.

"Get inside, Lexi." His voice was deep and firm. I'd only experienced that side of him on a few occasions and I knew he meant business.

"But, Dad..." I resisted, trying to pry his hands off my arms. My feet stumbled as he dragged me across the sidewalk. Anger tainted my blood and I couldn't believe my parents were treating me that way in front of Raven. "Stop! Please."

As soon as we were inside, my dad released his firm grip. He slammed the door shut and stood with his arms crossed and his legs spread, barricading it. "Where the hell have you been? With that guy?" Dad pointed outside.

"Um...yeah, I've been with him the entire week." I decide it was time I stand my ground. My decision had been made, I wanted to be with Raven, and I wasn't going to let them take that away from me.

"Do you know anything about him?" My dad huffed, clamping his hands around his waist. I'd never seen my dad so upset. It was usually Mom that did all the disciplining while Dad just stood by and agreed with whatever she did. I couldn't even imagine what my mom was telling Raven at that moment.

Thinking that my parents would have accepted Raven was a total disaster. I should've never went home.

"Yes," I straightened, "I do."

The whites of my dad's eyes bulged. "And you want to associate yourself with that type of person?"

"And what's wrong with that?" My blood boiled and my fingers tightened into tight fists. I seriously needed to punch something before I exploded. "No one's perfect, Dad. Not you, not Mom, Luke, or Ashley." I made sure to bring attention to my sister that they constantly reminded me did no wrong.

"No, we're not perfect, but Lexi," his voice lowered, and he neared me, "that guy has been involved with drugs and who knows what else."

"How do you know that?" I took a step forward, pressing my position.

"Because it's public information. And don't question me. I'm telling you that guy is no good for you and you need to stay away from him."

"What?" My breath hitched and it felt like I'd been jabbed in the stomach. "You can't tell me not to see him."

"I'm your father and I have every right to tell you who you can be with." He pointed outside. "And you will not be with that guy ever again!"

Rage ripped through me and I had to take a deep breath before I completely lost it. I couldn't believe my dad was acting that way with me. The best thing was for me to leave and never come back. "I knew it was bad idea for me to come home. I should have just stayed with Raven."

With determined purpose, I shuffled past him. I had had enough of their shit. As I reached for the handle, the door flung open and hit me in the arm. I stumbled back, clutching my forearm. My mom pushed through the entrance with my bags and purse in tow.

"And where do you think you're going?"

"I'm leaving." I reached for my purse and bags, but she jerked them away before I could grab them.

"I don't think so." Mom had a stunned expression on her face, as though completely surprised that I would even challenge her orders. "You're staying right here."

"No, I'm not." My breathing increased and I gritted my teeth together. I was a grown woman and it was time I made my own decisions. Good or bad. "I'm leaving and never coming back." I latched on to the handles of my purse and tugged hard.

"You will do no such thing." She dropped my bags, wrapped both hands around the handles of my purse, and pulled hard. I tightened my grip as I fought to keep hold.

"Let go, I'm leaving. And no one can stop me." We continued struggling to claim the rights over my purse. The next thing I knew, the handle snapped and the contents of my purse spewed on the floor. "Great. See what you've done!"

I dropped to the floor and began shoving my stuff back into my purse.

"What are you doing with these?" She bent down and picked up a string of condoms. Her eyes widened with disbelief and her bottom lip trembled. The color drained from my face and my mouth fall open. Could things get any worse?

"What the heck?" Dad took the plastic packages from her hand and stared at them for a moment.

"Oh my God." Mom covered her mouth and her eyes filled with a look of devastation. "Did you have sex with that boy?" Her hand shook and her nostrils flared.

The words caught in my throat and I didn't know what to say. Without much thought, I said, "It's none of your damn business." I yanked the condoms from my dad's hand, tossed them into my one-handled purse, and flung it over my shoulder.

"You will not talk to me that way. You hear me, Lexi Ann Thompson," my mom scolded, shaking a finger in my face.

"I can't believe you did that." Dad shook his head. "Did we not teach you anything?"

"I'm sorry, but I'm an adult and my choices are for me to make, not you." I bent down to grab my bags and my mom kicked them out of my reach.

"You're not going anywhere." She snatched my purse from my arm, snapping the other strap. My hand flew to my shoulder, trying to ease the pain that shot straight to my bone. She grabbed my backpack and bags and went to the kitchen. I followed her, yelling along the way, "What are you doing? Give them back to me."

Dad remained silent as he watched my mom toss my stuff on the kitchen counter. Nothing had changed. She was still the overbearing, overpowering, and controlling mother that I had grown to hate. She unzipped one of my bags and flipped it over, empting the contents onto the marble. All my personal items were in clear view. Clothes flew up in the air as she dug through my stuff as if in search of something.

"What are you doing?"

"Search her purse." She shoved my bag in my dad's hands. My dad let out a heavy sigh and set my bag on the counter. Unlike her, he slowly went through every pocket and compartment. I couldn't tell if he was afraid that he might find something he didn't want to or if he was frustrated that things had gotten to that point.

"What are you looking for?" My eyes darted between them.

"Drugs!" My mom's voice shook and her eyes narrowed. The demon in her was coming out. "Are you doing drugs?"

"What? No! I'm not doing drugs. Why would—"

Suddenly, it was clear to me. They thought I was strung out on dope and had lost it. "You two need to chill."

I reached for my clothes when my mom yelled, "Don't touch anything." I retrieved my hand, terrified that my mom was the one on drugs. I watched my parents investigate my personal items and I wanted to cry. I crossed and uncrossed my arms, unable to stop them from ripping through my things. I'd never felt so violated in my life.

"What the hell?" Mom exclaimed when she opened my second bag that had the Victoria Secret undergarments that Raven had bought me. With the tips of her fingers, she held up the black nightie that had the thong attached. "Did you buy this?"

"Mom!" I snatched it from her hands and stuffed it into the other bag. "Quit going through my stuff." I reached for the sack and her eyes widened. Her hand flew back and I braced myself for what was to come.

"Olivia, don't! Dad caught Mom's hand a few inches from my face.

The last time she'd hit me was when I was little, but based on the way her body was trembling and the wrath circulating in her eyes, I didn't trust her. I took a step back. Slowly, she lowered her hand and looked away. Fear pulsed through my blood and my throat tightened. The threat of tears hit my eyes and I blinked them away.

"Did he buy these for you?" She held up the bras and matching panties that Raven had picked out for me. "Answer me, Lexi. Did he buy these for you?"

"Yes. Yes, he bought them for me," I admitted, not knowing what else to say. What the hell was her problem? Was it so wrong that I had spent a week with a guy that truly cared for me and wasn't afraid to show it? Unlike Collin.

"That's it." Mom gathered all my lingerie in her hands and marched to the living room.

"Wh-what are you doing? Where are you going with my stuff?" I followed her, picking up the trail of panties and bras she dropped along the way.

She flung open the glass doors to the fireplace and I screamed, "No, Mom! Don't!" I tried to stop her from tossing my brand new underclothes into the blazing fire, but she was like a mad woman on mission from hell. Tears streamed down my face as I watched her throw everything that Raven had bought me into the flames.

Pain and sadness pounded at my heart. I felt like I had lost a piece of Raven. Even though they could be replaced, it upset me because he had helped me pick them out. He had bought them for me. They were gifts from him. And now they were gone. I slumped to the floor as the flames consumed all of the fun memories I had shared with Raven earlier that day. Tears dripped from my eyes as the material turned to ash. They were gone.

Burned.

"Hand me her backpack." I heard my mom tell my dad.

I turned around to see my mom remove my laptop. "Why are you taking my computer?" I cried out as I crawled across the living floor, trying to stand.

"And her tablet, too." She extended her hand to my dad and he placed my Kindle in her palm.

I stumbled into the kitchen as my mom gathered all my electronics, including my phone. "You can't do that." I wiped the tears from my face and tried to think of a plan. I'd be damned if she was going to take away every method of contact I had with Raven.

"I've got her wallet," Dad commented as he walked out of the kitchen.

"No! You can't do that," I called, but he ignored me, as if on a mission. "Mom, give me back my phone," I demanded, following her as she left the kitchen. "Mom, don't do this." Cords dangled at her feet as she walked straight to her room. "Mom!" I yelled as she slammed her bedroom door in my face.

I spent the remainder of the night crying and regretting returning home. Even if I would've come home earlier, it wouldn't have stopped my mom from going berserk. Talking to my parents about my relationship with Raven couldn't be done in a rational manner like I'd hoped. Why couldn't they act like grown-ups? Their reaction was beyond insane and the worst I had ever seen from them. No wonder Luke had warned me. I cursed him silently for not being there to help bail me out of the situation, as I had done for him on so many occasions. But like he said, he wasn't getting involved. I guess I couldn't blame him.

I couldn't help but wonder what my mom had told Raven. I had to call him and find out, but most of all, I needed him to pick me up. I refused to stay there and I didn't care if my parents disowned me. They were the most stubborn, irrational, controlling people I knew and I hated them. I searched through my drawers for my old cell phone and cussed when I realized it was at my dorm.

Covering my face, I fell onto my bed. Trying to clear the fog from my brain, I thought of several different ways to get of my house. I couldn't believe that I was a twenty-year-old woman running away from home. It was ridiculous that my parents had treated me like a child and stripped everything from me.

I considered taking one of the cars and driving to the store to call Raven. That idea failed when I couldn't find the spare keys. They probably had them locked in their room. Running to the store was another idea that popped in my head, but I snubbed it when I saw that it was raining outside. I'd freeze to death by the time I got there since the nearest store was at least a mile away. I told myself I'd leave as soon it stopped if no other options presented themselves.

Burying my head in my pillow, I raked my mind and raised it when I thought about Luke's room. Surely, he had an old phone in there somewhere. He hadn't returned home and I figured my parents had sent him to his apartment or to a friend's house. I waited until the middle of the night when my parents were in a deep sleep and crossed the hall to Luke's room. I shut the door and flipped on the light. I searched through his drawers and closet, praying that I'd find his stash of old phones, but I couldn't find anything. I was out of luck.

Damn!

Chewing on the edge of my thumb, I continued to think of how else I could get ahold of Raven. Then, it dawned on me to go to the office downstairs. My parents had a desktop computer and I could log into my Facebook account and message Raven. I flipped off the light and pressed my ear to the door, making sure it was still quiet. Silence filled the air and I carefully opened the door. The wooden floor creaked as I tip-toed through the hall. I treaded carefully with every step I took. The planks moaned against my weight, forcing me to stop every few feet to make sure my parents remained asleep. I finally made it down the stairs and to the family office without waking them.

I shut the office door and sat down. A cream colored envelop with the name of my sister's firm name caught my attention. I picked it up and slowly opened it, pulling out the thick bundle of papers stapled together. As I unfolded the papers, my eyes scanned the report that had court hearing information and charges. My eyes drifted to the top and my stomach dropped. Raven Renee Davenport was listed in bold. I flipped through the pages, noting the drug charges that had been filed against him at the beginning of the year.

I closed my eyes and took a deep breath. Even though I knew Raven had been suspended from PHU because of drug related charges, it sucked to see the actual paperwork laid out in front of me. But I didn't care. He meant too much to me and I didn't want him to return to the lifestyle that had nearly destroyed him. He needed me and I needed him.

Folding up the papers, I stuffed them in the envelope. The disappointment quickly transformed into anger when I knew my mom had asked my sister, Ashley, to obtain the reports. I started to rip the envelope, but instead, placed it next to me so I wouldn't forget to take them.

I turned on the computer and cringed when the motor spun and the monitored beeped as it powered up. The familiar tune of Windows sounded and I quickly turned down the volume on the small speakers. I prayed my parents didn't hear it and waited in terror for the door to spring open. After several long minutes, I was convinced they were still asleep and it was safe to continue.

The screen flashed through several booting protocols before it landed on a log in screen. I clicked on my profile and was prompted to enter a password. I didn't recall setting one up and I was certain that my parents had done it. I tried a few options, but none of them worked. I switched to Luke's profile and cursed when it asked for his password. I guessed until it locked me out. Desperate to get in touch with Raven, I selected my mom's profile. I was ready to punch the screen when it said the same thing. *Password incorrect.* I flipped to my dad's login as a last resort, screaming internally when I got the same response. My parents had password protected the computer, purposefully. I had no way of contacting Raven.

Shit!

I stayed in my room for the next two days, away from my parents and the rest of the world. Looking out the window, I cursed the cold rain that beat against the glass. Another winter storm had rolled through north Texas, bringing cold, freezing rain which made it impossible for me to run away from home. Every night, I sat by the window, holding on to the dove around my neck, waiting for Raven to show up, but he didn't. I prayed that Delaney would come over so I could take off with her, but she never did. I was sure she'd already left with her parents to Arizona for Christmas.

Life totally sucked. I had never felt so alone. I had gone from Raven's warm bed and his comforting arms to a cold, brutal home that showed me no hope for a better future. A knock sounded on my door and it startled me. I knew it was either my mom or dad, so I didn't bother to respond. They'd come in regardless, since my door didn't have a lock. Another one of my parents controlling mechanism for 'keeping us safe'. Everything was pointless while I was living under their roof.

"Lexi," my mom called as she opened my bedroom door. "Can I come in?"

I snickered under my breath, wondering why she was asking when she would do whatever she pleased. I continued staring out the window, hating life more with each passing second. How could the holidays go from the best to the worst ever?

"Are you going to come and eat some lunch? It's after one and you really haven't eaten anything since you came home."

A sour taste filled my mouth and my tummy sunk in from the emptiness of my stomach, but I didn't care if I ever ate again. I wanted nothing from my parents. Food, water, shelter, you name it. I was done.

"I brought you back your things." I watched her set my laptop and Kindle on top of my dresser. I eyed her suspiciously, wondering what had prompted her to return them to me. She eased onto my bed and held my phone in her hands. A somber look draped across her face, making her appear older. A tiny part of me felt bad for making her worry about me, but I let it go, reminding myself that she'd brought it on herself. I had done nothing wrong. And if they weren't willing to accept the fact that I was with Raven, then we would continue to be odds with one another.

I continued to keep a tight lip. Not having anything to say to her. When I didn't move away from the window, she said, "I thought you might want to read this."

I turned when I saw her hand my phone to me. Had something changed in her heart? Was she willing to accept the fact that I had chosen to be with Raven? A flutter of hope lifted my spirits and I slowly crawled toward her. I extended a shaky arm and took the piece of equipment I had been dying to get a hold of the past two days. The phone displayed a message from Raven and I blinked a few times, making sure my eyes weren't playing tricks on me.

Sitting on the back of my legs, I began reading his text message:

Raven: Lexi, I'm so sorry that I got you in trouble with your parents. I never intended for anything like this to happen. That was the last thing I wanted and I definitely don't want to come between you and your family. That's why it's best if we go our separate ways.

My throat tightened and a lump formed at the back of my throat. My eyes stung and quickly filled with tears. Was Raven breaking up with me? I scrolled through the message, making sure it was from him and not some trick my mom was playing on me. After verifying what number it came from, I returned to reading the message.

I knew all along that you were too good for me and it would never work out for us. I'm sorry I strung you along but the truth is, I can never walk away from the lifestyle I miss and love. You're better off without me. Like I said, I'll destroy you and I don't want to be responsible for that, so go back to Collin because he's the one for you. I hope you have a wonderful life and take care.

The weight of the phone increased and my hand hit the floor. My shoulders slumped forward and the tears poured from my eyes. The words repeated in my head, clouding over me and causing me to go completely numb. Everything I had been holding on to was completely gone. Raven wasn't coming for me. He didn't want to be with me. With one message, he had ended our relationship.

Raven and I were no more.

He had left me, again.

"I'm sorry, darling. If there's anything I can do for you, let me know." My mom gave me a gentle smile as if saying she knew it all along.

I stared past her, not knowing what to do or say. Everything Raven and I shared together — was it a lie? Was it all make believe?

The promises.

The memories.

The love.

Were they even real? I hated myself for being so vulnerable and reckless. And to think, I gave my virginity to him. But he tossed it out the door, as if I were another one of his hoes.

The Raven's trap had destroyed me and I'd never be the same again. Ever.

Σ

Chapter 18

Christmas came and went and I was in complete and utter shock. I barely ate, barely slept, and cried day and night. I hated life and truly wanted God to take me. But I had no one to blame but myself. I knew what Raven was about and I that he was trouble from the first day I met him at the writing lab. I fell for his contagious smile, his charming personality, and his hot and sexy body, just like every other girl he seduced. I was no different than Macy, the Silicone Triplets, or Reece. We were all victims to The Raven's trap and addicted to him like a drug we had to have and couldn't live without.

"Lex, are you going to get dressed? It's already five." Delaney struggled to zip up her dress. I motioned for her to come to me so I could help her. My parents were having a big New Year's Eve party so I invited her because I knew she wanted to spend time with Luke. However, all I wanted to do was stay locked up in my room forever. I didn't even care to go back to school because I knew that everything would remind me of Raven and Collin and that was the last thing I wanted or needed.

"Put it on so we can go and eat." She handed me a black jumpsuit with a velvet top that my mom had bought me.

"Okay, I'll get dressed." I tossed my long waves over my shoulder. If it weren't for Delaney, my hair and makeup wouldn't have been done and I would've settled for the au natural look with a messy bun. I had no one to impress and didn't care how I looked.

"Have you tried to call him?" Delaney handed me my brand new stacked heels. I sighed when I looked at them. They were the ones I had bought when I went Christmas shopping with Raven. Why did everything have to remind me of him?

I nodded and pressed my lips together, trying to repress the tears that once again, threatened to take over my life. "Yeah, but he doesn't respond." I stuffed my feet in my shoes, hoping that I'd break a heel and have to trash them. "I text him daily, but I get nothing in response." I sighed heavily and closed my eyes, knowing what I had to do. "I just need to move on, that's all there is to it. It's over."

Delaney dug around in my jewelry box and handed me a set of gold bangles and a long necklace that had a tassel on the end. "I just find it hard to believe that he's willing to end it... just like that." she motioned for me to turn around, "I think there's more to it."

"I doubt it." I tucked the silver dove underneath my clothes, refusing to remove it, and adjusted the long chain against my velvet top. She handed me a pair of earrings and I put them on. "I mean, this is the second time he's told me that we don't belong together." I sighed, trying not to recall the conversation at the football stadium and the text message. "I just need to accept the truth and forget about him."

"But why are you still wearing the necklace he gave you." She cocked a brow. "Huh?"

I shrugged and turned away, slightly regretting that I'd told her everything that happened while I was with him. From the great sex to us playing in the snow, to our little Star Wars Christmas tree, and the near drug incident, I'd spilled my guts to her and cried and cried until there was not a drop left in me. And she held me, like a good friend was supposed to until I was somewhat better. Raven had definitely brought me and Delaney closer, even though I wished it was him instead of her.

"Hey, I've got a surprise!" She shuffled to her bag and pulled out the familiar white liquor bottle. "This will help take away all your sadness."

I looked at the bottle and turned away. Even that reminded me of Raven. "Maybe I like feeling sad. Let's me know I'm still alive."

"What? You gotta be kidding me." She plummeted to my bed. "No one likes feeling depressed. And I definitely miss my new roommate."

"Yeah, I miss her, too." I checked my phone, hoping that maybe, just maybe, Raven had sent me a message. As expected, nothing had been received. What he was doing? Was he getting ready to go out? Had he already been drinking and partying with his friends? Had he resorted back to screwing his hoes and snorting his drugs? The thoughts sent shivers up my back and I didn't want to think the unthinkable.

"I think we need to find her again." Delaney showed me the bottle through the mirror, hugging it like it was sacred or golden to her.

I let out a half smile. "Maybe later. But you better hide it in my closet. If my parents find it, they'll kick you out."

Delaney jumped off the bed and darted to my closet.

"Damn, that was fast." I turned around as she closed my closet door.

"What do you expect?" She adjusted her skirt and fixed her hair. "I haven't seen your brother since the week before Christmas. I'm dying for a piece of his ass."

"Ewww." I covered my ears and said, "I can't hear you. I can't hear you." I repeated it over and over again, not wanting to hear what she wanted to do with my brother.

She shook her head. "Okay, I'll stop."

I uncovered my ears. "Thank you."

She grabbed my hand and led us out of my room. We went downstairs and were promptly greeted by a room full of family and friends. Soft holiday music played in the background and the room sparkled with tiny white lights strung around the stairwell, arches, and posts. Garland decorated the house and several Christmas trees in a variety of sizes were still up. The smell of rich, food wafted in the air and a wave a nausea hit me.

"Oh, wow. That smells so good." Delaney inhaled deeply like she hadn't eaten in days.

My stomach tightened and bile rose in the back of my throat. I covered my mouth and swallowed a few times, trying to dissipate the sick taste. A waiter appeared and offered appetizers along with alcohol free punch.

"No thanks." I turned my head when he held the tray up to me.

Delaney took several crackers with slices of smoked salmon that had white stuff speckled with green. The look of it made me want to barf. I grabbed a glass of punch and downed it just in time.

"Is it that good?" she teased as she picked up a glass and sipped the light colored liquid. "How boring." She rolled her eyes. "But I know how to make it ten times better."

The waiter looked at both of us suspiciously before walking off.

"What's wrong with you?" I elbowed her. "Do you want someone to hear you?"

"Sorry." She put on a fake smile and then walked to the living room where my parents lingered among the crowd of people. I knew she was trying to make a good impression so when she and Luke finally told them they were together, they'd accept her. Based on the comments my mom had made, I knew she had some work cut out for her if they were going to be okay with her dating their son.

I visited with a few of my aunts and uncles, catching up with them. Most of them lived in California, where my dad was originally from, and some lived in the area. I steered clear of my sister's husband, Ryan. He held a captive audience as he bragged about his law firm. It was sickening, to say the least. After an hour of torture, I finally decided I had had enough.

Luke and Delaney had magically disappeared and I didn't want to be forced to say anything in case my parents caught them.

I walked up the stairs but instead of going to my room, I headed to the game room. My niece and nephew were in there, along with several of my younger cousins and a few other kids from my parent's friends. My sister's nanny and one of other girl were playing games with some of the kids, while the older ones competed with each other on one of Luke's video games. And again, it reminded me of Raven. Why couldn't I stop thinking about him? Why did everything have to be a trigger?

I collapsed into the recliner and kicked off my shoes, pulling my feet underneath me. It didn't take long for my niece, Payton, to crawl into my lap. Her curly blonde hair and stark blue eyes made the four-year-old girl simply adorable. As I watched her play with her baby doll, my mind conjured up images of Raven and me with baby. Who would they look like? Would they have dark, wavy hair like him? Would their eyes be brown like mine, or hazel like his? My eyes watered and I quickly reminded myself that would never happen. I held on to my niece, rocking her until we both fell asleep.

"Lexi," my mom called and I slowly opened my eyes.

"Here, I'll take her," the nanny said, taking Payton from my arms.

"Are you feeling okay?" My mom touched my forehead and I placed the back of my hand on my cheek.

"Yes." I blinked a few times. "Just tired, that's all."

Her lips parted in a perfect smile, but I knew it wasn't genuine. I could see it in the depths of her eyes and feel it in the pit of my stomach. "Its ten-thirty. We decided that we're going to bring in the New Year early."

I stretched and shifted, trying to work out the stiffness in my back. "Why would you do that?"

"There are a few people who want to leave early." She rearranged my hair and I eased to the side, trying to get away from her hand. I didn't want her touching me. "No to mention, the streets are dangerous after midnight." Mom really wasn't a big fan of driving on New Year's Eve after she'd been in an accident when we were younger. I didn't remember much since Luke and I were only eight at the time, but it left a big scar on both her and my dad. They didn't talk about it — they pretty much avoided it like the big elephant in the room — so everyone just kept quiet, pretending like it never happened.

"So, we're going to pretend its Eastern Standard Time?" I asked.

"You got it." She continued fixing my hair and I searched her eyes, trying to uncover her true motive. "And I would like for you to play Auld Lang Syne on the piano."

A pain struck the center of my chest and my heart crumbled. The notes from the music I played for Raven echoed loudly inside my head, making me scream internally. They crashed into each other, clanging and banging until they stirred up every memory. Playing the piano was the last thing I wanted to do. It reminded me too much of Raven and how we had sang to one another. I wouldn't be able to handle it. It was too soon.

"Um, I don't know, Mom." I pushed her hand away and got up from the chair. "I haven't played that song in a while and it's not like I can go and practice with everyone downstairs." I put my shoes on and headed out of the game room. She quickly followed me.

"Lexi, it's only a couple of chords." Her voice deepened and I knew what she was about to say. "I know you can do it."

"I don't want to play." I turned around and faced her. "Not tonight."

"Lexi Ann Thompson," her eyes narrowed and her hands flew to her hips, "I'm not asking you to play, I'm telling you to play."

My blood pressure rose and I took a deep breath. "Mom, please—"

"Olivia, Lexi, can you please come down stairs? Some guests have arrived."

Gritting my teeth together, I unwillingly agreed. "Fine." I stomped down the stairs like a kid, pissed that I'd given in to her request. I hated being at home and I wanted to leave, but I had nowhere to go. I flew down the stairs so fast that I didn't see the group of people standing near the entrance. "Sorry," I said as I avoided a near collision. "I... um—" My breath hitched and my eyes froze. Standing in front of me was Collin and his parents.

"Hello, Lexi, it's good to see you." Pastor Clifton extended his hand and I stared at it for a few seconds.

My mom elbowed me and I stuck out my hand. "Hi, nice of you to bring your family." My voice clashed with the words I spoke, but I didn't care. The Norris' were the last group of people I wanted to see. Especially Collin.

I shook Suzanne's hand and then gave a quick wave to Collin. What the hell was I supposed to do? This was more than awkward and totally sucked.

"You look beautiful, as always," Collin said and I had to keep from rolling my eyes at him. It was a little too late for him to play Mr. Nice Guy. He had his chance and totally blew it.

"Lexi, why don't you get Collin something to drink?" my mom offered.

The words *why don't you do it* neared the edge of my tongue, but I held them back. I narrowed my eyes at her, knowing that she had invited them. I hated to think of what else she had planned for the night.

Reluctantly, I said, "Come on." Collin followed me in silence and I was glad. I really had nothing to say to him and seeing him only made things worse for me.

"How have you been?" he asked as I poured him a glass of punch.

Was he serious? We hadn't spoken since I told him it was over. Why did he want to know now? I was certain that my mom had told him what had happened and he was just being cordial, so I did what I was raised to do. I answered, "Alive, last time I checked."

"Oh, I see." He took the drink from my hand and his fingers brushed across mine. His eyes searched my face and I saw a sadness I'd never seen before. His lips parted and I could tell that he wanted to say something to me. I waited, giving him yet another opportunity, but he pressed his lips together and remained silent. Nothing had changed.

I really didn't want to engage in conversation with him because I was still angry at him for not fighting for our relationship. Yet, a part of me almost felt sorry for him. After the break, I hadn't tried to contact him or even check on him. Maybe it was wrong of me and I should have — after all, we had known each other forever — but I honestly felt like he should've been the one calling and begging me back. Since he never did that, I did what I had to do and moved on. And showing up at my house on New Year's Eve wasn't the answer. Especially since I was trying to get over Raven. The last thing I needed was old feelings for him to resurface, too.

I crossed my arms and leaned against the kitchen bar, deciding to show him some courtesy and praying I wouldn't regret it. "What about you, how have you been?"

His eyes lifted as he sipped his punch. It was as though he was waiting for me to open that door for him. "Getting by."

His remark told me he had so much more to say, but I didn't want to hear it. Maybe because I feared what he might tell me? I turned around, poured myself half a glass of punch, and downed it. I really needed some alcohol to get me through the night. I considered refilling my glass and going straight to my closet. Delaney was right — being depressed sucked and I needed to get on with my life. A little liquid encouragement might just do the trick.

"How were finals?" He broke the silence and I did a double take, making sure I heard him correctly.

Shrugging, I said, "Okay. I guess."

"I didn't see you in Spanish class, what happened?"

I stared at the small circle of punch at the bottom of my glass. Tilting my glass, I swirled the liquid around, contemplating if I should tell him the truth or make something up. Maybe he'd see that calling it off wasn't that easy for me. After all, what did I have to lose? Raven had dumped me, so I knew how he felt. *Karma's a bitch* reverberated in my ears.

"Um, I dropped the class."

Collin coughed a few times, clearing his throat. "You did what?"

I waved a dismissive hand in the air, like it was no big deal. "I took an incomplete."

"Why would—"

"Excuse me, Collin." My mom approached me and I sighed internally. "Lexi, I'd like for you to play some holiday music for our guests." She flashed me her fake smile and my stomach rolled again. With her hand placed firmly behind my back, she pushed me toward the baby grand piano. My legs stiffened and my feet cemented themselves to the ground. My favorite thing to do had now become the thing I despised the most.

"Mom, I'm not feeling well," I stalled but she pressed me forward.

With a fake smile plastered across her face, she bit out, "Just a few songs, Lexi, that's all I'm asking you to do."

"Mrs. Thompson, we have a slight problem." One of the wait staff appeared, looking fairly nervous. "Can I please see you in the kitchen?"

"Yes, of course." Mom turned to me. "Lexi, I'm asking you, please."

"I guess," I huffed. I walked out of the kitchen and stopped when Luke and Delaney entered through the back door. Her hair stuck to the sides of her face and it looked like she'd been sweating. Her dress was wrinkled and her tights were missing. Luke quickly ran his fingers through his disheveled hair and checked the buttons on his shirt. It was obvious what they had been doing and if I had to guess, they were in his car.

Gross.

"Hey, man, what's up?" Luke exchanged a handshake with Collin. "Glad you could make it."

My head quickly spun in their direction. Had Luke invited him and not my parents? After everything that happened, why he would do that to me? Anger bubbled up inside of me and I couldn't wait to rip him a new one.

"Hi, Delaney." Collin smiled but his greeting didn't sound welcoming or sincere.

Delaney shot me a quick look and then said, "Hey, Collin."

Thankfully, Luke and Collin started talking and I was able to slip away without having to speak to him further. As soon as we were out of hearing distance, Delaney spun me around.

"WTF! Who the hell invited him?" Her eyes widened when she saw Collin's family, "And his parents?"

"I don't know." I sucked in a deep breath. "Maybe Luke, maybe my parents... who knows."

She shook her head. "That's just wrong."

"Tell me about it." I trudged toward the piano and she followed me. "I so need that drink."

"Aww, so now you're okay with me bringing along some fun," she hiccupped and I glanced over my shoulder.

"How much have you had?"

She licked her lips and wiped the excess lipstick that spread beyond her lower lip. "Enough to give me a good buzz and show your brother how much I missed him."

I shuddered and held up a hand. "TMI, Laney."

She winked and smiled. "Sorry, I can't help it. Your brother is so damn hot." She eyed him from where we stood and when he caught her gaze, he flashed her his one and only dimple.

"Ohhh," she moaned, "see what I mean."

"You want me to agree with you?" I rolled my eyes and turned away. "That's incest, you know."

"I forget." She giggled and placed her hand on my shoulder as she pulled the strap of her shoe over her ankle. "Just ignore me, I'm drunk." I looked at her and then glanced around, hoping that no one heard her. Thankfully, no one was near us.

"Great." I pulled some of my song sheets from the bench and began to look through them. "Just don't throw up or make a fool of yourself, please."

"Don't worry. I won't." She began fixing her hair in the large mirror behind us. "Besides, I have to make a good impression, right?"

I laughed. "It might be too late for that."

"What?" She spun around. "Are you serious? Did your parents say something?"

Focusing on finding the right music, I didn't answer her.

"Lex, tell me. Did they say something?"

"No, not really. But if you want them to accept you, you're going to have to work really hard at making them believe you're good enough for Luke."

"Oh, great." A horrific look covered her face. "Like that's even possible."

"You're telling me." I sighed and then sat on the bench. My fingers trembled as I opened the cover to the keyboard and stared at the keys for a long minute.

"Is everything okay?" Delaney asked as she leaned against the piano.

My eyes began to water and I quickly wiped the tears away. "I haven't played in a while... since I last saw Raven."

"Oh. Sorry." She placed a hand on my shoulder. "Then don't play. Why torture yourself?"

"I don't have a choice." I gave her a pitiful look because it was all I had and deep down, I needed someone to feel sorry for me. "My mom told me I have to play."

"WTF." Her hands flew up in the air. "What's wrong with your mom? She needs to chill."

"You're telling me." I fanned my eyes. "I'm so ready to get out of here."

"School starts in two weeks and the dorms open late next week, so you don't have long."

I nodded and then stared at the music, trying to visualize playing the notes, even though I really didn't want to. I did that for a couple of songs and Delaney quickly busied herself with her phone.

"Oh my, it's almost eleven o'clock." Mom rushed into the formal area and Delaney shot me a confused stare.

"She wants us to bring in the New Year like we're in New York."

"Oh." Delaney gave my mom a quick once over and then turned to me. "Why?"

"Long story. She doesn't like being out after midnight." I rearranged the music on the backboard. "That's when all the drunks are out and accidents happen. And she knows because she was in one when we were little."

Delaney's face turned three shades lighter. She grabbed the edge of the piano and I prayed she wasn't about to barf. "Delaney, are you—"

"Lexi, it's almost eleven. Are you ready?" Mom motioned for everyone to gather near the piano and Delaney quickly darted through the crowd toward Luke. I figured that maybe the alcohol had hit and she wasn't feeling well. I just hoped Luke would be the one taking care of her, because I really didn't want to.

I sighed and positioned my fingers on the keyboard. Taking a deep breath, I began playing the notes to the song. It took me a few bars before my fingers finally loosened up and I convinced myself that I would be okay. The piano was something I loved and I wouldn't allow Raven to take that from me. He'd already stolen enough of my life in the short time we had been together.

The waiters finished dispersing the champagne and the crowd began the countdown. Each number struck a chord deep within me and I hated being alone. Just days ago, I was loving life and now I had no idea where my life was going. I caught Collin staring at me and it made my cheeks flush, but I managed to keep my focus. Never had I seen him stare so intently at me and I couldn't help but wonder what was on his mind. Why didn't he ever look at me like that before?

Guys! Ugh! Impossible!

"Three. Two. One! Happy New Year!" The crowd erupted and I began playing the song louder so everyone could hear it. Even though I knew it wasn't midnight yet, my mind continuously ventured over to Raven. Wondering where he was and what he was doing. I could only hope he wasn't doing anything stupid.

My parents gathered around the piano, hugging each other tightly as they sang the lyrics to the song. Instead of feeling euphoric, I began to feel sad and lonely. Nothing had turned out the way I had hoped or intended. Everything was so screwed up and I didn't know how it would get better. Tears welled in my eyes and dripped down my cheeks. I continued playing, not caring if anyone saw how messed up my life was.

"Lexi," my eldest uncle yelled, "play *For He's a Jolly Good Fellow.*"

I laughed at his request and it relieved a little of my sadness. Repositioning my fingers to the appropriate keys, I played the song for him. At his age, I knew it could be his last celebration. The least I could do was give him that request.

My uncle sang loudly and everyone joined in, swaying back and forth with arms laced around each other. Thoughts of Raven and me flooded my mind and I recalled the first time I played for him and we sang. My lower lip quivered and the tears reappeared.

"Lexi, play *Lean on Me*," one of my dad's friends announced and my fingers crashed against the keys.

The memories collided inside of my head and everywhere I turned, I saw Raven and me together. I heard his voice, his laughter, and felt his touch against my skin. I embraced myself and began rocking rapidly back and forth. His presence surrounded me and there was no escaping it. The Raven's trap had consumed me again and I was its victim for the umpteenth time.

"No! No! No." I pushed away from the piano and ran toward my room.

"Lexi!" I heard Collin yell as I darted up the stairs. "Wait."

I didn't stop, just kept running until I threw the door to my room open and flung myself across the bed. The tears gushed and sobs escaped from my mouth. I missed Raven and I needed to see him. Being without him was like living without air. It hurt to breathe and it hurt to exist. The pain was unbearable and I couldn't take it any longer.

"Lexi, what's wrong?" I heard Collin enter my room. He'd never bothered to step foot in it before and I couldn't help but wonder, why now? I wanted him out.

"Just go, please." I covered my face with my pillow and motioned for him to leave me alone.

The bed sank and his warmth surrounded me. Why was he there? Didn't he see that I needed to be alone?

"I'm not going anywhere until you tell me what's wrong." He placed his hand on my arm and I flinched.

"Please, Collin. Go," I whined louder, feeling the frustration ripple through me.

He kept his hand on me. "Lexi, I know you've been through a lot, and I'm not sure where things went so wrong," he stalled and I slowed my crying.

His hand eased down my arm and his fingers wrapped around my hand. With a gentle motion, he tried to pull the pillow away, but I held on to it. I didn't want him to see me crying. Especially since I wasn't grieving for him. He continued to tug and I resisted, hugging the pillow tighter. Why was he acting like he cared when I knew he didn't? Finally, I allowed him to remove the pillow from my face. Collin sat next to me, staring at me attentively. His eyes were filled with unshed tears and his lip quivered.

Why the hell was he about to cry?

"I know this might not be the ideal time to tell you this, but I love you, Lexi." His hands cupped my face and he stared deep into my eyes. "I love you more than anything and... and I'm sorry that I was so stupid and I didn't tell you when I had the opportunity."

My breath hitched and my heart stopped for a moment. Was he freakin' serious?

"Please forgive me for being such an ass. I... was just doing what I was brought up to do." His eyes lowered and his chest heaved up and down in slow, paced movements. "I thought you needed some space so that's what I gave you. I never thought you'd run off with some guy and throw everything we had away."

He pressed his lips to mine, but I didn't respond. I was in total shock. Why did he wait so long to tell me? Nearly three months had passed since we had broken up and he waited until I wasn't with Raven to finally express how he truly felt about me? He wasn't making things any easier for me.

"Lexi, please, say something," he spoke against my lips and then pulled away.

"Oh, God, Collin," I moaned as I sunk deeper into the mattress. My heart was longing for Raven, not for him. But how did I tell him that? The pain clawed at me, tearing a new hole that I knew would leave a permanent scar. I was certain I didn't love Collin. The lack of yearning and need for him wasn't there, it was practically non-existent. There was no fire, no flame, and no excitement inside of me. Collin wasn't the one that held my heart, it was Raven.

"I'm..." I heaved a huge sigh, still trying to control the sobs. "I'm sorry, Collin, but I don't feel the same. Not anymore."

The tears released from his eyes and rolled down his clean-shaven face. In the six years I had known him, I'd never seen him cry. I didn't want to hurt him, but I had to be honest with him and myself. I wasn't going back to something that I knew wasn't real. It would be the worst decision of my life.

"Please, Lexi," he latched onto my hands, "give me one more chance to prove my love to you."

I closed my eyes, searching deep within me for something — anything — that hinted there might be a chance for us, but there was nothing. "Collin... Collin..." I wiped his tears with the pads of my fingers. "I wish I could—"

"Lexi!" Delaney darted into my room, screaming a frantic cry that made my hairs stand on end.

"What? What is it?" I darted upright, feeling my heart drop to my stomach.

"It's Raven. He's been in an accident." Her eyes were wide and she looked distraught. She paced the floor as she held her head.

"What? When?" I jumped off the bed, totally abandoning Collin's plea for my love. "Is he okay?" My insides tightened, forming a thick knot threatening to slice me in half. If anything had happened to Raven and I wasn't there to save him, I'd die.

"I don't know." Delaney scrolled through her phone and then started dialing a number. "I don't know." Tears filled her eyes and she lowered her phone. "It's happening again. It can't be." She covered her mouth with her hand and sobbed quietly.

Why was she so upset? Did she know something I didn't?

"Calm down, Laney." Luke pulled her against his chest. "You're freaking out Lexi and everyone else."

I raced to her side, unable to catch my breath. "How did you find out?"

"Shelby sent me a text." She showed me her phone and my eyes blurred as I tried to focus on the words. The letters jumbled together and my left eye twitched, making it nearly impossible to read the message. My ears rang loudly, blocking everyone's voice in the room.

Raven had been in an accident. What kind of accident? Was he alive? Was he dead?

Shelby: Raven's been in an accident. OTW to the hospital. Call u when I know more.

My hands shook uncontrollably as atrocious thoughts ripped my mind in two. "Call her, ask what hospital." I handed her back the phone and held my breath.

Delaney quickly dialed Shelby's number and held the phone to her ear. My heart bashed against my chest, threating to tear through me.

"She's not answering."

"Shit!" I clenched my head between my hands, trying to think of what to do.

Her phone chimed and I grabbed it from her hand.

Shelby: He's at Harris Hospital downtown FW.

"We're going." I ran toward my dresser and grabbed my purse.

"What's going on?" My mom entered my room, looking at me, then at Collin, and finally at Luke and Delaney. "Why's everyone yelling?"

"Um, there's been an accident. I have to leave." I pushed by her and she grabbed my arm.

"Who's been in an accident?" Her fingers dug into my skin and I twisted my arm, trying to break free.

"A friend."

"Raven?" Her voice raised a few octaves. "Is that who you're talking about?"

"Why does it matter to you?" I yanked my arm from her grip and pushed past her.

"Lexi, if you walk out that door, don't you dare come back."

"Fine." I pivoted on my heels, feeling the rise of anger within me. I was tired of being a prisoner in my own house and I was sick and tired of them ruling over my life.

I was done.

"If that's how you want to treat your daughter, then it's your loss, not mine."

"Lexi Ann Thompson, how dare you talk to me that way? I'm your mother, for crying out loud."

"Then act like it!" I threw my hands up in the air. "And you're taking me." I grabbed Luke's hand.

"What?" Luke stalled.

I started to drag him out of my room when my dad stopped us, blocking the doorway.

"And where do you think you're going?"

"We're leaving and no one's stopping us." I stood toe to toe with him, feeling the rise of determination overcome me. Not my mom, nor my dad, would control me any longer. I was calling the shots now.

He braced himself against the doorframe, spreading his arms wide. "It's too dangerous and people will be drinking and driving."

Luke looked at me and then at my dad. My dad shot him a warning look and Luke shuffled his feet while he rubbed the scruff on his chin as though contemplating what to do. Listen to my father or help me.

Errantly, I stepped forward. "That's a chance I'll have to take."

My dad dropped his arms and stepped aside. "Be careful. Both of you."

"What? You can't allow them to leave," Mom snapped at Dad and they began arguing.

"Lexi, you really want to go after this guy?" Collin voice startled me and I spun around.

"What?"

"I'm telling you...I'll do anything for you, anything to prove my love, and you're not going to even give me a chance?" Disbelief laced his voice and his body flanked on the edge of falling down to his knees. Was he ready to beg me?

Please don't!

"Lexi, listen to Collin," my mom pleaded and I grimaced. "He's the one that loves you, not that loser."

I gritted my teeth together, trying to keep calm amongst the opposing forces preventing me from doing what I wanted.

What my heart wanted.

Raven.

It was Raven that I loved, not Collin. I pressed my lips together, finally coming to realization that all the feelings I had amounted to one thing.

Love.

I was madly and irrevocably in love with Raven and nothing was ever going to change that. Ever.

Turning toward Collin, I took several steps in his direction until I stood in front of him. Our gazes met and I gave him a heartfelt apology. "I'm sorry, Collin. But I don't love you."

"This is what you want to go running to?" He held up his phone, showing me pictures of Raven with several girls. I immediately took his phone from his grip and scrolled through them. For the past several days, Raven had been posting pictures of himself on Facebook with several girls. I cringed when I saw Macy and Reece. His eyes were small and he looked seriously messed up. The pain reappeared in the center of my chest, cutting off all oxygen. My body heaved forward, but I told myself it was only because he was drunk or high. I wasn't there to stop him and he had reverted to the deadly lifestyle that was waiting to destroy his life.

"I don't care." I shoved the phone in his hand. "He needs me."

"You're making the biggest mistake of your life." Collin shook his head. "I can't promise that I'll be around when he breaks your heart again."

I sighed. "I know and I don't expect you to."

"So, I guess this is it?" Collin shoved his hands in his pocket. His shoulders slumped and his entire body deflated with one breath.

"I'm sorry, Collin, I really am, but...I have to go."

"I wish you the best. I really do." Collin leaned forward and kissed me on the cheek. "Bye, Lexi."

I pressed my lips together, fighting back the tears. I may not have loved him, but I did care about him and I wanted him to be happy. I wanted both of us to be happy and we didn't equal that. Our equation was better split in two. "Bye, Collin."

I sucked in a silent breath and turned toward my brother and Delaney. "Let's go."

My mom stepped in front of me. "If you leave, you're not welcome back."

Adjusting my purse, I said, "Good. I don't want to come back to this prison."

I walked to my closet and grabbed the bag that I had packed when I was planning on running away from home. I quickly stuffed a few of my personal items inside and zipped it closed. My dad kissed me on the forehead. His eyes glazed over as though he felt sorry for me. If he did, he didn't say anything. I figured I'd never know unless he was waiting to tell me in private.

We walked out of my room and were promptly greeted by my sister. "Where the hell are you going?" She lifted her wine glass and moved out of the way.

"She's going to see that no good, SOB," my mom snapped.

Anger ripped through every muscle fiber in me and it took all my effort not to punch my mom in the face. I was ready to knock the words out of her mouth so she never spoke them again, but I kept my focus and darted down the hallway. She wasn't worth it.

"Oh my god. Are you still hung up on that loser?" My sister's voice trailed behind me.

"Screw you. That's none of your business," I barked as I flew down the stairs.

"You really are a disgrace to this family, you know that?" she yelled, calling everyone's attention as we passed into the living room. "He's a druggy and it's rumored he has a kid. But I'm sure you already know that."

I stopped and turned to face her. Biting down on the inside of my cheek, I drew blood to keep from lashing out a string of expletive words. "Go to hell."

"To each their own." Ashley threw her head back in laughter. "Just wait. He'll end up in prison, being someone's bitch for a very long time."

"What?" I had to catch my breath because I couldn't believe what she'd just said. "Would it kill you to—" I stopped when I remembered the background check and court documents. She'd been helping my mom all along. It all made sense. My mom had her dig up stuff on him.

"You've really gone too far." I shoved my finger in her face. "You better be careful, I'm warning you."

"Oh, like I'm so scared." She pressed a hand to her chest and I pushed her out of my way, heading straight to the garage. "You'll be going down, just like your loser boyfriend. Mark my words."

"Whatever!"

"Shut the hell up, Ashley. You always think you're so perfect when in reality, you're like every other attorney I know," Luke commented as he followed me out the door.

"What's that supposed to mean?" She raced after us and Luke slammed the garage door in her face.

Luke started the car and we got in. My parents stood in the garage, watching as we backed out into the street. I wasn't certain if my mom would keep to her promise of disowning me and never allowing me in the house, but that was the least of my worries. Raven was my number one concern.

Σ

Chapter 19

I pulled out my phone and hit Raven's number. I knew he probably wouldn't answer, but I could only hope that his mom or someone else would. With each ring, I squeezed the edge of my seat tighter, unable to contain the unease stirring within my already upset stomach. It rang and rang before finally going to voicemail. I considered leaving a message but hit the end button instead.

"Anything?" Delaney turned around in her chair as she checked her phone.

"No, nothing." I shook my head and tried to keep calm, but between the beat of the music and the pounding of my heart, I was spiraling into a full-fledged panic attack. I took several deep breaths, trying to ebb the tension tightening every muscle in my body, but it was pointless.

"Hurry, Luke." I leaned against the front bucket seat, unable to sit still.

"I am. I am." Luke's fingers gripped the steering wheel and the hum of the motor increased as he sped up.

"Don't get pulled over and please don't wreck." Delaney sighed as she continued checking her phone. "Damn, no one's posted anything. What the eff is social media for if you're not going to give updates?"

"I don't know." I watched the lines of the freeway race by as I kept my focus on the road in front of us. The lights blurred in the night and the green signs faded quickly as Luke passed them at a high speed. I said a silent prayer, asking God to get us to the hospital safely and to let Raven be okay.

He had to be okay.

I kept telling myself that everything would be alright once I got there, despite every vibe telling me that it wouldn't. I leaned against the back seat, battling the voices of defeat. Closing my eyes, I thought about all the special times we had spent together. Tears seeped from my eyes and I let them fall as I released the worry eating away at me. I smiled as I reminisced the first time we met at the writing center and how I despised the fact that Dr. Connor forced me to help him. My body tingled with excitement as I recalled how he'd awoken a need in me that I never knew existed.

The time we spent in the stadium suite was magical and I'd never forget it. Especially the way he teased and flirted with me, but maintained a level of respect that was not common or familiar for him. There was something special between us; we were direct opposites of each other, but perfectly crafted for each other at the same time. I needed him and he definitely needed me.

I wrapped my arms around my body as I imagined the week I spent in his strong arms. My skin was marked with the memories of his touch and scent. All of it was embedded deep into every cell of my body. Raven owned a part of me and I was glad that I had given it to him. There were no regrets and I would hold onto every encounter we had of making love to each other. Nothing would ever take that special bond away from us.

Not my mom.

Not my sister.

And definitely not Collin.

One thing was certain. I loved being hooked in The Raven's trap. It was the best damn trap I'd ever experienced. I prayed that I'd be able to have more of it, because one thing was certain, I was never releasing myself from it again. No matter what.

I'd fight for him.

I'd fight for us.

"Lexi, I'll drop you off at the front," Luke announced and my eyes popped open.

"Okay," I said, grabbing my phone.

The car tilted to the right as Luke took a hard turn and the tires screeched against the pavement. I slid all over the backseat, trying to stay put as he drove like a bat out of hell. He flew over several of the speed bumps before slamming on the breaks and coming to a stop at the emergency entrance. Delaney flung the door open and we toppled out of the car. Weariness filled my muscles and my legs felt heavy as we rushed inside. I managed to pick up my pace, not letting the fear keep me back. I had to see Raven. I had to know if he was okay. I didn't care if he didn't want to see me or wanted nothing to do with me. And the more I thought about what Delaney said, the more my intuition told me that my family might have had something to do with our breakup.

Delaney kept up with me as we darted toward the information desk.

I skidded to stop, trying not to twist my ankle in my stacked heels. "Ra-ven Daven-port." I gasped for air, taking in big breaths. Delaney rested on the counter, drawing in air to her lungs as we waited impatiently.

The lady behind the desk adjusted her glasses. "When was he admitted?"

"I don't know. A few hours ago, maybe."

"Okay, let me check." She typed in some information on her computer but before she could respond with any information, I heard a familiar voice call my name.

"Lexi?"

I spun around and saw Raven's mom, Trish, heading toward me. Her eyes were red and her hair was matted. She had on an oversized sweatshirt and sweatpants and it looked like she had literally crawled out of bed and went straight to the hospital.

"I'm so glad you're here." Her arms wrapped around me and she began to cry. "I can't believe..."

Embracing her, I tried to calm the panic and worry in her yelps. "What happened, Trish?"

Delaney looked at me and then grabbed a handful of tissues and handed them to her. "Is Raven okay?"

Trish nodded and my body shifted from a feeling of nervous hope to one of excitement.

Raven was alive!

"What happened? We heard he was in an accident."

She released me and wiped her eyes and nose. "They found him passed out in the bathroom at one of his friend's place."

"What?" My stomach rolled and I wanted to throw up again. The blood drained from my face as I imagined Raven high on cocaine and drunk from alcohol. Covering my mouth, I swallowed several times, pushing the bile down. "Did they say why?"

Her eyes drifted to the floor and she gave a slight shrug of her shoulders. She either knew and didn't want to say, or was too embarrassed to tell us.

"Lexi!" Shelby barreled through the front doors with Josh following her. They were dressed like they had been at a New Year's Eve party. Shelby had a long, formal, black dress on and Josh's ensemble was missing the bow tie and tuxedo jacket.

"We came as fast as we could." Josh ran his fingers through his short, blond hair. His brows knitted together, forming deep indentions on his forehead. "Do you have any details?"

I shot Trish a quick glance and she sighed. "All I know is that they found him passed out on the floor."

"Who found him?"

"I did."

We turned to see Shawn standing behind us. He rested his arms against his chest. "At Jared's place."

"Shit." Josh's nostrils flared and his face reddened. "I told him to stay the hell away from that guy." He placed a hand on Shawn's shoulder, leaned in, and said, "Was he back at it?"

"I'm not sure." Shawn gave a slight roll of his dark brown eyes.

"No." My heart dropped and I swayed to the side. I leaned against the wall, until the dizzy spell passed.

"He wasn't supposed to be there." Anger laced his words and he gave me a disapproving look. I wasn't sure if he was insinuating that it was partially my fault for not being there for him, and although I wanted to tell him something, I was grateful that he'd saved Raven.

"Fucking idiot!" Josh growled, and stomped off, cursing under his breath.

Trish placed her hand on Shawn's arm. "Thank you so much for helping my son. If you wouldn't have brought him here, he might not be alive." Tears dripped from her eyes and her voice cracked.

"He's my friend, so I'm going to watch out for him," Shawn reassured her and she started sobbing harder. Gradually, he took her in his arms and held her as she wept.

Tears rolled down my cheeks and regret furled inside of me. If I would've stayed with him, none of that would have happened. We wouldn't have gone back to Jared's. That entire night could've been avoided if I had only stayed with Raven and ignored my parents. I hated that I wasn't there for him, especially after I promised him I would be. Some friend I was.

We sat in the busy waiting room, waiting for the doctor to come and talk to us. The hospital buzzed with traffic as one incident after another filed in. We even had a little excitement when a man started yelling, demanding that they allow him to see his wife. The security guard had to restrain him and eventually they took him away. We wondered if he was able to see his wife, but based on his behavior, we figured that he was taken to a holding cell for evaluation.

The clock moved slowly as each hour passed and I waited with baited breath. We leaned on each other for support, but most of all, for hope. All we could do was pray that Raven would be okay. He had to be okay. I refused to believe otherwise.

"Everything's going to be okay." Delaney held on to my hand as I sat, curled in a ball.

"I feel somewhat responsible for what happened," I whispered, not wanting anyone but her to hear me.

"But it's not your fault." Luke handed her a cold Coke Zero. "Thanks," she said as she tried to open it. Luke motioned for her to hand it to him and he twisted the cap with a flick of his wrist.

"Do you want anything?" Luke asked.

"A Sprite, please. My stomach feels like crap."

"I bet," Delaney said in between sips. "It's been one messed up night."

"I should have never went home." I shook my head.

Tucking my hair behind my ear, Delaney said, "Quit harping on the past. What matters is that you're here. And you're going to tell Raven how you really feel about him."

"But what if he doesn't feel the same?" I squeezed my eyes, not wanting to cry. "I mean, he's the one that broke up with me."

"I know he cares about you. And I bet he did all of this because he couldn't handle being without you."

"Do you really—"

"The family of Raven Davenport." A man wearing a white coat walked into the waiting room.

Everyone stood and Trish and I rushed toward the double doors. "Yes, I'm his mother." Trish held on to my arm as we waited to hear news about Raven.

"I'm Dr. Ghatalia, and I've been overseeing the treatment of your son. The good news is that we were able to stabilize him. Thanks to his friend Shawn, we knew exactly how to treat him and more than likely, that's how we were able to save his life."

"Thank you, doctor." A huge weight lifted from my chest and I released the breath that I didn't realize I'd been holding. My vision cleared and the ringing in my ears subsided. Every muscle in body relaxed and I thanked God for saving him.

"Thank you, thank you," Trish whispered repeatedly as tears streamed down her cheeks.

I pulled her in my arms and we embraced, crying together over the same man we both loved and cared for unconditionally. The same man that had taken us to hell and back. I couldn't imagine what she'd gone through, and at that moment, I understood her last comment to me at the mall. Raven was a handful, and I wasn't sure how if I could handle going through another ordeal like that one again. All I knew was that I loved him, cared for him, and was willing to give up everything for him. I would hold to my promise. I would be there for him, no matter what it took. I wouldn't let him throw his life away to drugs — he was too precious to me and I had to make him see that, because apparently he didn't appreciate his life.

"My son's alive," she sobbed in my ear and I cried with her.

After a long minute of releasing all the pinioned worry within us, we turned to the doctor.

"When can we see him?"

"You can see him now." The doctor swiped the screen of his tablet. "But only for a short while. He's been through a lot and needs to rest. We will move him to a room within the hour and we will keep him here for at least a day. I need to make sure his vitals are stable without medical intervention." He straightened and took in a slight breath. "Based on his history, I will have to recommend him for treatment, you understand, correct?"

His mom nodded. "Yes, I understand."

"Thank you, doctor." I hugged the man, even though I didn't know him and turned to Trish. "If you want to see him first, I understand."

"It's okay. You go ahead." She wiped her eyes and sniffed. "He needs to see you, not me."

"Thanks, Trish." I gave her another quick hug. "I won't be long."

"Go." Her quivering lips formed a lopsided smile as she pushed me toward the double doors.

"He's in room sixteen." The doctor smiled and stepped aside.

I raced down the hall, dodging a few nurses on the way as I looked for his room. A sign on the wall pointed toward the end of the hall and I ran toward it. The hallway seemed to extend with every step I took and I increased my speed until I finally reached the door.

The large door was slightly ajar and a low light filtered through the crack. I slipped through the opening and gasped when I saw Raven laying on the hospital bed with wires connected to his arms as several monitors kept tabs on his vitals. His eyes were closed and he looked peaceful as his chest rose and fell in steady movements. Thank God, he was alive.

I tiptoed to his bed and eased beside him. Taking his hand in mine, I held on to it and raised it to my lips. I kissed his fingers and then pressed his palm to my cheek, dying to feel his touch. His hands were cold and didn't hold the usual warmth that I had grown accustomed to. I figured it was because he'd nearly died and it would take a while for his body temperature to get back to normal. Damn, he made me so mad. I wanted to yell at him and kiss him at the same time.

As I lowered his hand, he stirred and his eyes cracked open. "Le-xi?"

Tears streamed down my cheeks and my heart leaped at the sound of his voice. It felt so good to hear him call my name. "Yes, it's me. I'm here."

He cleared his throat a few times as if struggling to talk. "What are you doing here?"

"Shh." I rested his hand next to him. "You're going to be okay."

He shifted and kicked the thin sheet that covered him. "Is it really you?" He cupped my cheek with his hand and sighed.

"Yeah, babe, it's really me." Instinctively, I placed my hand on top of his, relishing in his familiar touch.

It felt so good.

So right.

"I never thought I'd see you again." He blinked slowly as he flashed me a lopsided smile.

"Well, here I am." My heart soared and unfettered emotions flayed from me. Never had I cared this way about anyone before. It made me only want to get closer to him and never leave his side.

"Come here." He held open his arms open wide and I crawled into the bed, wrapping my body around his. The coldness of his body made me shiver, but I refused to let go.

I promised myself I'd never let go.

Never again.

He took long, slow breaths as the monitor above us beeped in perfect tune with his heart and I rejoiced at the sound. His fingers threaded through my hair and I rested my head against his chest. We kept a steady gaze on each other and it released the familiar feelings that I'd been missing over the past week.

"What the hell happened?" Slowly his eyes widened as he took in his surroundings. "Where am I?"

"You're in the hospital." A lump formed in the back of my throat and I looked away, trying to hold back the tears. I didn't want to upset him. "Shawn brought you here."

"Aww, hell."

"Just rest." I gave him a gentle smile even though I was ready to rip him a new one. "You're going to be okay."

Silence filled the air and he closed his eyes for a moment. His jaw tightened and his nostrils flared. The beeps on the monitor increased as his breaths quickened. He opened his eyes and darkness filled them. "Why are you here, Lexi?" His body shifted as he gently pushed me away. "You're not supposed to be here."

An unwanted agony gnarled and twisted inside of me and my heart stilled. Did he really not want me to be here with him? Was he truly done with me? I knew that it wasn't the right time to discuss what had happened between us, but I couldn't help it.

"Raven, tell me that everything you wrote me was a lie. Tell me it's not true. All that we've shared and the time we've spent together, tell me it wasn't for nothing. Tell me it meant something." Tears poured from my eyes like a fountain turned on high. I couldn't repress the feelings I had for him. He had to know exactly how I felt. "Please tell me that I didn't walk away from everything for nothing."

His eyes glazed over and he took my hand in his. He pressed his lips together and then took a deep breath. "It was all a lie, Lexi. Everything I said in that text. I didn't mean one word."

I squeezed my eyes tightly together, trying to stop the waterworks from freefalling, but nothing would stop them.

Raven did want to be with me.

"Then why did you tell me that? Why did you leave me?"

His chest rose and fell and his face twisted in confusion. I couldn't tell if he didn't want to tell me or couldn't remember. I was willing to give him a reprieve after everything that he'd been through. I was just relieved to hear that he didn't mean it.

"It's a long story and I'll explain it to you later." He pulled me in his arms and drew my face to his. Our gazes connected, binding us together like when we first made love. "I'm sorry about everything, but know this, I love you, Lexi Thompson, and I'm going to prove it to you, over and over again, just so you know and never forgot."

The entire room spun around me and I felt like superwoman in his arms. Raven knew how to make me feel bullet proof and I was going to do whatever it took to protect us from the world that was trying so desperately to tear us down. I wouldn't allow my mom to keep us apart and no wrecking ball, no matter how big, would destroy us. I would stand strong and not let anyone or anything in this world come between us ever again. Even if we were broken, I knew that together we could have all that life promised us. All we had to do was fight for our love, and I was willing to do that as long as he was.

I stared him deep in the eyes and said, "I'm going to fight for you. As long as I have you by my side, I promise to give my life to you. Because I love you, Raven. I love you more than anything in this world and I'm going to stay right here next to you, just to make sure you know it."

Our lips reunited and I knew that together, we were invincible.

Σ

To be continued

in

The Winning Side

Book 3

from the University Park Series

From Best Selling Author
CM DOPORTO

THE WINNING SIDE

UNIVERSITY PARK SERIES BOOK 3

About the Author

Born and raised in the United States of America in the great state of Texas, CM Doporto resides there with her husband and son, enjoying life with their extensive family along with their Chihuahua, Mexican Redhead Parrot, and several fish. She is a member of Romance Writers of America, where she is associated with the Young Adult Special Interest Chapter. To learn more about her upcoming books, visit www.cmdoporto.com and sign up to receive email notifications. You can also like CM Doporto's fan page on Facebook and follow her on Instagram, Twitter and Pinterest.

Other Books by
<u>CM Doporto</u>

YOUNG ADULT

The Eslite Chronicles

The Eslites (short story prequel)

The Eslites, The Arrival

The Eslites, Out of This World (Summer 2015)

NEW ADULT

The Natalie Vega Saga

Element, Part 1

Element, Part 2

The University Park Series

Opposing Sides

The Same Side

The Winning Side

A Different Side (March 2015)

My Lucky Catch (June 2015) - Luke and Delaney's Story